The Light of the World

The Light Series

Tara Brown

ISBN-10: 0987941097
ISBN-13: 978-0987941091

I dedicate this book to my mother, my very own Willow

Thank you to Claudia and Catie at Phatpuppy Design for doing an amazing job on this one!! Thank you to Andrea Burns and Blue Butterfly for the editing job. I realize most of the words I force you to keep are tots annoying and only really legit in the urban dictionary. Muah!! Thank you to Triple M and J&G for being such awesome Internet friends. Thanks to Katy and Mani and Roof, for being my homies and helping me to figure this crazy world out.

To the bloggers and reviewers and fans, I bow before you. Thank you for making this fun.

Thank you to Nick and Amillia and Erralynn, love you.

Yes, love indeed is light from heaven; A spark of that immortal fire with angels shared, by Allah given to lift from earth our low desire.

Lord Byron

Chapter One

Dreams speak to you about the things in your day that your brain feels are unfinished. I know this because my mom is a dream analyst.

If I ask her about my dreams, she always tells me something crazy, like the bear in my dream tells me that the female side of my body lacks something in some way.

It's not about sex or wearing perfume though. It's always something mysterious and intangible, like I avoid being a woman and need to make womanly decisions because I still act like a girl. A bear wants me to know this. Apparently in dreams, bears are girls. They are also incredibly judgmental.

If I could 'le sigh' and move past it, I would. But I can't. She is relentless.

Instead of acknowledging she is crazy, we make a dream board, which are essentially pages cut from a magazine glued to a poster board. This tells her my fortune. She is a picture reader too.

When I was eight, she was a palm reader. Several times she has toured with groups of psychic spiritualists. I don't believe in a lot of things, but I swear the things I saw with those women have still not started to make sense. They're always with us, her spiritual friends.

She isn't a bad mom and she isn't a flake or a fake. I just am not entirely sure I believe the things she might be. The things people, who want to see and need to see, see.

Which is why, instead of backpacking across Europe for the year like she suggested, I chose university. The battle over university was brutal. To the point of me nearly running away…to school. What kid runs away from home to go to university? Deep down I wonder if there are other kids out there like me, kids of the flower children and hippies. Kids running away to school. Overprotective isn't the right word for her. Security detail might be a better way of saying it.

Like I said, she isn't a bad mom. She just isn't much like a mom. She's more of a spiritual guide. She felt 'spiritually' I needed Europe and to be with her. I think she just wanted to meet up with me in Italy or Norway. She has friends everywhere. Followers. Like Gandhi. With my luck and her attitude, I think she might have actually come for the entire trip. Fun.

I climb the stairs with my box of belongings in my hand and try to ignore her rambling on behind me.

"Nene, this place has no sauna, no steam room, and no pool. There isn't a yoga studio for twelve blocks. How are you going to get there six days a week if it's that far? I think you should rethink school and start next year."

I glance back at her and run into something with my armload. "Stop. Just stop. This isn't the place for this argument. Please. They have a vegan menu and reusable water bottle fountains. It's just like home. We talked about this. You can't keep controlling my choices. Remember the bear told me to make womanly choices?"

She shakes her head. "The energy in here is bad, kiddo. Really stuffy. I have some white sage in the car. I'll be right back."

She turns and runs back down the wide stairwell. I try to shove forward, but the box is still stuck. I heave again and try to peer over the edge of the massive box. Fortunately, it's light.

A muffled voice speaks as I push forward once more. "Please, for the love of God, stop shoving that into my back."

I lower the box and lose my grip. It tumbles from my hands and takes a blonde girl to the ground. Her hands are full too. I drop the box and put a hand out. She looks annoyed.

"I'm so sorry," I mutter.

She takes my hand and raises an eyebrow at me. She stands and gives me the up-down. Dropping my hand, she sneers. I haven't seen a sneer in forever. Hers is a decent effort. She disapproves of me for whatever reason. She bends and picks up the things she dropped. She scowls and moves to the side of the hall.

I grab the box and squeeze past her. "Sorry."

She blows her blonde bangs out of her perfect oval face and glares at me with dark blue eyes. Great, a mean girl. Nothing like pissing the mean girls off on the first day. I've seen this movie and am fairly certain I will be hazed savagely.

"Nene, come hold my hand. It's stronger if we both do it." I hear my mom calling me from the bottom of the stairs. I cringe and wonder how bad the hazing is going to get when my new dorm-mates see her? I suspect she's filling the halls with white sage smoke and waving her hands around in circles. I suspect this because I've seen her do it a millions times. I'm not even exaggerating. Well, maybe by a couple thousand.

I walk/run down the hall, struggling with the gigantic box. The numbers fly past me. Finally, I arrive at my room. I drop the box and slide the key in and trip over the box trying to slide it. I fall into the room. A girl with dark hair and a somber look scowls at me from the bed on the left side of the room. She is prim and proper, and I suspect she already hates me—her and the blonde mean girl. Great first day.

I hear people in the hallway with my mom. I don't dare poke my head out and look. She either has them all waving their hands and smudging the air (like in a musical), or she is being laughed at. If it's the latter, she will shake her head and tell them how she just saved them from wicked karma and bad juju. She doesn't care when people laugh at her. I wish I had inherited that from her. Instead my face is flaming red and my stomach is aching.

I lean into the box and sigh. "Shit."

The moody-looking brunette gives me another look and then pulls her headphones over her ears better. She doodles like all angst-ridden people of my generation. Only the truly misunderstood know how to be sullen and doodle, like Bella Swan. In reality, she looks a lot like Blair from Gossip Girl. She is evidently my new roommate.

I blow my hair out of my face and push the box into the room, sliding it along the hardwood floor.

The room smells. It's not the Gossip Girl look alike that stinks. It's an older smell. Something that only happens after floors and walls are lived in for hundreds of years. Beer has been spilt and food has been heated in microwaves, and all of it has left a scent in the walls and floors. Like decay.

"Nene, come on out into the hall. I have a few of the others doing a meditation to clear the air and change the vibrations of the building. We need to create a harmonious space for you all."

I look back at her standing in my doorway. I cringe when I notice how unbuttoned her shirt has become with all the smudging she has been doing. She has mad cleavage everywhere. It's appalling that there are stores called Forever 21 for cougars like her to shop at, but to wear it around twenty-one-year-olds is horrid. I know she didn't mean to wear a tiny button-top t-shirt from that store to my new university. She doesn't ever mean to be sexy. It just doesn't change the fact that she is sexy.

Had I not been near vomiting with nerves when I left our house, I might have noticed our t-shirts matched. God hates me, I am convinced.

We match.

My t-shirt is light blue and hers is lilac. Her jeans are nicer than mine though. So she actually looks better than I do. She is fit for forty, but she is forty. It's not fair.

Blair Waldorf's stuntwoman loses her glare as Willow leaves the room. Yes, I call my mother Willow.

Gossip Girl raises an eyebrow. "Is that your mom?"

I want to say no. My lips form the word but my head nods, dejectedly.

She takes her headphones off and raises both eyebrows. "Damn, dude. I thought I had it bad. My mom's a gyno."

I grimace and like her instantly.

I kick the door closed and stand up.

"She looks like she could go here."

"Yeah." I sit on my bare bed and wonder what kind of perversions have occurred on it before I got here. "She's a vegan. They don't age fairly. All the healthy eating and water and steam baths have pretty much stopped her from aging. In fact, she could be getting younger looking instead of older." My voice is exhausted and hollow.

"She could be your sister. Is she for real leading mediation out there?"

I shake my head and lick my lips. "No clue. Most likely."

She puts her headphones down and looks out the window. I can tell she wants to go see. Everyone wants to see what Willow is doing. She has a way about her. You can't help but like her, love her even. People follow her, stare at her beauty, and enjoy the feeling of her energy. They can't fight it.

"I'm Rayne."

She laughs and nods. "Of course you are."

I glare.

She puts her hands up defensively. "Sorry it's just your name is

Rayne and your mom is leading group meditation. Is she wearing your clothes?"

I laugh with her. "Yeah, we share clothes. This is nothing though. Wait till Halloween. She'll come here and try to party with us. She has no concept of age. She loves clubs."

She laughs and I laugh and we never mention the 'us' I threw in there. I'll admit it was premature, but I like her. Even if she is trying to look like Blair Waldorf. She even has the headband and the lip gloss.

"I'm Mona." She stands up and opens the door a crack. She peeks and shakes her head. "Amazing."

"They're sitting cross legged, aren't they?"

She nods and closes it. "Wanna go get a drink so no one knows that fiasco belongs to this room?" I don't have hurt feelings. As far as parents go, Willow is more than a fiasco. She is crazed when it comes to being away from me or me leaving the house or me having friends she doesn't approve of. But then in the same breath, she is mellow and calm and totally a hippie. Her garden is insane. She actually grows weed, but we aren't allowed to smoke it. It's for medicines.

I stand and pull my phone out. I text Willow and let her know I forgot some crap at the house and went to go buy replacements. I'll stop and buy something on the way back…if she's still here. I'm scared she's going to move in.

Mona sneaks out the door and I follow. She creeps to the left, not the way I came in with the box. Apparently, a fire exit is three doors away from our room. We run down the stairs like we have escaped from prison. When we leave the hall and the fresh air hits me, I feel it.

The freedom. Finally. It's blowing in the air and dusting the control off of me.

I always imagined it would feel amazing and it does. More than amazing. It might be my first spiritual moment…ever.

Well, except when Willow's friends make me channel, but I pretend that never happened. I pretend I can't hear them. I don't talk to the dead anymore. Willow doesn't ask and I don't tell. Even when I don't mean to hear them, and they tell me something crazy, and then it happens. Sometimes they make the air sparkle, but I ignore that too. Willow's weird spiritual blood flows in my veins. As far as possible outcomes are concerned, I will take hearing the dead every now and then. It could be so much worse. I could read palms or pictures or hear live people's thoughts.

Mona is funny and sarcastic. She tells me about her parents' divorce as we cross the greens to College Street. Her stepdad sounds like a real treat. I'm glad I don't have stepparents. I don't even have a dad. Willow says he is a man she would rather not discuss.

The pub we go to is hopping. Back to school means chaos and constant noise. I don't mind it, but I can't focus on one thing. My eyes dart constantly. I've never been exposed to this much chaos in my life.

She natters on, "So anyway, me and my dad moved here a year ago. He gets a good rate for me at the school, and I pretend I don't see him. I'm not in any of his classes. I'm for sure not that smart. Not in languages."

I watch her sip her float. She's so pretty.

"You meet any billionaires in this town yet? Maybe one named Chuck?" I smile.

She frowns and then laughs. "For the record, I looked like this before that show came out."

I point. "No beaver teeth or gap though."

She laughs again. "Yeah, I got braces."

I notice the guys at the pool table smiling our way. "So, you single?"

Her eyes dart at me. She blushes and winks at me. "I am, but I'm not into that. I'm all about boys."

I look back at her sharply. "No-my-God. No. I mean, I get it - yoga teacher-democrat-vegan mom and my name is Rayne. Yes, I could be a classic case, but I'm not a lesbian either. My bestie back home is a lesbian though. Her parents are both republicans and teachers, so you never know. Actually she just moved to Canada and got married." I'm talking too much.

She gives me a look. "That's weird. Anyway, yeah I'm really into angst-ridden boys with poetry and dark hair and internal conflict. Delish. Have you read any of the Bronte Sisters' books? Love the gothic romance heroes like Heathcliff."

I shake my head. "Yeah, not really my kind of books. I'm more a Harry Potter kind of girl or Vampire shows. Anyway, the reason I was asking if you were single was because the guys at the pool table are eyeballing you."

She tilts her head. "Yeah, pretty sure it's you. They can't see me."

I roll my eyes. "Dude, you look like a movie star. I look like I'm one AWOLNATION song away from cutting myself."

She snorts and root beer froths from her glossy lips.

I pass her a napkin and smile. "Sorry. I always crack a joke as someone puts something in his or her mouth. I'm thinking dentistry for my future."

She wipes her face. "For real."

I shake my head and sip my root beer. "No, that was another joke."

"That one wasn't actually funny." She glances back at the guys at the pool table and looks back. "Yikes. Seniors. We need to steer clear of them."

I look at them and frown. "How can you tell?"

"Beer. Real beer. They don't serve minors here."

My phone vibrates. I look down at Willow's message.

'Try to stay in the dorms as much as possible. Don't sleep at other people's dorms, Rayne. Bed Bugs are a real problem in places like this. I love you so much. No sex, no meat, and no boys. Promise. Stay in the dorms, okay? Kisses!!'

Relief fills me and wrestles with the guilt. I shouldn't be so excited she is going home and will miss me from a distance.

I glance over and smile at the dark-haired guy in the group trying to get our attention. His hair almost matches mine. Dark brown, almost black. Willow says I'll go gray before her, because of the dark hair. Her naturally strawberry-blonde hair doesn't have a single gray, at forty.

I probably already have them. Probably because of her.

Pool table senior smiles, and my stomach knots. I can't help but think about what Willow said, 'No boys,' and roll my eyes a little bit.

"Those seniors are trouble, for real. I heard last year about lipstick parties with the freshman girls and pass-around girls."

I frown. Apparently, I've been under a rock for a hundred years. "What's that?"

She leans in and mutters. "If you date them, you have to do stuff for their friends. You know. They pass you around." She presses her tongue into her cheek, and I fight my WTF face.

"Oh my God. Seriously?"

She looks severely serious. "I knew a girl, a freshman last year. Did everything her senior boyfriend asked and then he dumped her anyway. Gross."

"Harsh."

"Way harsh."

He smiles at me, but I furrow my brow in disgust. He looks offended and puts his arms up defensively. I almost laugh, but keep my brain focused on the girl who got dumped. Gross.

"So, where you from anyway?"

"Near here. Just in Plattsburgh. Close enough, anyway. So your dad is a French prof? I'm actually bilingual. I took French immersion. I guess he'll be one of my teachers."

"Next year. He teaches second year linguistics. Sometimes German or Spanish or Russian or French."

"He is my hero. He speaks all of that?" I ask and then glance again at the dark-haired guy showing off for me. He leans in and takes a shot when he sees I'm watching. His butt wiggles slightly. I laugh and feel the heat in my face. He looks back and shoots, but maintains eye contact. I roll my eyes at him and look down into my float.

"Yeah, he's like all about languages and history. Boring. Anyway, you going to the big tent party tomorrow?" she asks. Luckily, she is texting and not paying attention to the fact that I'm flirting with danger.

"Yeah. I think so." I clear my throat and decide to just ask the question that will determine whether we will have a friendship or not. "You pledging any houses?"

She shakes her head and looks up from her phone. "No. Those girls become PTA moms and shit. Parents To Avoid. No, Stepford has never really been my thing."

I can't help but laugh; she looks Stepford. "Me either. I did some studies, and most of the time they end up with lower grades and comprehension levels. I want to work for the United Nations as a linguist. I am competing against nations with better schooling and smarter kids. No TV or texting or Xbox."

She puts her glass in the air and grins from ear to ear. "To the loser nerd girls, who will never be accepted and never be the toss-around girl in a frat."

I clank my glass and try not to notice the boy vying desperately for my attention.

"Wanna go?" She looks around at the pub starting to fill up. She is probably as nervous as I am.

"Yeah, I should go set up. I'm praying Willow brought my crap from the car."

She sighs. "Really? Willow?"

"Yeah, and I'm not allowed to call her Mom."

"Wow, dude, she's probably in a frat house right now."

I laugh. It isn't bitter or angry. "If you knew who you were talking about, you would laugh. She is clueless. Has no idea she's hot. None. She is a complete moron when it comes to guys. She does meditations and eats leafy greens and presses on people's stomachs to help them straighten out their organs' placement inside of them. She doesn't do social graces. She doesn't believe in sex. She gardens."

Her jaw drops. "She looks like that and doesn't have sex?"

I nod, raising my eyebrows. "She follows the six poses from the Fountain of Youth. It's a Buddhist yoga practice. She channels her sexual energy."

"Okay, you're screwing with me." She leans in on her elbows. Her dark-brown eyes sparkle with curiosity and sarcasm.

I shake my head. "Nope."

"You know, it's not like we need to have sex. We could do the poses too. So we don't get urges to... you know. I don't want you getting urges in our room and letting the dark-haired guy at the pool table come over and help you out with them." Her dark eyes glint, and I laugh at her.

"Totally not my type. Mock all you like, but she'll probably live to be a thousand." I shake my head.

She nods. "She looks like she's already off to a good start. You don't seem to be much like her though."

I shake my head and try not to be offended. "I'm not. I don't want to live forever, and besides, urges are normal. Poses are not."

She makes a face. "No urges in the room."

I laugh again. "I don't really think I'll get urges here anyway. I see the guys here and can't help but think that they've already been around the block. Our beds have probably all seen more action than a brothel. Let's be real. I'm not losing my virginity in a dorm room. Gross and cliché." In my excited rant, I failed to notice how pale her face had gotten. Her glint was gone. She was trying to tell me something with her eyes. Feverish heat covered my body, as a deep voice cut into the tense air.

"So, I was going to see if you wanted a drink, but I can see my efforts and my dollars would be wasted. Celibate college girls seem to be big this year."

I don't turn my head. I don't need to. I know the hottie with the dark hair and the sparkly blue eyes is standing next to me. The sexy, deep voice mocking me...of course it would be him.

I look down and press my lips together. He hits me in the arm. "It was a joke."

I look at Mona and shake my head.

She shakes her head and looks at him with a grin. "Not funny."

I look up at him and try not to stare at him. "Not funny."

Mona smiles sweetly and looks just like Blair, plotting something. "We were discussing a movie scene about virgins. It was a line from a movie."

He smirks at her. When he looks back at me, I stare him down. "Yeah, I'm a virgin. I'm not ashamed of it. I'd be more ashamed of myself if I'd done half the things I can imagine you've done."

He leans on the back of my booth and smiles like he's Prince Charming. "Maybe I like girls who aren't ashamed of being innocent. Maybe you've misjudged me. You don't know me."

I feel my brow knit; the bullshit is being laid on thick.

"Innocent?" I laugh. "I'm not a nun. I'm just not a whore. I'm also not some bimbo who's going to be passed around by dirty frat boys. Look at you with your charming schoolboy looks and smooth moves. Please—like I'm going to have a drink with someone who has used his best moves on every other girl in the room. Yummy. Nothing like being last in the line up."

He looks confused. I'm instantly afraid the pass around thing is not true, but I've already gone with it. I've gone too far. His eyes are cold and his schoolboy charms are gone.

"A drink. That's all I was going to ask. You women's lib chicks are hard-core. But hey, I'm all about pride. Enjoy your date, ladies." He backs away making a peace symbol and walks back to the pool table.

I look at Mona. She is blushing and trying to stifle a laugh. "That was amazingly humiliating."

I want to crawl under a rock. "We need to leave. Can we leave now? Like this second?"

She cranes her neck to look over to where he's gone. "He's super hot."

I throw down ten dollars and walk out. I don't look back. The giant carrot shoved in my ass prevents me from turning around to see if he and his friends are laughing at me. Thank God it's a big campus.

Outside, I feel sick. The air is still muggy, and I'm hot and uncomfortable. I've been feeling sick all day. I thought it was my nerves. My day has sucked, so nerves could very well be the answer.

"He was super hot."

I want to cry. I feel the hopelessness crossing my face. "Oh my God, Mona. He was so hot."

"You were so mean. That was awesome."

I shake my head. "No, not awesome. So mean. I don't know what happened. I panicked. He was hot, and I was such a bitch."

She laughs and nods. "Yeah. Pretty much. You're having a rough first day. Between that and your mom, dude."

Day one of college is new and embarrassing, and I haven't even made my bed yet.

Chapter Two

The big tent party isn't as much fun as I thought it would be. It's good clean fun, but not fun, fun. The houses seem too tame and the teachers seem to be everywhere. Everyone is too polite and too nice. I imagined it more as seniors with paddles running after a freshman with a sore ass. Hazing isn't what it used to be. I am grateful.

Three separate groups of girls have offered me sheets, pledges and clubs. I didn't bite on any. Instead I wander and try to get my bearings.

"Rayne? Rayne Phillips?"

I turn to see a girl with long, blonde curly hair and a beautiful face. Her hair is in a side ponytail, with a huge yellow flower in it. She doesn't look like anyone I would hang out with.

"It's me. Michelle. From home. From Plattsburg." She smiles wider.

I shake my head. Home was small. I would have known a Michelle. Especially one who wore side ponytails.

She takes a step closer, and I feel heat creep up my face. Michelle used to be Michael and she/he is so pretty and different suddenly. I can't seem to find the words to say hello.

"You must remember me?" she says, almost afraid. I put my arms out and take her in.

"Oh my God, how are you? I didn't recognize you at all. You look incredible." It's been fourteen months since we graduated, and she has completely changed in that short time.

She pulls back and blushes. She's so pretty. I can't stop staring.

"So you go here?" I ask. She's wearing the campus shirt.

She has boobs. I'm staring. I'm a moron.

"I do and I just got those." She sticks her chest out more, almost in my face.

I blush harder and look up to meet her bright-blue eyes. "Oh my God, I'm so sorry. I'm so sorry. I didn't mean to stare. It's just so different than before. I mean, I always knew, but..."

She puts a long, manicured finger on my lips. "Shhhh. It's okay. I know I look different. I just feel like the right me now. No more small towns and small town people."

I cover my eyes and shake my head. "I'm being such a dick." I pull my hands away and smile. "Let's start over. Hi, Michelle. How are you? What did you do this summer?"

She laughs a girly giggle and points at her chest. "I got my surgery this summer. I took the drugs, but they only grew to an A, so I got them bumped to a C."

I nod. "Okay, never mind. I love them. They're fabulous. Very beautiful."

She hugs me again. Our chests press against each other, and I am excited for her. Weirded out slightly, but happy.

She whispers in my ear, "I'm so excited you're here. I know someone else. Yay."

"I know right. My roomie is awesome, but beyond that, I don't know anyone." Awkwardly, I sputter, "So which hall are you in?"

She points to the other side from mine. "The Living and Learning Center. PRIDE rooms."

"I'm pretty sure I heard that. I'm glad you have somewhere to stay." I feel like an asshole. My verbal diarrhea is just non-stop. "You know, so you can be with your people." My face is on fire. I clamp my mouth with my hands.

Michelle laughs hard. "Oh girl, I missed you. You're always so funny when you get nervous. How's Willow? I'm amazed she let you come here."

"Good." I don't want to let my mouth open for longer than the second it takes to say 'good.' I don't trust my lips.

She links my arm with hers. "Come on. Let's walk. You need to get used to the idea that I have the same parts as you."

I squeeze her arm and notice her muscles are gone. She feels like a soft girl. "It's remarkable. You're a girl."

She looks so proud and smirks. "Yup. I got it ALL done."

I look down. "All?"

She laughs again. "All."

I stop. "But how, if it sticks out—how does it go in?"

She laughs and bends at the waist. "You're crazy. Everyone else is so fake about it. I love you. I've been on the drug therapy for a long time and working toward this. I've had the Adam's apple shaved, and the progesterone, and estrogen, and everything. Then I went six months ago and got them to do the surgery, where they invert everything. It was a process, let me tell you."

"Invert?"

She gives me a wide but pretty smile. "Invert."

"So you have a same…as…me, you know?" The words stumble from my lips.

"Vagina? Yeah. Honey, you are stunned. Have you never heard of this?"

I shake my head, but then a light comes on. "Oh my God, I did. Nip and Tuck. Willow hated the show, because Christian was such a slut. I loved it. Mostly because Christian was so hot."

She laughs. "Oh, he was. God help me, may I never meet a man like that."

I laugh. "Me too. She was right. He was a slut."

"Speaking of slutty hot men, who is that hottie? I guarantee he's trouble. Look at the charm oozing off that man." I look up to see the dark-haired guy leaning against a lamppost, smiling at me. My face instantly flushes.

"Oh my Christ. He's, um, no one." If I say it fast enough, it might be true.

Michelle laughs. "That doesn't look like a no one to me. He wants to say hi to you. I can tell." I look up at her and frown. She winks. "I'm going to go find my people."

My already-red face burns hotter. I am confident my skin is melting off. I squeeze her arm. "I'm so sorry. That was an accident. I'm a moron. I'm really happy you're here. Really. I'm your people. You're my people."

She kisses me on the cheek and laughs. "I know. You're crazy. Say hi to Willow. Come find me in the PRIDE rooms. Slumber parties and shit. Eek." She hugs me again and then saunters off, not nearly as drag queen-ish as I would have imagined. She is a girl. She walks like a girl. More than I do. I've never actually seen her this alive. It's a weird but spectacular moment.

The moment is ruined by the hot dark-haired guy standing in front of me. He looks expectantly at me, with a grin I hate instantly.

I wrap my arms around myself and walk through the couples on the sidewalk. I stop a good distance from him. "Following me is pretty creepy."

He smiles and I have to force myself to focus on not drooling. The dark night does nothing to diminish the dark-blue eyes or sexy smile. He shrugs. "I was just walking when I randomly happened upon you and your friend."

I look over to where she is turning the corner and shake my head. "Random, huh?"

"I meant what I said before."

I smile. "That Women's Lib girls are hardcore, and you're all about PRIDE?"

He laughs and runs a hand through his hair. It's thick and dark and I want to touch it. "No. I meant that I like girls who are proud and not easy." His smile turns dangerous. "I like a challenge."

I take a step back and gulp. "I'm not easy. I'm not easy at all. I'm like expert level hard." Which is totally true. Willow has actively lobbied for the chastity belt.

He takes a step forward. "I'm not an expert." Bullshit. "But I would like to buy you that drink."

I watch his face and nod after a minute. "Okay, fine. One drink."

Why am I saying yes?

He puts a hand out for me. "Wyatt."

"Like Earp?"

He smiles and blushes. "Yeah, like Earp."

I take his huge hand and let it swallow mine. "Rayne." His skin is fiery and sparks slightly against mine.

"Like puddles and rubber boots?"

I laugh and try to pull my hand away, but he doesn't let me. He holds it and pulls me along the sidewalk.

My stomach twinges. "No, like R-A-Y-N-E. My mom's a weirdo, well, a hippie."

He points with his free hand. "You made fun of Wyatt Earp, with a handle like that one?"

I jerk my hand free and watch as he flexes his hand and balls it. "Rayne is nice. It's soft."

He nudges me with his shoulder. "Unless it's a downpour."

I cross my arms. "Whatever."

"You must be a freshman. You pledging?"

I shake my head. "No. It's not for me. Frats are weird. Archaic."

"I'm in a frat." Huge shocker there. "It's been the thing that kept me sane these last four years."

"What's your house GPA?" I mock him with my grin.

"2.89."

I whistle and nod. "Yeah, exactly the reason I won't join. Lower GPA's and less focus on school. I'm good being a loner in a dorm."

We turn down a path I haven't walked on before. I look up at him. "Where are we going?"

He points. "There. My house is that way."

I stop.

He laughs and turns to face me. "I promise, no funny business. We can't drink out in the streets, and you're too young for a bar."

His eyes seem honest. Something about him makes me feel weird. I stop and back up.

"I have to go. I forgot I was meeting my roomie, Mona."

He looks hurt. "You can trust me."

I shake my head. I start to back up on my shaky legs. "I bet you say that to all the girls. Dude, stranger danger. Thanks anyway." I turn and walk away. What was I thinking almost going for a drink with a stranger? One I insulted, no less.

I don't go to my place. Instead I turn to the Living and Learning Center. Gays and Asians and hardcore Goths file around the rooms and halls. It's like being in the city or a multicultural fair.

It reminds me of San Francisco, Willow's favorite city.

I see a blonde head and push past a group of black kids wearing bright colors. They're laughing and speaking Yoruba. I smile with pride at being able to recognize it. I haven't heard many of the languages of Nigeria, but I know this one and Hausa. My dream is to know twenty languages.

"Michelle."

She turns and smiles, but when she sees my face, she stops smiling. She grabs my hand and pulls me into a room. It's hers, for sure. James Dean posters and the entire cast of Twilight are all over the wall. Robert Pattinson makes appearances on a few walls. I can't deny his hotness, but his role in Harry Potter was hotter for me.

She looks at my face and shakes her head. "Your eyes."

I look at her mirror and jump back. "Oh my God, what is that?"

In the mirror my long, dark hair and heart shaped face, which normally stand out, are muted by the bright, glowing color of my eyes. I have gray eyes. They aren't amazing and colorful. They're plain and gray but against the dark hair and my slightly tanned skin, they usually look okay. Now instead, they sparkle like gems are inside. I put my fingers up to my face and touch gingerly. "What is that?"

She shakes her head. "It looks like a flashlight is shining from behind. Like your eyes are the flashlights."

She flicks the light and it's the most remarkable thing I've ever seen. I can see perfectly. Like a cat.

In the mirror, they look normal. They don't glow in the dark. They don't look different or anything, but I can see every aspect of her dark room as if the light were still on. I can tell it's dark because the room is black in my peripheral, but in front of me, the room is almost lit up.

"They look normal without the lights on," she says.

I don't tell her that I can see the weird face she is making.

She flicks on the light and my eyes don't need to adjust. I can see flawlessly.

"It's gone." She sounds stumped.

I look back at the mirror and nod. "Weird."

I smile in the mirror. "That was creepy."

She looks suspicious. "You been drinking?"

I shake my head. "No."

"Drugs?"

I tilt my head. Michelle knows me better than that. We were best friends all through elementary school. She was a he, and he was my best friend until we got older. Then he clammed up and stopped talking. I can't imagine the internal struggle he has endured. I knew he was gay. Everyone knew. I just never knew that he should have been a she. Seeing her the way she is now makes more sense. She always was a she and now that it's official, it makes sense. She is alive for the first time, ever.

I, however, am beat.

I yawn and stretch. I have never been so tired. I yawn a second time and my eyes water. "I'm going to bed. See you tomorrow." I rub my eyes.

She points at her bed. "You look like you're already asleep. Wanna sleep here? You can sleep with me. Like a slumber party."

I think for a second. The walk back to my place feels like a pilgrimage, and I'm exhausted. I nod and kick my shoes off and climb into her bed. She sits beside me and turns the light off. She turns on a movie. I can see it flickering in the dark.

I snuggle into her bed and get comfortable. I like her room better than mine. Her room is new and smells clean. My room still smells old and musty, and my bed stinks.

I don't know if I closed my eyes or if I slept with them open, but my dreams come instantly.

Chapter Three

'You'll be dead again before this day ends.'

It's a chant. I see Willow's lips moving as she chants on the floor in lotus pose. The words are not spoken in her voice, but they come as she moves her lips.

'You were born dead.'

I shake my head and plug both my ears. I'm standing amongst graves, which are in the living room at our house. She chants and mouths the words in a whisper. Even with my ears plugged, I can hear them.

'You were dead already this morning, and you'll be dead again.'

Her green eyes open and lights shoot from them. Her lips move slowly and I can hear exactly what she whispers, *"You're dead, Nene. You're dead. I just forgot to tell you."*

Chills cover me, and I wake. Not with a start or jumping up like I should after a crazy nightmare. I always just open my eyes and look around the room. For a moment it feels like I am being watched, but I'm alone.

The whispers still seem to be there. Chanting. I shiver and climb off the bed. I put on my shoes and stretch. Michelle's room is neat and tidy and new.

In the mirror, my eyes are bright again. I close them and rub. When I open them, my mascara is flaking everywhere. I look like hell, but at least the color's normal again.

The halls are empty when I leave. I still feel like I'm being watched, but no one is there. I can't shake the feeling from my dream. I'll have to text it to Willow. I'm afraid she'll have some 'I told you so' moment and make me come home.

I decide telling her can wait. I texted her yesterday to tell her Michelle was at our school. That made her happy. She seemed relieved. Her texts and constant nagging are getting to be annoying.

The fresh morning air is thick. Late August in Vermont is muggy. It's always muggy. Then mid September hits and it's cold. It's like a switch.

A guy's voice interrupts my thoughts. "Wow, that explains so many things."

I stop and look at him. He nods at the guys he's walking with and comes over to where I am. He grins and crosses his arms smugly.

I frown. "What?"

He nods at the building. "You're making the walk of shame from the lesbian building. I for sure called that, huh?"

I look back and laugh. I hug myself and walk toward him. "Sometimes I wish I were a lesbian. You're stalking me, aren't you?"

He laughs. "Yes. Definitely. If you're gay, I'll have to double my efforts. Try and win you back."

I scowl. "You're an idiot. You can't change gay people. My friend lives in there. I'm not gay. I'm just not into dating the first three days of school either. I know you frat boys have competitions and shit, but don't include me in the sport, okay?"

He looks angry again, but the look I saw on his face the night before isn't there. "You're really sort of rude. You know that? Not all frat boys are the same." He shakes his head and walks away. He looks back and scowls. "My GPA is 3.89."

He's gone down a path, and I feel stupid. He always makes me feel stupid.

When I get back to our room, Mona gives me her best death glare. "I looked everywhere. I was worried sick."

"I slept at the Living and Learning Center," I mutter.

She raises an eyebrow.

I shake my head. "My friend lives there."

"Well, next time text me."

I shrug. "Okay. How was the night?"

She looks me over and grins. "Not as good as yours. You're making the walk of shame. PRIDE rooms or not, it counts."

I scoff. "Mine sucked. Pretty sure I've offended that Wyatt guy brutally and spent the night sleeping in a girl's bed. Minus the girl when I woke. I'm not even sure she slept there last night. I suspect she might have had a good night."

"Is she gay?" she asks.

I shake my head. I don't know how to explain without sharing her secret, if it's a secret. "Complicated."

Mona laughs. "Not a college girl?" She sits on her bed and looks at my eyes. "Your eyes look different."

I yawn. "I'm super sleepy. I think I'm gonna crash again."

She gets up and walks to the door. "I'm going for the pancake breakfast. Want a plate of food?"

I nod and lie down on my bed. I kick my shoes off and pull my jeans off. I curl into my blankets and snuggle in.

My phone starts vibrating just as my eyes get heavy enough that I can't open them. I drift off and ignore it.

When I wake, it's dark. I've slept through the entire day. I sit up and look around. The room is dark, but I can see clearly again. I'm going to have to have an eye test. A plate of cold pancakes sits next to me on my bedside table. Mona is gone. I push my phone, but the screen stays black.

"Crap." I plug it in and lie there. A knock at the door startles my thoughts. I climb off the bed and open the door.

Michelle is dressed to the nines and giving me a worried look. "You sick?"

I shake my head. "I don't think."

She taps her heel on the floor. "Then get the eff up and come party. It's the second to last Saturday before classes start. Oh, and Willow sent me a text. She got the number from my sister. She wanted to know why you're ignoring her and if she should come and see you."

I roll my eyes. "My phone is dead. Jesus."

Michelle gives me a serious look. "Well, I told her you were sleeping a lot. She said that was good. She's weird, dude."

I nod and open the door all the way. When she comes in and sees me in my panties, she laughs. "Nice. Who buys your underwear?"

I look down at my beige underwear and scowl. "What?"

"Beige granny panties. Really?"

I tug at my t-shirt and climb back into my bed. I rub my eyes. She turns a light on and looks at me funny.

"Your eyes are doing it again." She points.

I nod. "I know. I think I must have like glaucoma or something."

She rolls her eyes. "Please. It's probably your ghost-hunter ancestry going nuts in this spooky ass old dorm. With a mom like Willow, you're doomed."

I snort. "Ghost hunters. Please. Charlatan's maybe. Where did you sleep last night?"

She smiles softly, like she is remembering something. "With Benny."

I raise an eyebrow. "Benny?"

She nods. "He's so awesome. He's a senior and he's a bio major."

"Smart, huh?" I ask.

"Going to be a doctor."

I laugh. "I can totally see you as a surgeon's wife. Little Miss Suzie Homemaker."

She bats her eyelashes. "I know, right? He's sweet. And he's cool with my history."

I flinch. "You told him?"

"Of course."

I feel confused. "Isn't the whole point to being a girl, not telling people you used to be a boy?"

She nods. "Duh, but I'm not going to lie. What if it gets serious and I have to tell him, and then he breaks up with me because of it, and I end up with a broken heart? It's not like I can have babies. Plus, I take more shots than a crack addict. No. Telling the truth is better. Besides, he likes it. He's always been sort of bi-curious."

I shrug. "Okay, good call. Just seems weird to have a conversation like that on the first night."

She laughs. "We've been dating for two months."

I am totally confused. "How did you meet?"

"Group therapy."

I feel confused. "For what? Does he want to be a girl, and then you'll both be hetero-lesbians?"

She crosses her thin arms and frowns. "None of your business...smart-ass nosy parker. Anyway, everyone is going to some club tonight. Wanna come? Or we could just stay in and continue to make fun of minorities and alternative lifestyles?"

I shake my head. "You're a dick. I wasn't making fun."

"You coming out with me or what?" I have totally inappropriate 'coming out' jokes, but now I'm scared she won't think they're funny.

Instead, I look at what she's wearing and dread the effort it would take to get me to that standard. I know it's going to be too much. Like surgery for me, too.

I shake my head. "No I'm beat. I haven't been this tired, ever. I think I got mono from thinking about kissing that frat boy."

She rolls her eyes and walks to my closet. She moans when she opens it. She looks back. "Do you own normal girl clothes?"

I frown. "Yeah."

She shakes her head and mutters to herself whilst filing through my clothes. "No, you don't."

She grabs a khaki skirt and a white tank top. "Ugh. Put this on. It'll have to do." She grabs some flip-flops from my closet and throws them at me.

The door opens and Mona walks in. "Hey."

I smile. "Hey. Michelle, this is Mona, my roomie. Mona, this is Michelle. She's from my hometown. One of my best friends."

Mona stops and smiles. "Oh my God. Congratulations."

Michelle looks at me, confused.

I shake my head. "No, not this friend."

Michelle puts her hands on her hips. "What?"

I give Michelle a flat look. "She thinks you're Trudy."

Michelle crosses her arms. "I look like a lesbian? In this?"

Mona looks at me for support, but I laugh. Michelle is wearing a pink halter with a silver mini skirt and huge shoes that look like they belong on a Bratz doll. She actually looks like a Bratz doll. Her long blonde hair is shiny and smooth.

"No?" Mona looks at me again. I laugh harder.

Michelle slaps her arm. "I'm totally kidding. Anyway ladies, let's get some cute clothes on and bust a move. We're going out. You coming?"

Mona nods. "Sure."

Michelle walks to Mona's closet and grabs a purple shirt and a black skirt. "You have seriously cute clothes."

I scowl. "Nice."

Mona grins. "Thanks. Where are we going?"

Michelle shrugs. "Not sure. Some club."

I pull on the tank and slide the skirt on. I look like I should have a bathing suit under my clothes and be wearing a straw hat. I look over at them and frown. "I can't go with you guys."

Mona is 'smoking.' She looks more like Blair than ever. Her dark hair is shiny and around her shoulders in soft waves. Her lips are glossy and plump. Her eyes shine and her skin is pale and flawless. She and Michelle could be models. Both are crazy tall in their huge shoes. I feel like a hobbit next to them in my flip-flops.

They both look at my clothes and grimace.

Mona shakes her head. "Yeah, you look really casual."

"I've never been to a club." I say it like it's an excuse.

Michelle raises an eyebrow. "Neither have I, but I still have clothes that would suit the occasion. Your closet looks like it belongs to a nine-year-old."

"I shop at trendy places," I defend myself.

Michelle points at me. "You shop at trendy places, and somehow, come out with the plain shit that no one else wants. Those knit t-shirts you wear are pajamas tops. Don't even start with me." She's exasperated.

I look at Mona, but she puts her hands in the air. "I'm not getting involved." She turns and faces her closet. When she turns back around, she is holding something dark blue.

Michelle squeals, "Yes. Oh my God—that would be perfect."

Sometimes I miss my mom. This is one of those moments.

I pull off my clothes and look at the blue thing. I don't really know how to put it on. I try pulling it on, but it's got shorts instead of a skirt.

Michelle snatches it and holds it in front of me to step into. She pulls it up my body, launching my granny panties into my ass.

"Oh my God." I squirm away and pull it out of my butt.

Mona laughs. "It's a romper. Don't frown like that. It's pretty. You look pretty."

Michelle brushes my hair and Mona attacks with the makeup. I try to protest, but they move fast and talk over me.

I turn and look at myself. I look different. It's not bad different or good different. It's just different, and I'm instantly uncomfortable. I hug my arms around myself.

Michelle pulls my arms to my sides. "No fidgeting. Haven't you seen Pretty Woman? It makes you look taller when you don't fidget."

Whatever a romper is, it's uncomfortable. It's giving me constant a wedgie, and I feel like it's going to fall off my boobs at any second. It's a strapless one piece with shorts instead of a skirt. The shorts are short and the top is low cut. I feel naked and reach for a sweater, but Michelle swats my hand. "No. No. Ewww."

Mona hands me a pair of heels.

"Delicious choice. Navy, sling-back kitten heels look amazing, and she shouldn't fall in that low of a heel."

They examine me and I shake my head. "This is a bad idea." I don't wobble in the heels, because contrary to popular belief, I can walk in them. I practiced a lot in Willow's one pair.

Michelle grabs my hand and drags me from the room. Mona follows us and I instantly want to turn back.

My stomach has the uneasy feeling from the night before, and I'm exhausted.

Chapter Four

Clubs suck.

This is a discovery I made while being groped twice on the dance floor and shoved as I tried to wind my way through the crowds. I fell into another girl and someone spilled a drink on my foot. My shoe was sloshing with booze on the way to the bathroom.

Now sitting on the toilet cleaning my shoe and foot, I lean my head against the wall. I want to go home. The light in the bathroom flickers.

I have a funny feeling in my stomach. It's the one from the other night, when Wyatt scared me.

I swallow and put my shoe back on. My toes stick to the inside, but at least it isn't wet anymore.

I reach for the handle on the door, but have a terrible feeling I shouldn't open it. I hesitate and watch my fingers tremble.

My mother's words float into my mind, 'your stomach has magic, Nene. When it tells you someone isn't good, you run. I don't care where you are or who you're with. You run and you don't stop until the magic stops.'

I feel a shiver come over me. I step up onto the toilet and crouch down. My shoe almost slips off the seat, but I manage to hold myself still.

I hold my breath and wait. The air grows cold. I expect to see my breath, but I don't. Instead, I hear girls laughing and stumbling into the bathroom.

One of them laughs and says, "Oh my God, he's such a loser. I can't believe she is hooking up with him."

I feel like it's the only chance I'll have to leave the bathroom. I open the door and run from the stall. I wash my hands quickly. I never take my eyes off the other girls. They primp in the mirror and give me weird looks.

I run from the bathroom and get lost in the crowd again. Suddenly the club doesn't feel so bad. Something in the air makes me happy. The music feels like it's getting under my skin and creating energy.

The lights are flashing and pulsing to the music. It's bright for me, even though I know it's dark. My eyes are doing the weird thing again. The eerie feeling from the bathroom lessens, but my nerves are getting the best of me. I miss Willow and the quiet of our house. Maybe school was a bad choice. Maybe I should withdraw and go home.

I shake my head at myself. Maybe I should stop being such a pansy. Classes haven't even started yet.

A voice speaks softly into my ear, "You want that drink now?" A hand grabs me and spins me. I turn and face Wyatt, and for a moment I'm so glad to see him. I let him pull me into him. He's been drinking, I think. He's too affectionate. Too grabby.

I put my hands on his chest and try not to notice the way his hands feel on my bare back. Jolts of energy or sparks hit my skin where he touches. He bends down and kisses me softly. It's unexpected, but it feels right. His lips meet mine with gentle sweetness. He presses me against him. I feel the softness of me melting into his hard body. Our lips make sparks on my mouth. I let him devour me.

His tongue parts my lips and I push him back. He pulls me with him and I feel my feet lift off the ground. I shake my head. "No, stop." I am breathless. I can taste his drink on my lips when I lick them. He grins at me, cocky and confident.

"I like you," he says plainly.

I look at him and feel like my world is about to explode. "You don't know me."

He nods. "I know, but it feels like I do. It feels like we've met before. Like our souls know each other."

I want to roll my eyes and mock him, but he has described how I feel exactly. I'm trembling. "You probably say that to all the girls," I say. My voice doesn't sound like I'm convinced.

I bite my lip and feel lost in his eyes.

"Your eyes look weird," he whispers, mesmerized by them. He is really drunk. He slurs his words, "I like them."

I shake my head and look away. "Something is wrong with them. They keep glowing."

He smirks. "Like a cat."

I feel sick. My stomach clenches, and I double over. He looks worried. "You okay?"

I feel myself heave. He lifts me up and carries me. I don't know where we are going, but I feel my feet hitting people and my shoes sliding off. The pain is everywhere all at once.

The air hits when we get outside. He puts me down, and I throw up everywhere. It splashes on my feet and my bare legs. People in the line-up to the bar groan, "Get her outta here."

His arms are behind me, pushing me along. My stomach is clenching again.

"Come on." Heat rips through me again, and I throw up a second time.

I feel his arms circle around me. I hobble along.

"What did you drink?" he asks.

"Water."

He looks at my face. "Did you put your drink down?"

I shake my head and feel my eyes starting to flutter.

"Fuck, I think you have the flu or something." He picks me up. Just as he lifts me, everything goes black.

I wake to the sound of water. I look around me, but there is no one.

My head is pounding, and my mouth is dry. I try to sit up, but I'm weak. The room spins and in the movement, I see something. A man is sitting in a chair watching me. It's not Wyatt, and no matter how hard I try to stay awake and focus, I can't. He watches me in silence. Like he is debating something.

I wake the second time in a puddle of sweat. Something is on me, weighing me down. I struggle to get it off. When I move, it moves with me and ends up covering me more. Then it moans and I almost leap from the bed.

"Rayne?" Wyatt mutters into my back. I remain frozen and try to gather my wits. My brain struggles to remember the last things I'd done. My blue shorts-wedgie outfit is on the floor beside me. Wide-eyed, I lift the covers expecting to see my naked body. I have a bandeau and my granny underwear on. I wince.

"Rayne, you awake?"

I turn over to see him. He looks horrified. "How are you feeling?"

I frown. "Fine, why?"

He laughs. "Your makeup is all the way to your cheekbones."

I catch a glimpse of his boxers and avert my eyes. "How long have I been here?" I'm glad he never slept in the sheets with me.

He stretches. "Two days. You slept mostly. You had a high fever and threw up a lot. I think you had the flu."

"You never thought that maybe you should take me to a doctor?"

He shakes his head. "No, your friends came and said for sure you were just sick. They said you'd been coming down with it for a few

42

days. I phoned the nurse hotline. They said sleep and fluids. Apparently it's going around campus."

I move my head and notice I feel better. Amazingly better. "I'm starving."

He leans in and kisses my shoulder. "Good. Me too. I have hardly eaten. Luckily, I keep rations in here."

I'm not comfortable with the shoulder kiss.

"You stayed the whole time?" I ask.

He looks wounded. "Of course. I wouldn't have left you alone in here." He grins and his face looks cocky. "Not wearing what you're wearing."

My eyes narrow. He laughs.

"Who was the man watching me from the armchair?" I feel a chill when I see the chair and recall him.

"What man?"

I point to the chair across the huge room. "The man who was in that chair. It was dark and he was sitting there. He had his legs crossed and he looked annoyed. Older with a sweater on."

He shakes his head. "There was no man. No one has come here except Mona and Michelle. You must have been dreaming."

I let it go, but I know I wasn't dreaming. The man was real. He was creepy. His eyes looked like mine. They were gray and I swear a light came out of them.

He pulls me into him and kisses my neck. I feel frozen and not caught up in the instant relationship we seem to have. The sparks start where he touches me. My stomach hurts. I pull away and wrap myself tighter in the blankets.

"You okay?"

I look back at him and shake my head. "No. I know I owe you for taking care of me, but I don't want to owe that. This. Whatever this is."

He frowns. "You're kind of a bitch, you know that? I'm being nice and trying to help and you act like I've got a hidden agenda. I'm not doing it to get into your granny panties." He smirks again.

I cover my face. "Oh my God. I need to go home. I need to borrow some clothes."

He hugs me and kisses the top of my head. "You smell. You should shower first."

I shake my head. "I'm not showering here. This is a den of sin. I can sense the virgins who have come here only to have their innocence stolen. I don't even want to think about this bed and the things you've done in here. You guys probably have Wiserhood meetings in here."

He laughs. "You're weird."

I laugh. "You're weird. And in a frat. Which means you're slutty, probably."

He nods toward the bathroom. "And she's bitchy again. Take that shower." He leans in. "You smell. It's almost vomit, mixed with something like honey or beeswax candles maybe. Your breath is bad. Use my toothbrush."

I look horrified. "What? Eww. No. Dude. Never share toothbrushes. You can get plaque bacteria from other people and mess up the Ph in your mouth."

"Kissing can do it, too."

I blush. I remember the kiss. I remember him holding me and his lips pressed against mine. I remember his hands on my bare skin and his tongue in my mouth. I remember liking it. All of it.

He pushes my hair back from my eyes. "I have a shower in my room. It's the suite. Only the seniors get it. Go jump in, and I'll put some clothes in the bathroom."

I nod at the wall and point. "Turn around."

He laughs. "I saw all there was to see when I was taking the vomit-covered clothes off of you."

"I wasn't aware of it then. Now I am. Turn around."

"You always wear granny panties?" he asks.

I snarl. "Yes. Turn around."

He turns around. "You need to go underwear shopping. I can come if you need help choosing."

I slap my hand against my face and cringe. "You're an asshole, and I don't want new underwear. Mine is organic unbleached cotton. It's good for my body."

I creep from the bed and run into the bathroom, closing the door. I look at myself in the mirror and almost scream. My hair is sticking up all over. Makeup is all over my face. A fake eyelash is stuck to the side of my face. I never even knew that I was wearing them. My fingers shake as I pull the other one from my other eye.

I turn on the shower and peel my clothes off. The hot water feels amazing. I can't help but be pissed at my friends. Mona is new, so she is kind of off the hook, but Michelle has been my friend since we were five. How could she leave me here? They should have made him bring me home.

He has no conditioner so I wash my hair twice with his Axe shampoo and body wash. I smell like a dude and will have to condition my hair at some point. I climb out and grab a towel. I smell it to be sure. It's got the Bounce freshness my friends' houses always had. Not like my house, where the laundry always smells like tea tree oil. I towel off and pull on the huge black shirt and boxers he has left me on the counter. I ball my underwear and bandeau up in my hand and hang the towel up. His bathroom is nice. It's pretty clean for a twenty-one year-old guy. I scrub his toothbrush with antibacterial soap and brush my teeth. It feels amazing to be clean and have fresh breath.

I leave the bathroom, nervous. Nervous of being alone and clean. I make a silent pact that I will not lose my virginity in his dirty frat bed. No matter what. Not matter how I seem to feel about him.

He is still in his boxers on the bed. I notice for the first time he has tattoos. A black band around his left bicep and a blade coming up the underside of his right arm. His chest has a tribal-looking thing in a circle. It's big and black, with something red in the middle. It looks like there is writing on the other side of the chest tat, but I can't see it because he's lying on his side.

He smirks. "You look better."

I shake my head. "That was gross. I never wear makeup, so I had a tough time getting it all off. Axe is apparently not makeup remover."

I look at the door and the bed, and my romper on the floor. I pick it up and roll it into the ball of clothes I'm holding.

"Well thanks, and I guess I'll see you around," I mutter.

He smirks. "You don't want to climb back in here and repay me? I mean, you owe me, right?" He smiles like the wolf would to the bunny.

I laugh and shake my head. I pick up my one shoe and look around for the other. I hold it up. "I have to get going. Where is the other one?"

He makes a face. "You lost it on the way out of the bar."

I grimace. "Shit. Not my shoe. Mona's gonna have a fit." I walk to the door barefoot and smile back. "Thanks again."

He looks pissed. "Stay."

I shake my head. He scares me. His intensity scares me. The way I like him scares me. I don't know him. "No. I can't. I have to go. I haven't called my mom in a while. She's going to freak. I need to get ready. Classes start soon, so... see ya 'round. Thanks for everything. I owe you dinner or something. Something friendly."

I open the door and make the walk of shame. It's almost the run of shame. I know I look like the biggest slut ever. One shoe, a ball of vomit covered clothing, and leaving a frat house in an oversized black t-shirt and men's underwear. The guys in his house smirk, smile, grin, and make every face imaginable. I get a couple whistles and a few catcalls. I ignore them.

Thankfully his house and my building aren't too far apart. I keep my gaze ahead and try to piece together my missing two days.

If my mom smudging my building didn't almost kill me, walking the hallway was going to. Everyone smirks and nods. The blonde with the mean-girl glare laughs and gives me a thumbs up.

I almost fall into the room. I slam the door, press my back into the closed door, and wait for it.

Mona smiles. "Hey you. How are you feeling?"

I frown, not what I was expecting. "I lost one of your shoes."

She points to the closet. "I got it back at the bar. They had it in the lost and found."

I toss my dirty clothes into a pile on the floor and look at her. "You left me at his place?"

She bites her lip and smiles. "He's so sweet and nice, and I think he's really into you. When I got there, he was putting cold cloths on your forehead, and you were smiling at him and passing out. You were really sick."

I flop onto my bed. "Yeah, I should have seen a doctor. I wouldn't have left you with some random dude."

She looks confused. "He's not some random dude. I saw you making out with him, and I know you were sober. Michelle said you guys kinda had a thing going on."

I cover my face with my hands. "School hasn't even started yet. For Christ's sake. I shouldn't be this into a guy—the first guy that looks at me. Ahhh. I'm becoming one of those girls. You know. The girls who lose their virginity in a frat bed."

She laughs. "Eww, you were sick. You didn't? Not while you were sick?"

I shake my head, with my hands still covering my face. "No, I didn't, but, oh my God...I wanted to. What is wrong with me? He was laying there with boxers and tattoos and I thought dirty thoughts. Lots of them."

I lift a hand and look at the shit-eating grin crossing her lips. "You need to do some poses, Mrs. I-Don't-Get-Urges."

I laugh and rub my eyes.

She laughs it off. "That is normal for a girl like you. You're sheltered and now, for the first time ever, you're partying and making out with boys."

I shake my head. "Eww. No. I don't want to have this talk."

My phone vibrates and she scowls. "Dude, that thing has been making ungodly noises all effing weekend."

I pick it up and see the hundred texts from my mom.

Yikes.

'Nene, call me'

'Nene, where r u?'

'Okay, I'm getting worried now'

'Look kid, you call or I'm coming there'

'Fine, be there at lunch'

'Is your phone dead?'

'Fine, be that way. Be the irresponsible kid who breaks her mother's heart when she goes off to college'

'Dammit, Nene'

'I had a bad dream about you last night. There was a man watching you sleep in an armchair, and he was evil'

WTF! How could she have had the same dream as me? That's never happened before.

'I think it means you are feeling sad about a boy'

'Nene'

I stop reading and dial home on the phone with shaking fingers.

Mona snaps me out of my panic attack. "You okay?"

I glance at Mona and nod.

Willow doesn't answer the phone like she normally would. Instead, she screams so loud Mona can hear her.

I hold the phone away from my face as she blasts me, "What the hell is your problem? How can you leave for college and not send me a message or a phone call for four days? I've been worried sick."

I sigh. "Hi, Willow."

"Hi, Willow. Hi, Willow. Are you kidding me?" She is pissed.

I go on the defensive immediately. "Mom, stop. I was sick. I got the flu. I've been asleep for two days."

She snaps louder. "Don't mom me, Rayne Willow Whynde Phillips. I was worried. Who is the boy?"

I sigh into the phone. "His name is Wyatt. He's nice. He helped when I was sick."

She sighs back. "Okay, well you better be sure he's nice, and you better not be doing anything you shouldn't be doing."

I rub my temples and plot how to tell her about my night. "Mom, I'm nineteen-years-old. I can do things that I want to do. I can choose for myself. I didn't do anything. I was sick."

"Rayne, please stop calling me Mom. You know how I feel about labels. I'm sorry I called you 'kid.' Did you sleep in your room every night? No meat or sex, right? You know it'll age you and waste your chi."

I pinch the bridge of my nose and count backwards. "I was sick, Willow, and my phone was dead. I slept in my room." I glance at Mona, who stifles a laugh.

"What did you have for dinner? Did it have active plant enzymes or bacteria?" She starts her harping.

I nod and lie. "Yeah, it did. Vegan menu, remember?"

She sighs. "I love you and miss you. I just think maybe this was too soon for school. Most studies show the most successful career choices are made when a person is in their thirties."

I shake my head. I'm done. "I love you and I will call next weekend, okay?"

"A whole week?" She sounds like she's getting pissed again.

I can't do this. "Four days, Willow, not a week. It's Monday. I will call Saturday."

"Fine. I'll send a care package."

I know it's pointless to argue. "Okay. I'd like that."

"Want the carob bark?" she asks sweetly.

I nod rapidly, as if she can see me. "Yes. Yes please. Love you."

"Love you, too."

I put the phone down, and Mona bursts into laughter. "She is so awesome. I want to be friends with her. She is intense."

I give her my best eff off look and lie back down. "You wouldn't make it through the colonics."

Chapter Five

I'm not avoiding him as much as I am avoiding myself. I grip my books tight the first time I see him. I think he's watching me, but I can't be sure. He is talking to someone, and I see his eyes dart my way. I bow my head and almost break into a run.

"Rayne, wait up." He says goodbye to the guy he's talking to and then runs to where I am. He looks sexy. He has a dress shirt on and the sleeves are rolled up. Some of his tattoos stick out through the bottoms of the sleeves. His forearms are big. He's very muscled for someone as tall and lean as he is. I blush, remembering the way he looked all messy and in his boxers. I want to touch his tattoos.

His dark hair and blue eyes suit the pale-blue dress shirt and dark jeans. I bet he smells good.

"Hey." I mutter it and pick up the pace. I just want to pretend I barely know him... that I've not made out with him or slept in his bed. In my granny panties, no less.

"Where have you been?" he asks.

I don't say the Living and Learning Center or anywhere I think you won't go, which is what I'm thinking. Instead, I shrug nonchalantly. "Around."

He looks confused. "I tried calling you a few times."

I never gave him my number. "What?"

51

He nods and looks around. "Yeah, I got your number from Michelle. You never answered."

I swallow hard. "I never saw the calls." I'm lying. I don't know why. Just like I don't know why I never answered his calls. I didn't know it was him, but the calls made the magic in my tummy hurt. Something about him makes me feel unclean. I can feel it now.

"Want to have dinner tonight?"

I shake my head. My stomach starts to feel uneasy. "I can't. I have a night class." I don't really. I have a study group. It's our first night.

"Night class. Which one?" He is annoying me.

I shake my head. "Study group."

"So, not a class?" he asks.

I shake my head again. He makes me nervous or I make myself nervous when he's around.

He puts his hands on my arms and pulls me into him. "Hey, are you mad at me? You know I was joking, right? You don't owe me anything. Especially not what I was joking about. I mean, unless you want to owe me. In which case you can start repaying me anytime."

I scowl. "Ewww. No, I have to go. I have stuff to do."

His grin is boyish again. "I'm kidding. You're so tense. Really, you aren't mad at me, right?"

I can't be. His boyish charm and cocky smile have me beaten down. My arms spark from his touch. It almost burns. My belly starts to feel funny. I'm starving.

I shake my head. "No."

"It's been two weeks and I've gone to your dorm, phoned you. Why are you avoiding me?" he asks softly.

I shake my head and notice the tension in his fingers on my arm. "I'm not. I swear. I've just been busy and trying to figure out classes and stuff."

His eyes burn when he looks at me. I gulp.

He bends his face and kisses my cheek. "Let me walk you to your next class."

I feel heat everywhere. "I have to go home. My classes are over till later. Till study group. I need to get ready for study group." I am a moron and a bad liar.

He puts an arm around me and leads. I feel my legs walk with him.

He grins. "Let me take you to an early dinner."

He swallows my hand in his and pulls me along the grass. If I'm not careful, I think he will swallow all of me up.

His car is nice. Nicer than I thought it would be. I never thought that he would be rich, but when I see his car I know he is. It's a sleek-looking white-silver Lexus. I don't know anything about cars, but I know this one is expensive. It has three mufflers in a triangle and says LFA on the back. The interior is blood red and black. It looks futuristic. I want to touch everything, but instead I watch him.

He drives sporadically. Fast and then slow. Jerky and then calm. It's like he's trying to hide his true speedy self from me. He talks about his frat brothers and how the freshmen were a great selection this year. I don't pay attention. I watch him. Him and the conflict he is trying to hide.

The restaurant is a pasta house.

He smiles at me from across the table. I don't know what he's grinning at.

"What?" I ask.

He shakes his head. "You seem weird. You sure you're not pissed at me?"

I shrug. "Yeah. I'm just, you know. Embarrassed. I don't know what happened those two days. I woke up in your bed smelling like barf and sweat, and I'm embarrassed."

He leans across the table and his sweet boyish smile makes my stomach ache. "I swear I never touched you and all you did was sleep. In and out of sleep. Your friends came and got water down your throat a couple times and then you would sleep. Once you ate broth that Michelle made. You don't remember?"

I shake my head and drag my finger up and down the condensation on the glass of cold water in front of me.

"You're safe with me. You were then, and you are now. So, can we move past it?" I realize his thumb is massaging my palm. Our hands are stretched across the table. I don't remember letting him touch me. The heat and sparks are making me feel funny. I'm starving and my stomach is hurting again.

I pull my hands away and sit up properly. "I'm not going to have sex with you."

He laughs. "I know that. I never asked if you wanted sex. I just want you to give me a chance."

I cock an eyebrow. "You asked if I wanted to repay you."

"I never said sex. Maybe I meant helping with my essays or cleaning my room. Besides, you're not really my type."

"Why dinner and phone calls and taking care of me if you don't like me? Seems like a lot of effort for a girl you don't like?" I'm being a bitch again. I try to offer a smile at his incredulous look. I know he can't believe I'm so rude. I can't either. Something about him creates conflict.

He shrugs it off and shakes his head. "You're under my skin. Every minute of hanging with you so far, is locked away and tormenting me slowly. It replays constantly. You in my boxers or dancing or walking down the path."

I blush. "Sounds painful." Sounds like you're stalking me.

He taps the table. "It is painful." He looks pained.

The server places our bruschetta appetizer down on the table. She licks her lips when she looks at him. "Hey, Wyatt." She seems nervous.

"Hey." He looks up for a second but then back at me.

I smirk. "Thanks." But she leaves and ignores me.

"You know her?" The question is really, 'Did you sleep with her,' but I'm trying to be more polite.

He shrugs again. "She graduated last year. We hung out a couple times. She's kind of strange. She dated a friend."

I change the subject. "I love that our economy is so great that she finished her undergrad and is still a server."

He laughed. "I think it's a pretty common theme. You should try some of this. It's good."

He puts a piece on a plate and passes it to me.

I have never eaten it before. Willow doesn't do wheat. Ever. I lift it to my lips and take a bite. I moan before I can catch myself. "Oh my God," I mutter, trying not to spit food at him.

He nods and takes his bite. Watching him eat is better than I imagined it would be. His blue eyes sparkle and his jaw flexes. "You like me. I know you do."

I laugh. "You're too cocky for your own good."

"I'm just cocky enough. You want another?"

I wipe my mouth. "No, thanks. I don't do much wheat. My stomach can't handle it."

He gives me his charming smile. "I wouldn't have brought you to a pasta house if I'd known that."

I brush it off. "No worries. I'll just have a protein shake with enzymes later."

He laughs. "You're weird."

I narrow my eyes. "You've said that already."

The waitress comes back to take the plates. "So how's senior year?"

He shrugs. "Good. Can't complain. The house got great pledges and we have a full house. A lot of the freshmen never went Greek, so we got lucky."

She ignores me completely. I feel uneasy around her. She glances at me when he looks down at his phone. He picks it up and stands. "Sorry, I have to take this." He leaves the table and walks to the back of the restaurant. She watches him leave and whispers, "Run."

I frown. "Sorry?"

She looks at me and her eyes are fiery red. "Run."

I get up from the table and back away. "What is wrong with your eyes?"

Her voice gets creepy. "It's not me you need to worry about. You were dead when you were born, Rayne, and when he knows it, you'll be dead again."

The words are from my dream. I back away from her. "How did you know that was in my dream? How do you know my name?" I almost stumble. Fortunately, no one else is in the restaurant.

She gives me a frightening look. "When they know what you are, they will come for you. You were dead when you were born."

I turn and run and don't stop. Not even when I reach the campus. I'm in better shape than I thought I would be. I'm winded, huffing and puffing, but I'm still alive. I didn't know I could run farther than a block. I push it up the stairs. My hand shakes when I finally get the key in the lock. I throw open the door and let out a huge gasp as I close it.

Mona looks confused. "What are you doing?"

I shake my head and try to catch my breath. I huff and puff a few times and then nod. "Running. For sport. You know, exercise."

She doesn't look convinced. "Well, Wyatt called like two minutes ago looking for you. He said you ran out on him. You left your phone in here again. Willow called too. I told her that you were at class. Why did you run away from Wyatt?"

I shake my head and wave my hand at her. "No." I struggle to get my breath. "No. I just ran off the meal. Big, carby, pasta lunch. Too many carbs."

She crosses her legs, and I can see her underwear. I turn my head away. "Dude, skirt." I almost need to take a knee, I'm breathing so hard.

She looks down and straightens her legs and skirt. "He said you acted funny. Some waitress he knew scared you off."

I frown and can't believe it's taking me so long to get my wind back. Maybe I'm not in good shape. "You guys had quite the grand old chat."

She laughs. "Well, I told him it was weird that he took you to a restaurant at three in the afternoon. He's kinda weird. Who eats lunch this late?"

I shake my head. "I don't know how to feel about him. I'm conflicted. I think I like him, but I feel weird about him. You're right. He's kinda strange."

I shake my head and walk to my bed. I sit and look at her. I want to tell her about my encounter with the waitress, but I know she's going to call me a weirdo. She will mock me, and I won't actually feel better or accomplish anything by it. The red eyes and the dreams are messing with me. I don't believe it, and I was there.

"What are you doing?" I try changing the subject.

She sighs. "Going through photos from the other night. We took a ton." She hands me her phone and smiles. "Look at this one."

I take the phone from her. I can't help but smile, seeing the three of us dressed to the nines and looking fabulous. Michelle looks the prettiest. She really has blossomed since we moved away from our old hometown. I took the first year off after high school to work. She did it to cocoon and become the beautiful butterfly she is now.

"Michelle is so gorgeous. I wish I had her legs. She's so thin and yet meaty. You know?" she asks.

I nod. "She is stunning. She's lucky. Good genes."

I hand the phone back. "She probably has an amazing metabolism."

The flux in her tone gives it away. "She told you?"

Mona laughs. "She did."

I shake my head. "She keeps telling everyone. She's crazy. I would lie."

Mona shrugs. "I guessed."

I give her a curious look. "How? She looks impeccable. I didn't even recognize her. Not even a little."

She looks down. "Too perfect. She has no flaws. No fat in weird spots or a muffin top. She eats like a pig. Typical guy metabolism. Plus, the Adams apple isn't all shaved away."

I laugh. "That's funny. I never noticed."

"What was she like before, when she was a guy?" she asks.

I shake my head. "Lost. Like he never fit. This is what he's supposed to be now. He is a she. She makes sense. He never did."

Mona fidgets with the end of her skirt. "I think all girls feel that way."

I nod. "Yeah. I think it's pretty much the standard for our generation. Too many options."

As it was just about to get deep and she was about to open up to me, a knock interrupted our little chat.

I look at the door and then her. She grimaces and nods. She mouths, 'It's probably him.'

I nod back.

Shit.

I stand and walk to the door. I don't know what to say. 'A waitress with flames in her eyes knew exactly what I dreamt about and told me to run away from you.' It sounds crazy to me and I was there.

I put a hand on the doorknob. He bangs on the door and shakes it in my hand. "Rayne, open up."

His fist against it feels almost violent. Fear runs up my spine. I look back at her.

Suddenly, he speaks softly into the door, "I know what she told you. She had a crush on me last year. It was no biggie. Nothing happened."

I swallow hard and keep my hand pressed against the door. "It's okay. She isn't all there, Rayne. She's really crazy. She dated a friend to try to get to me. That's all it was."

He has no idea what she told me. He thinks I'm acting like a jealous freak.

Now I'm annoyed. I open the door just as he pounds on it. I look at him and try to see the asshole. I try not to notice the chiseled jaw, gorgeous face or boyish smile. I try to focus on the cocky grin. I try to remember that he makes the magic in my tummy hurt.

He leans on the door, taking up the entire frame.

"Where is she?" he demands.

Mona looks at him and then me. She raises an eyebrow and points at me.

I wave a hand in front of his face. He doesn't flinch.

"I'm right here. What are you doing?" I say.

He growls. "Mona, stop playing with me. Where is she?"

I look back at her. "He can't see me?"

She doesn't look convinced. "Dude, she's right there."

"Funny, Mona. Where is she? Did she call you?" He looks

agitated. He has sweat on his brow.

"She is right there. She is in front of you. She is there." Mona looks annoyed.

I push him but he pushes off the frame at the same time and points at Mona. I tumble forward into the hall past him. He looks angry. "You're really funny." He turns and walks away.

I look back at her and the words of the waitress float through my mind, 'You were dead when you were born.'

"What the hell was that? Why are you messing with me?" She's obviously infuriated. She gets up and storms from the room. I'm alone and confused. I close the door and run after him.

He is across the greens when I finally catch up enough for him to hear me.

"Wyatt, what the hell are you doing?" I shout after him, "What was that?"

He stops and looks back at me. "What is your problem?"

I point back at the dorm. "I don't know what that was, but I was standing there. You…"

He looks crazy angry. "You didn't have to run out on me, Rayne. I was just getting the phone. She is nuts. I swear."

I cross my arms and watch his eyes. They don't turn to flames. They don't flicker even. He's normal. I'm the not-normal one in our relationship that isn't a relationship; my eyes see in the dark and I'm always sick and hallucinating.

He looks at me with his head cocked. "Why did you run out?"

I point back at the room. "Why did you pretend you couldn't see me in my room? You think I'm acting nuts? Well, what about you? I was standing in my room. I watched you talking to Mona. Why are you screwing with me?"

His face drops. "You? You were in the room? I couldn't see you in the room."

I shake my head. "I was there. I was. I saw you. I tried to touch you, but you ignored me. You honestly couldn't see me? How is that even possible?"

He is pissed. Whatever I've said has made a vein in his head bulge and he crosses the gap between us in a step. He grabs my arms hard and shakes me. "WHAT ARE YOU?"

I feel like my brain is going to explode. "I-I-I don't know what you mean!"

He slaps me hard. I see stars. My vision goes dark for a second and suddenly I feel it. The heat rushes through me. My vision gets a haze. I see his hand come up to slap me again, but this time when he swings, I block it.

He stops. His face is horrified. "No."

I'm huffing and disoriented. I don't know what is happening. I've never been struck a day in my life. My cheek is burning and it feels like my blood is boiling. I gingerly put my fingers to my face. I taste my own blood in my mouth.

"Never come near me again," I whisper.

He shakes me one last time and releases me. He backs away from me. He is breathing like flames will shoot from his lips any second.

I fall to my knees. The muggy air feels cold suddenly. I swear a piece of my soul breaks off and follows him across the greens.

Chapter Six

Two months is a long time to wait for someone to apologize. Especially when the man-whore who should apologize dates everything that moves. Not even dating... flaunting and screwing.

I feel sick most days.

It isn't that I mean to let him be everything, even after he attacked me. I'm stronger than that, and I have more self-respect than that.

It isn't that I mean to let him ruin my life. My life is more important that that.

It's that I can't shake him. He's shaken me like it was nothing. I was nothing. I feel like nothing. Depression isn't the right word. All consuming is the right way to say it.

Michelle is curled around me, twirling my hair. Mona is making a collage of the pictures of us on poster board. If my mom could read it, she would be disappointed.

I don't need magical picture reading skills to see the lost hollow look in my eyes. Even in the pictures I don't remember, because I was so drunk, I can see it.

The look.

No matter how hard I try and no matter what I do, he is everything. He is my life. The piece of my soul that broke off and went with him was bigger than the piece that stayed, and I am broken. The farther I am from him, the more I want him. It's painful and mysterious. Like Stockholm syndrome.

"You know that guy you slept with last month?" she asks.

I glance up at Mona and nod. "Matt?"

She shakes her head. "Eww, what? Matt? No, the guy from the bar who gave us drinks all night. You slept with Matt too?"

I blush. "What? I was drunk."

She rolls her eyes. "Yeah, glad to see you aren't getting too out of control."

Michelle pulls my hair. "Sam. The one that took your V-Card was Sam. The fact you can't remember means you're drinking too much and having too much sex. This isn't you. Willow would freak."

"You've slept with more guys than I have." I tilt my head at her and give her my 'duck lips'.

She grins. "Gay guys don't count."

I frown. "I can have sex if I want to. I'm in college. I need to experiment. Sam was hot anyway."

Mona smiles lazily. "So hot. He looks just like Ryan Gosling in this pic. Imagine him in a suit?" Her eyes glaze over.

I look over and moan. "I need to go see him again. That was fun, I think."

She rolls her eyes again and mouths nasty words like 'slut' at me.

I sneer but Michelle pulls my hair again. "No, didn't you hear? He got beat up. Bad. Like a month ago. Jumped on his way home. My friend Marcie got a job at the bar to replace him."

I gasp. "No. Oh my God. It must have been right after we slept together. That's horrid."

She grins. "If you even make a joke about making him feel better, I will throw up. Or slap you."

I laugh.

It's hollow.

Like my heart.

The only time I feel better is after sex. It's not even because of orgasms either. The only ones I have are when I'm alone, which is not something I want to discuss.

At all.

I feel good after sex, but it's more like when you eat a lot and feel satisfied, but then the remorse hits. Then you have to unbutton your pants and everything feels uncomfortable. I feel good at first and then the discomfort and self-hatred starts.

Daily, my goal is to make it through the day without sex. I've slipped up four times in two months—at least half of the number of times Wyatt's 'dated'. With him, it's a new freshman every week. I can't help but wonder if he slaps them around or pretends he can't see them or acts like a crazed, stalker nut? I can't help but wonder if they feel like they will die without him, after he's discarded them?

Like I do.

Mona hates him, and Michelle's worse. They both swear I'm not allowed to have contact with him or be alone with him. Ever.

It doesn't matter.

He doesn't try to be alone with me anyway. He doesn't make eye contact with me except to glare at me. Like I hit *him*. Like *I* acted crazed.

I have vowed I will let myself get past him. Willow would hate him and kill me if she knew. Two months of 'I'm fine' has been taxing, and she doesn't buy it anymore.

The only vow I have kept in losing my virginity was where. I vowed not to do it in a frat house bed and I kept that one. I lost it in the bed of a local guy. I had meaningless sex and walked away unscathed. I like to pretend it's unscathed, but I hurt afterward. I hurt in my soul. Like I've traded a piece of it to feel the full feeling.

My phone vibrates.

I ignore it.

I almost always ignore it.

I can't face Willow. Not after everything I've done. I don't know how to face either of us. Instead I ignore us both and seek companionship in shallow places, where I don't have to face them either.

Mona picks my phone up and looks irritated.

I wince. "I can't. She's been super needy lately. She wants me to come home for Thanksgiving, but I'm not sure I can. I've been eating meat and having sex. She'll smell it on me."

Michelle laughs. She knows it's true. I look back at the TV and try to get lost in the movie. Scream 3 isn't my favorite movie. I prefer the first one.

"So, you still planning on being a Vampire tomorrow night?" she asks.

I nod once.

She sticks her lip out. "Please be Witches of Eastwick with us."

I laugh. "No. I don't want to be noticeable." They know what I mean. I have enough trouble as it is.

Michelle scowls at me. "Fine, be that way. You could take one for the team, you know."

I look at Mona's pout and shake my head. "Last time I took one for the team, some creep read me poetry in the corner while you bitches danced and had fun. No. There will be a million vampires. I want to blend in."

We fall asleep in a bundle of legs, arms, and fleece.

My dream is disturbing, as always.

I'm walking in a maze made of corn. Just like the one we just went to in Quebec last week with some random guy Mona likes. I had to lie to Willow and say I was spending the weekend in a study group in my common room. She's been nuts about me staying in my dorm. Anyway, I'm in a corn maze but I can't find anyone. Smoke is rising from the ground. I try calling for them. No one answers, but when I turn a corner, I bump into him. He steps back and bows his head slightly. "Forgive me." He looks ashamed.

I try to fight the tears but I can't. I put a hand out. I'm scared of him. He brings his hand back and slaps me hard. My cheek burns, and he does it again. I'm trembling and crying out his name. When I look up at him through the swinging arm, I see the dead look on his face. His eyes are dead. He whispers, 'I knew you were already dead, Rayne.'

I wake as always. I open my eyes and look around calmly. No one is there. A note sits on my pillow with a red wig and pair of glasses. Susan Sarandon's character.

I sigh. I am scared of Wyatt and yet attracted. Somehow, through the slap and the fingers that dug into my skin, I am attracted to him. It makes me ill.

My attraction to him bothers me.

The dream bothers me.

It'll bother me all night.

It'll be worse when I see him at the bar with some slut.

Not that I can really throw that name around anymore. They're my people now.

My phone is dead again. Willow has been blowing it up. I plug it in and make a mental note to call when I get a chance. I curl back into a ball and pray for good dreams. Not that they ever come.

I sleep all day again. Saturday has quickly become a sleeping day for me. I seem to need it. I am exhausted all the time.

I wake up to a whisper and look around. The room is empty, but I can see perfectly. The eye thing is worse than ever. I pick up my phone and dial home.

She answers on the first ring. "Are you okay? Are you in your room? Honey, you need to call more often. I need to see you.

There is something I need to talk to you about." She sounds tired.

I sigh. "I know. Sorry. I'm just busy and stuff. School is hard."

She sighs back. "You're eating meat, aren't you? I can hear it in your voice. You're tired. Are you having sex, too?"

I cough. "Willow, jeeze."

"Don't try lying to me. Just tell me what's been going on. I can hear it in your voice. Your chi is down. It's bogged. Is it still that boy you liked? That Wicker or Whilom or whatever? Did you have sex with him?"

I burst into tears. "Wyatt. I love him still, and I don't know why. Something is wrong with me. I can't make it stop. He doesn't talk to me." I heave slightly. "I can't get him out of my head. He was cruel to me, and I can't get over him. He's over me, and I'm a feeble weak loser."

"Nene. You're not a loser. You just love more than regular people. Baby girl, you need to come home. Want me to come get you now? Did you have sex?" she asks.

I shout, "NO GOD! I NEVER HAD SEX! Er... with him."

"Okay, okay. Calm your energy, Nene. Just take a breath. How about next weekend? You want to come home next weekend?" She sounds concerned.

"Okay. Fine. Can we drop the sex thing though?" I beg.

I can hear her smile. "Yes. Yes, we can. I just worry so much. I hate that this boy has hurt you. I love you."

I sniffle. "I love you too."

"I'm sorry."

I cry softly. "I know. Me too. I didn't mean to yell. I'm just, I don't know."

"I'll come get you next Friday afternoon, okay?" I can hear her smile in her voice.

"Yup."

"Is that all?" she asks warily, the smile is gone.

"No, I ate meat."

She sighs again. "I knew it. How much?"

I cringe. It's better than telling her about the sex, so I tell the truth. "Everyday."

"Rayne Willow Whynde, what are you thinking? You need to stop that and restart the meditation and the poses. Don't forget the sixth one. I can tell you're not doing it enough." Or at all.

"Okay," I say.

"Promise?" she asks.

"Promise."

She smiles again. "I love you, Nene."

"Love you too, Mommy." I hang up the phone and feel a little better. I'm still exhausted all the time, and sometimes the dead whisper to me for no reason and my eyes glow, but I feel better. I have confessed half of the crap I've been doing. Next week, I'll tell her about the sex. I vow no more sex. At least until I tell her.

I pull on the Vampire costume and paint my lips black. I decide on a Gothic Vampire. My dark hair suits it. I don't even realize I'm doing my makeup in the dark until Mona and Michelle come in, and the light from the hallway filters in. "You in here?"

I put the makeup down. "Yup. Just woke up."

When they flick on the lights, they both frown.

Mona looks at my makeup. "You're doing shit in the dark again?"

I nod and stammer, "Y-yeah. Uhm, trying to get in the gothic mood."

They don't look like they bought it.

Neither does the Asian girl I don't know who is with them. Mona grabs the red wig and the glasses and passes them to the Asian girl. She pulls them on. I turn back to the mirror and finish my makeup. Michelle is Michelle Pfeiffer and Mona is Cher. The three of them look awesome and sexy.

Michelle inspects me. "You look creepy." Mona nods.

I smile at Mona and flash my huge fangs. They're the real-looking kind that fit snugly onto your teeth. I used plaster to mold them.

Michelle looks at me. "All that fabric and you'll still be the most popular girl at the bar."

It's true. I'm cursed. I believe it. Ever since that stupid waitress flashed her red eyes at me and the weird dreams have gotten worse, I've been like a dude magnet. A gay guy Michelle knows hit on me last week. I can't walk into the bar without guys offering me drinks or dances or whole tables.

I look at myself and nod. I'm wearing long, black pants with a black tank top and a cape. I don't have bare skin except my face, which is covered in white makeup, bloodstains, and masses of black eyeliner. I look scary and creepy, and I will still be turning them away.

We leave the room and walk to the Asian girl in the Susan Sarandon costume's car. She drives us to the bar. I feel anxious and excited to party. I like partying now. I leave a club feeling good for days. The beat of the music and the energy makes me high. I don't even really have to drink anymore. One or two but that's it. Otherwise I get trashed and sleep with someone. Then Mona calls me a slut and Michelle tells me I should start charging so we can afford dinner out more often.

The line is long but the bouncer is one of my adoring fans. I walk up and flash a toothy grin.

He pauses and then smiles. "Hey, Rayne. How's it going?"

I nod. "Good. Is it busy in there?"

He smiles seductively at me. "Very. Be careful."

I smile sweetly. "Always." He lets us in. The line bitches and complains, but one look from the huge lug is all it ever takes to quiet them down.

We climb the stairs and look at the crowd. It moves like an ocean. I feel instantly better. My stomachache is gone and my smile feels real. It only ever lasts until I see him. I don't look into the crowd. I walk out onto the dance floor and start moving with the music. Instantly a guy comes over. "Want a drink?"

I look at Mona and Michelle. They nod.

"Four beers." I lean in and whisper in his ear. I can smell his cologne. He smells good. I lick his neck. He pulls back and flashes me a grin. When he leaves for the beers, I catch a glimpse of Wyatt. He sees me and turns away. He looks angry. He always looks angry when he sees me. I close my eyes and let the music take me.

"Can I get you a drink?" I look up at a cute boy in a Spiderman costume with the mask up. I smile and shake my head. "No thanks."

"Wanna dance with me?" he asks sweetly.

"No thanks. My boyfriend is coming now." I point to the guy at the bar watching this guy hit on me.

Spiderman lifts his eyebrows and smirks. "Is he good enough for a hottie like you?"

I laugh and wave. "Bye." I hate being rude, but this won't be the only boy accosting me.

I close my eyes again and feel the beat.

The cold beer is pressed into my palm after a few minutes. I take it and flash a vampire smile. He passes the beers to my girls.

He grins at me. "You are sexy."

I laugh. "What's your name?"

He leans in. "Jon." He has dirty-blond hair, blue eyes, dimples and a sexy surfer look. He's actually dressed as a surfer, but I would bet he got the outfit from his own closet.

"I'm Rayne."

"I know. I'm Wyatt's frat brother. He told me to stay away from you or he would kick my ass." He bursts out laughing. I feel weird about the whole thing. I look at Wyatt and catch him staring at us. He isn't wearing a costume. He doesn't need one, except maybe some horns and a tail.

I grab the surfer shirt and press my lips into Jon. I moan and savor the smell of him. He presses his body against mine. I'm lost in him when something pinches into my arm. "Stop." An angry voice blasts into my ear over the music.

I pull away and see Wyatt's crazed face in mine. "What are you doing?"

Jon clenches his jaw and pushes Wyatt, "Back off, man. Don't grab her arm like that."

Wyatt looks at him and points. "Leave now."

Jon looks at me and shakes his head. "No. You're a head case, Wyatt."

Wyatt grabs his arms and sends him sailing through the crowd. People push him and shove him when he hits them. He trips and ends up lost in the crowd.

Somehow everyone notices Jon tripping and flailing. They miss Wyatt holding me by my arm and growling at me.

I glance at Michelle and Mona watching me. Michelle is in the arms of Benny. He gives me a nod, and I shake my head. They all look pissed, but I don't want a scene. No more than the one I'm in.

"Like he would stand a chance. Why do you insist on hurting these people, Rayne? Leave. No one wants you here. No one wants your kind." His words are venom in my ears.

"What kind, psycho? You're an effing nut, Wyatt. Stop watching me and talking to me. I hate you." I tear my arm away from his grip and walk away. I hurry to the bathroom and push on a stall door. When it flings open, I slide in and close it. I am twitching in agony. If the stall were bigger, I would pace.

I cross my arms and sit on the toilet.

I bite my upper lip and wait for the pain to pass.

"Rayne, you okay?" Mona asks from outside my stall.

I nod. "Yup." My voice is weak.

"You sure?"

I shake my head. "No. I never did anything to him. I know I didn't. I left our date early, that's it. He's been a miserable shit since the day HE hit ME. It wasn't even a date. It was an early dinner."

She shakes her head. "Stop worrying about it. He's such a dick. I threw my beer at him. That's why I'm hiding in here."

I laugh. Mona is crazy. "Did you hit him?"

She chuckles. "Yeah. In the chest. It spilled all over him. He came up and swore at me and told me I should move out of the dorm and not live with you anymore. I called him a cock and the bouncer came up. He threw him out. I just don't want to be thrown out for throwing a bottle of beer."

I open the door. "He's gone?"

She nods. "Yeah. He got bounced. Asshat."

I look at myself in the mirror and try to ignore my glowing eyes. "Total asshat. He's a douche canoe, that one." I act like I hate him, but truth be told, I am worried the bouncer hurt him.

Shit is wrong with me.

We leave the bathroom and head back for the dance floor. We dance and I end up making out with Jon some more. He apologizes for not sticking up for me. I tell him I understand. He would have been kicked from his house. He is a good kisser and he smells delish. I can't help myself. We stumble down the stairs at the end of the night, laughing and leaning on each other. I'm not drunk. I'm high from the energy.

"Wanna go for breakfast?" he asks. I want him for breakfast. I shake my head and lean in for a kiss. I may have my first sober sex, ever.

We walk up College Street and head home. My feet hurt a little. My black ballet flats are not made for hours of dancing.

"So, what's up with you and Wyatt?"

I shake my head. "No clue. We went on a date once. He's acted like an asshole ever since."

He looks confused. "One date?" I nod.

He shrugs. "Weird. He acts like you guys were serious. I saw you leave that morning in his clothes."

I shake my head. "I was sick. He let me sleep over. Nothing happened. I didn't want it to."

It's weird that then, when I had him attacking me, I didn't want him, but now he's mean to me and I want him more than food or air. My intense attraction/love for him started the day he hit me.

Shit is wrong with me.

"He's a dick. I'm probably going to get kicked out of my house for this. But I don't care." He laughs. He's very drunk.

I grab his arm. "Wait, he's going to kick you out for kissing me?"

He hiccups. "If he doesn't beat me bloody. He's a wicked fighter. I saw him kick the shit out of some guy a few weeks ago. The guy was huge and older, and he still didn't stand a chance against Wyatt."

I know about his anger. I've felt the sting of it first hand. Oddly enough, it wasn't enough to make me hate him, not properly.

"Yeah, he's weird about you. Any guys even mention you and he gets creepy. His eyes go all dark." He makes a spooky face and then laughs.

I laugh too, but I am stunned.

We walk and talk and I lose my interest in him. I decide to walk him to his place and make sure he gets home safely.

Halfway across the huge sprawling greens, I see him. He's standing under a tree, leaning the way he always does. Like our encounter is casual. Like he's waiting for me after school and just wants to chat. My stomach starts to ache because I know it isn't casual. It never is.

"Jon, you should probably walk that way." I point toward their house. He looks up and shouts, "FUCK YOU, WYATT! YOU FUCKER!" His speech is still a bit slurred. "I'll protect you from him." He walks out in front of me.

"No, just walk that way. I can take care of myself." I can't, but I can scream, maybe.

"No, I got this." He shoos me away.

When we get closer, I'm scared. Not just for me, but for Jon too. Wyatt looks savage in the shadow of the tree.

He points at me. "You have to stop this, Rayne. No more dating." He is angrier than I've ever seen him.

I have had enough. I shout at him. "SCREW YOU! WHO DO YOU THINK YOU ARE? YOU'RE NOT THE BOSS OF ME! Go fuck yourself or ONE of those whores you're ALWAYS with!"

He takes one of his massive steps. "I am trying to help you, Jon. Run. Get away from her. She is dangerous and damaged goods." His words kill me inside. I feel rage building inside of me. It makes my stomachache come back.

"Go home." He points to their house.

Jon sways and tries to shove him. "Leave her alone. You're the damaged goods, dude."

Wyatt pushes him and sends him sprawling on the grass. I try to run to Jon, but Wyatt grabs my arm and swings me. I fly out of his grip and land on my butt on the grass. He grabs for me but I pull away.

"ENOUGH!" I cover my eyes for a split second. "I am done with you touching me or mauling me. This is nuts. I'm calling the cops. I know it was you. You beat up Sam."

His eyes are dark. His jaw is set. His face is contorting into something. It scares the shit out of me. I reach into my bag and fish for my phone. It's in my dorm. I left it on the bedside table. I remember the call to Willow earlier and crying over this asshole. I'm stunned at the lengths I will go to make myself suffer. His mouth still makes me want to kiss it. His hands that look ready to strangle me remind me of the feel of him against my bare skin. I get a waft of him in the air. He smells like Axe cologne, but also the musk that he naturally smells of. My mouth waters.

He looks at Jon and points. "Go." Jon stands and stumbles off into the night.

My vision clears and I can see everything. I can see his eyes grow soft and concerned.

"You're screwing with me. You don't want to be with me. You only want to hurt me and make sure no one else wants me." I'm angry, sobbing in the grass.

"You don't know, do you?" He takes a step toward me again. He's out of control. One minute he's raging and now he's talking to me gently.

I stand and take a step away from him. "Screw you." I walk past him. When he reaches for me, I run.

I run until my stomach twists and I gag. I dry heave and clutch myself.

He's laughing behind me.

I try to walk fast while doubling over in pain.

His arms scoop me up and he plugs my nose. "Stop smelling me. Don't breathe me in."

I swat his hand away and plug my own nose. I hate to admit it helps. I turn my face away from him and drink in the cool night air. "Screw you."

He looks at me and smiles his boyish smile. "Rayne, you're going to be the death of me."

My hand drops and I take in a huge breath through my nose. I am instantly nauseous. I lean away from him and retch. He holds me out. I throw up all over the grass.

"You have to stop puking on me," he mutters.

I cough and gag, trying to stop.

Chapter Seven

I feel like death. "I think someone drugged me," I whisper into the darkness.

He looks worried. He's sitting in the chair across the room. The chair the man was sitting in when I slept here last time.

"Where does she live?" he asks, like I know the answer.

I rub my eyes and frown. "Who?"

"Your mother."

I lick my lips and swallow. "Plattsburg." I have to call her after I call the police… as soon as I get away from him.

"Get up and shower." His face is stoic. I have no idea what's going on. I need to get away from him.

"Are you bipolar?" I ask and wipe my mouth.

He starts laughing.

I climb out of the bed and stumble into his bathroom. The room is messy. The bathroom looks like a tornado has whirled through it. Nothing is where it was the last time. There is regular shampoo and soap on the floor of the shower. No body wash. I wash the soap until it's half its size and then scrub myself.

When I step out of the shower he's holding the towel out for me. I'm naked and dripping water. I hold the curtain over my body to hide my nakedness. "Get out." I'm terrified deep down, but something on the surface likes him. It wants to trust him.

He shakes his head and walks toward me with his arms out. He wraps the towel around me and hugs me. He's being sweet and gentle again.

He sounds crazy. "I don't know how to be with you. Not without killing you."

My arm hair stands on end and my lower lip trembles. "Are you going to kill me?" My stomach drops into my bowels.

He kisses my hands and shakes his head. "I'm going to find a way. I'm going to fix this."

His face is devastating me, just as it's confusing me. "Like taking meds?"

He laughs bitterly. "If only it were that simple." He points at the counter where he has jogging pants and a t-shirt folded for me. "I brought you those."

He leaves me alone. I look at myself in the mirror. My hair looks almost black against my ghastly white skin. My tan is gone. I sleep too much.

My gray eyes glow in the light. They're the only things about me that aren't weak and sick looking.

I look deep into my eyes and realize how cruel I need to be with myself. I need the cold hard truth.

I look into my gray eyes and whisper, "We can never be together. He's insane. It's not just regular, crazy boyfriend stuff. This is full-fledged, four-alarm bad."

It's breaking my heart, but he's shithouse-rat crazy.

He's probably poisoning me to keep me with him, weak and sickly. It's probably why I've been sleeping so much. I saw a special on 60-Minutes once where parents did that.

I dress quickly. I need a plan.

His bathroom has nothing I can use to hit him with and make a run for it. The idea of smashing him in the head makes me feel ill again, but I need to get away. My phone isn't here. I stand at the bathroom door plotting nervously, but he opens it and takes my hand. He drags me from the room. My stomach is worse instantly. His touches and kisses make sparks.

"I think I have stomach cancer or something."

He ignores me. The pain becomes too intense. My legs buckle, and he picks me up. I gag and he starts to run. His running doesn't make my stomach feel better.

He places me down when we get outside and walks away from me. I bend and heave into the garden next to his house. There is nothing in my stomach. It's burning from emptiness.

"I need a doctor. Please, please let me go to the hospital." I cough.

He is pacing beside me. He looks stressed. He's going to kill me now. I can see it in his eyes. He grabs my hand and pulls me along the greens. I can feel anger building inside of me.

"Stop pulling me. I'm sick. I need a doctor." I jerk my hand. Fire builds inside of me, and he lets me go. He runs to a guy walking on the greens and smashes him in the face.

I scream and fall to my knees. He drags the guy to me and places him on the ground in front of me.

I scream, "GET AWAY FROM ME! GET AWAY! YOU'RE FUCKING CRAZY! LEAVE ME ALONE!"

I swat at him, but he grabs my hands and puts them on the bare forearm of the unconscious guy. Wyatt's stronger than I am. I am trying to scream, but I can't. My throat is hoarse from all the throwing up.

Wyatt backs away and watches me. I can smell the cologne on the guy and something else. Something musty. I stop fighting it. I feel the injured man and let my senses take over. Something shifts inside of me. I hear a growling noise and realize it's coming from me.

I sniff the air around the guy's face and breathe it in. I feel a pull in my lungs. Like they are screaming for the air I'm breathing coming off the guy. My fingers shake and dig in, and I don't know what's happening to me. I don't know where I am. I just know my fingers are kneading him like a cat. My fingers are squeezing and twitching into the warmth of his flesh. I bend my face over his and inhale, like it's the first time breathing after being underwater my whole life. My lungs expand and the air that hits them is sweet. I growl on the exhale and suck in again. My fingers are warm and sticky, but I can't stop them from gripping him. I inhale a third time and my body convulses. I twitch and moan and it feels like I've had an orgasm, on the grass. Gross.

I shiver and open my eyes. The world is different. There is more color and the wind tickles me with whispers and promises. I feel a power coming off of me. It's intense and amazing. I can hear the dead instantly. No matter how hard I try to not hear them, they are everywhere. The air sparkles with them.

My eyes dart to where Wyatt stands, and I see something different about him. I see the thing I saw the night I was scared of him. The magic in my tummy becomes anger. His face looks more pronounced. His eyes are striking. They can see through me. They can see every thought I've ever had. I'm sure of it.

"What?" I snap at him.

He shakes his head and sighs. "Rayne, we need to go now."

I look down at the man in front of me on the grass. He's pale and his eyes are closed.

Wyatt looks around and grabs my hand. His skin burns mine, like a shock has jolted between us. I scream out but he drags me across the greens. We run until we reach his car. My skin is smoking where he touches me. He drops my hand. I hold it up and cry.

"What have you done to me?" I whisper.

He opens the door and shoves me inside.

He gets in and starts the car. He drives the way I imagined he would. He's fast and out of control, but in a way that seems like he's in control. I would bet his skills are unmatched, by even race car drivers.

"What are you?" I ask.

He ignores me and points. "Sit as far away from me as you can. Don't get too close. I'm making you sick. Press against the window."

I lean against the cold window and put my hand on it. The burn is feeling better, but it still hurts.

"What are you?" I ask again.

He looks at me as we race along the winding road. "The better question is, what are you, Rayne? What has she told you?"

I shake my head. "I don't know what you mean."

He sneers. "Your mother. She keeps it at bay with a macrobiotic diet and intense yoga, but she can't keep it at bay all the time. She must do nightclubs for the mini sucks. Let me guess, she never has sex? Never dates?"

I don't want to hear it. I don't want him to tell me things about her. "You know nothing about her or me."

He looks at me and his eyes burn a hole in me. "I know you. I know all about you." For the first time, I'm able to fear him properly. My lust for him has intensified but I can feel the fake pull he's giving off. He's making me attracted to him. He's making me want him. I'm not crazy. It's not real love.

After a while I ask, "Where are we going?"

He answers sharply. "Home."

"Where's home?"

He gives me a blank stare. "Your house."

I scowl. "You can't meet Willow. She's going to hate you."

He grins his cocky smile, and it makes my skin crawl. "Your kind always hates me."

I shake my head. "My kind? You're a dick. Why did you need to see my mom, Wyatt? You heard how hot she was, didn't you? Look, she's not like that."

He rolls his eyes. "I don't need to force myself on cougars, Rayne. Jesus. Thanks, though. You're always so full of nice things and compliments."

"Why do you want to go to my house?" I ask through my teeth.

He sighs. "We need to find out what you are and why you make me... uncomfortable."

I laugh bitterly and cry a little bit. "I make *you* uncomfortable. You burned me and made me hurt that man. Trust me, you make me far more uncomfortable."

He glances at me as he takes a sharp corner. "I doubt that."

I mock him. "Why did you beat me? Do you like hitting girls?"

His eyes look dead, and his lips fight the emotions he refuses for me to see. "I needed to see. Violence makes the change pronounce itself. When I hit you, the rage filled you and you couldn't hide it from me."

I feel fear crossing my face, because he is insane. I back away, closer to the door. "What do you think I'm hiding from you? I never changed. I'm the same. You're the one who's gotten crazier and crazier."

He clenches his jaw and says nothing. Maybe nothing is better at this point. He's fucking nuts. I'm not sure what that makes me. I need a plan.

I lean back against the window and watch the road. He's driving me home. He's going to kill me or Willow or both of us. He's unstable, and my cell phone is at school still. I can see it on my bedside table. I feel the panic starting to increase with every mile we get closer to home. I'm getting antsy.

I'm not hungry the same way I was before. I think about the man. I don't know what to think. It doesn't make sense in my rational brain.

"What did I do to him? The man." Tears stream down my cheeks. Everything feels messy. I look down at the dried blood on my fingers and feel dirty.

He sighs. I think he's annoyed with my question. He runs his hands through his dark hair. "You sucked him dry. I think you're a Succubus. But you seem different. You might only be half. I've never seen eyes glow like that on a Succubus. Like the light is coming from inside. Witches eyes glow and Angels'. But you would know if you were either of those things. Your eyes really glow."

I scoff. "You should have seen the waitress's."

He looks sharply. "What waitress? That's why you ran? Shit, I thought she told you about how she kept trying to sleep with me last year."

I make a face. "Gross. No. She was nice; she just knew my dreams, and her eyes were like fire."

"Fire Witch. Fuck. How…?" He clenches his jaw again.

My questions and confusion are overwhelming.

The rest of the short drive is silent.

I don't want any more answers.

The welcome sign to Plattsburg is not a welcome sight. I feel dread so thick in my belly, I feel like I might explode. I wonder what my chances are of getting away from him. My brain is formulating plans, but they all suck.

"Where is it?" he asks.

I stare straight ahead.

He shakes his head. "Rayne, I can find her on my own. I can smell her out. She has left a trail all over the town. I guarantee it."

I point flippantly. "You can smell vegan yoga instructors? Fine, go ahead. Sniff her out."

He grabs my hand and fire burns into me again. "Where?"

I jerk my hand from him. "Promise you won't hurt her? Please just take me wherever you want to take me and I promise I'll do whatever you want me to."

He looks disgusted. "Rayne." He grabs my shoulders and burns me, through my shirt. "I am not going to hurt you. She has some questions to answer, though. She owes you answers." His eyes burn.

He's crazed.

My voice cracks from the pain and trauma. "Promise you won't hurt her."

"No. Where is it?" His voice is filled with regret and emotion.

I press my lips into each other.

Fuck him. "Fuck you."

My eyes burn and tears flow down my cheeks in steady streams.

He revs the engine and makes a hard turn. He sticks his face out the window and drives. He makes another hard turn, sharp. It throws me against him. I lean into him and wince from the contact.

He drives for half an hour and then pulls up in front of our house.

I am stumped.

He climbs out of the car and walks up to our small house.

I don't get out. I'm shaking. The blood on my fingers is the tip of the iceberg of shit that's wrong. I can't let her see me like this. Maybe she won't answer the door.

He looks back at me and climbs the front steps. He bangs on the door with intensity.

The door doesn't open. I look up and see Willow in the window on the second story. She sees me in the car. She is staring at me with terror across her face. Her strawberry-blonde hair is pulled up in a bun. I can see her pulling out the knitting needle she has in there, holding it up. She wants me to see it. She bites her lip and puts a hand against the windowpane. I cry and look up at her. I'm ashamed my love of some freak is about to escalate.

I look at him banging on the door. He looks savage. He left the keys in the car. I press the door lock.

He glances at me and steps back from the door. She watches me from the window. He kicks the door open and walks into my house.

Her eyes never leave mine. I motion for her to run. I'm a coward. I should have gone in with him. I should be protecting her right now.

Why isn't she calling the police?

After a few tense minutes, I see him walking around behind her. He's feeling with his hands. He is calling. He doesn't see her. I don't know how, but he doesn't. She takes a step to the side. He comes to the window and looks down on me. She's in the window, right beside him. Her face turns psychotic and she raises the knitting needle. She drives it down on his throat. Her mouth opens just as mine does. We scream at the exact same moment, for completely different reasons. Crimson blood sprays across my bedroom window.

Panic, pain, and confusion are superseded by shock. I fumble with the door handle. The lock I clicked.

Panicking and sobbing, I push the lock and leap from the car. Her hand is still coming down on him. Slicing in the air. He's trying to fight her.

My legs push hard. I scream as I enter the house, "MOM, NOOOOOO!"

I run up the stairs inside, skipping stairs. I can't breathe. I can't get the air. Tears and sobs are blocking my airways. I burst into my room, which is now covered in blood spray. I slide along the floor to him. He clutches his throat wide-eyed. She licks the needle and glares at me.

"A fucking Van Helsing, Nene? Really?" she growls at me.

Her eyes are bright green. I've never seen them look so alive. She growls at him and slides the needle into his throat again.

I push her aside and hold his bleeding throat. My fingers press into the wounds. He gasps for air, but sounds like he is drowning. My tears are mixing with his blood. His skin is burning mine.

I'm holding him and rocking, and she is watching me. He growls and her eyes widen in fear.

Chapter Eight

He watches me from the corner of the room. His needle marks are filling in. My burns on my hands are healing. Willow is pacing like a savage.

He is still alive and that is the least weird thing I've seen all morning.

She seethes at me. "How the fuck? How? I can see it on his face, Nene. Jesus Christ. Jesus. You can't do this to me and to you. Your mother would…"

My face snaps up and she drops to her knees. She covers her face and sobs.

"What? What did you say?" I gasp.

She shakes her head and looks at him. "We need to run, Rayne."

He looks at her and then at me.

"How could you let her live without knowing?" His sentence makes no sense in comparison to all the other things in the air, floating around. I feel like any minute they will rain down on me, and I won't live through the shock of everything. I have a dreadful feeling that everything is a lie.

I feel like I'm in a dream or a movie.

"You said 'my mother.'"

She shakes her head, ignoring me. "You can't let them have me, Van Helsing. Kill me or let us run."

I put a hand out. "Whoa! Whoa! Wait a minute. You said 'my mother?' Who the hell are you? Aren't you my mother?"

She turns to face me and her face fills with rage. Her eyes are glowing green. She covers her face again.

"She isn't like you. She's a witch. She's an Earth Witch." His words are deadpan and cold. "I told you, their eyes glow."

She puts her hands out to him. "Let us run. I promise you'll never hear from us again."

He glances at me. "What are you?"

I spit at him. "What are you? What is she? What is a Fire Witch or an Earth Witch? WHAT AM I?"

He looks at her and points at me. "Look how you've raised her. She is defenseless."

I shake my head and scream, "SOMEONE EXPLAIN THIS TO ME NOW!"

She sobs in a heap on the floor. "I failed you."

He waits for her to speak, but she doesn't. "You're a Succubus of some sort, Rayne. She's your guardian I would bet. She is raising you the way you should live. Working to keep your powers at bay." His eyes dart to her. "But why? Who is she?"

She sobs louder and then her sobs become a fit of laughter.

She laughs like a crazy woman. She smiles at me and whispers, "I failed you, Rayne." And then she is gone.

"Fuck. We have to leave now."

I look at him. "I'm not going anywhere with you. I want answers. Actually, fuck the answers. Get the fuck out of my house right now. My mother just vanished, vanished. Did you happen to catch that? She stabbed you repeatedly, and yet, here you stand. What in the hell is going on?"

He laughs. "I will answer the questions. Just stop cussing and freaking out. You sound nuts."

I cry and laugh, mostly out of frustration. I want Willow and the answers to the questions I have.

"*I* sound nuts? *I* sound nuts? I wonder why. Maybe because you make questions and chaos." I'm a heap on the floor.

He stands and crosses the room in one of his huge steps. He looks down on me, threatening me with the sheer size of him. Double my size. Maybe triple. "We are leaving now. I'm not screwing around. If there is something you need, like absolute must have, get it now. I need to find her lair."

My lips tremble. "W-w-what?" I laugh hard. I am losing my mind. I want to pull my hair out, burn the fucking house to the ground and blow his car up. Then I want to turn myself in for killing the man on the grass. That's what I want to be able to do.

Instead I sit, frozen and lost. I sit and wait for things to make sense.

He looks around and walks to the kitchen. He plays with the cupboards. I glance over. He's standing in front of a doorway I never knew existed. It's a secret entry inside of the pantry. He looks at me. "You should probably come with me."

I don't move. My feet refuse. They need answers. Answers about the secret room in the pantry and the secret mom I've never met.

He walks to me and grabs my hand. I can barely get to my feet as he drags me across the floor. It burns where he touches me, but the feeling of the pain is becoming a comfort. I think it's the only real thing in my life.

He drags me down the old creepy stairs. They go down in a circular motion, like a castle tower would. The walls are brick, like the stairs. It's dark. My eyes light up instantly. I see perfectly.

I walk to a bench at the bottom of the stairs and flick a switch on the wall.

He looks around slowly. I don't get how he can be so calm.

"This is her lair."

I snort.

"Hey, don't laugh. She's probably in here with us. Earth Witches are crafty."

I look around but don't see her. When he couldn't see her, I could.

"Can she kill you?"

He shakes his head. "No. I'm death for her. My blood, my skin, my spit, my sweat, everything about me is designed to kill you. All of you." Watching him rip the knitting needle from his throat and grab her savagely was bizarre. The way he dragged her downstairs, burning her skin was beyond bizarre.

My skin shivers.

"What's a Succubus?"

He walks to where a huge shelf is lined with books. He grabs a book and carries it to me. He blows the dust off and hands it to me.

The writing is like nothing I've ever seen.

"What's this book?"

"It's her grimoire and journal. If anything can tell us what you are, it'll be that. She will have kept track of things with you. Changes."

He walks back to the table and mixes something. He starts a fire and points to the stairs. "There isn't anything in here. It's all just magic crap."

I look around and shiver. I grip the book to my chest. The room is small. Books and herbs and vials line shelves and sit amongst debris on the tables. There is no light or windows. The walls are the same bricks from the stairs.

I can see chalk drawings on the floor and walls. Like she had some sidewalk chalk and went crazy with it.

The fire spreads fast. I hear a vial break. He turns and pulls me up the stairs.

He drags me out to the car, and I try not to look back. I try not to see the happy house that I grew up in. The house I loved more than anything in the world, along with the mother I loved more than I loved myself. I try not to remember scraping my knee and the way she kissed it and bandaged me. The way she mothered me, but never let me call her mother.

She wasn't my mother. My heart is broken. Seeing the smoke start to creep out the windows and the broken front door is killing me. I want my mom. I don't care if she gave birth to me or not. She was my mom. Even if she never let me call her that. Tears burst from my eyes.

He starts the car and we drive away as the flames engulf the house.

I feel my life end. My old life is gone, and the mixed bag of bullshit that has become my new life needs to be sorted through.

I look at him and try not to love him. I try not to feel everything I feel when I look at him. I hate the way I make him everything.

"What's a Van Helsing? She called you a Van Helsing."

He pauses and watches me for a moment before answering. "Your natural enemy. I am the hunter of the things you all are."

I furrow my brow. "Wait, like Dracula vs. Van Helsing? Like the movie with Kate Beckinsale?"

He nods. "You really want to mock me after all of the shit that's happened?"

"The Wolfman?"

He looks pissed.

I laugh. "The Swamp Thing?"

"Keep laughing. Whoever was coming for you or hid you with an Earth Witch is going to be pissed when they find out you're missing."

"So, all of it's true. Vampires, Werewolves, Mummies? Witches and Goblins and Trolls and Faeries?"

"No mummies; that's stupid. No zombies or goblins. Try to focus on the plausible beings. They're all true. Like Vampires and Faeries. Shifters are what you would call werewolves. The shifters are the only ones you probably would get mixed up. They are either wolves or foxes or lions or other things. Some are cats and some are dogs and never do they fall in love." He looks at me and smiles bitterly. "Like things like us."

I know the pain in my eyes and the hurt crossing my face is visible. I don't care.

"Do you love me?" I ask.

He laughs. "I can't. Like I said, you're under my skin but I can't love, not something like you. I should have killed you the first time I realized." His words cut me. It's deep, and I know I will never heal from the way he says, 'something like you.'

"Why didn't you?" My voice is angry.

He shakes his head. "I don't know. I just know that I can't live without you."

I shudder. I just want to talk and not feel anything. I've pushed down my feelings about Willow. I can't let myself acknowledge his confession about his feelings. It's a path I don't want to tread upon. Not yet.

"When did you know I was different?"

"The day you ran away from me."

"When you slapped me?"

He knits his brow. "I can never redeem myself for that. I need you to know I am truly sorry for it. Truly. I wouldn't normally have hit you, a girl. You caught me off guard. I mean—I hit the things, like Vampires and Shifters and stuff. But not regular girls."

I believe him. Mostly because I want to. But I can't let him know that. "You're irrational. You beat up those other guys. The guys I dated. I know it was you."

He looks straight ahead and drives like a nut. "It was wrong. I know that. I was just so angry and drunk. I get angry thinking about anyone touching you."

My skin shivers again. "That's creepy."

He doesn't say anything else. I look down at my hands and the dried blood. Wyatt's blood is mixed with the blood from the guy I think I killed. No, I know I killed. I know he was dead when I left him there alone on the grass.

I look at the book and trace the weird letters. "Can you read this?"

"Some of it."

He puts a hand over mine and I wince from the pain. "We'll figure this out, okay?"

I pull my hand away. My stomach pains and the burning on my skin are too much to add to everything else.

We drive in silence. I glance over at him and wonder when I'll be able to be away from him. If ever. My sick obsession with being near him has been getting worse all day. It's overtaken the things I am truly devastated about. I have a sickness. I should be terrified of him. I should be running for my life. I should call the police. I need help.

I look out the window and see we're back in Burlington. He pulls up in front of a house. It's small and white and sort of looks like my house. My old house that now sits in a pile of rubble and ash. With my old life.

He gets out and runs up to the door. The waitress answers. The Fire Witch.

She looks at me as he talks. She looks defeated. He motions for me to come. I put the book down and climb out of the car.

I'm shivering. I hug myself and walk up the steps.

She glares her fiery eyes at me. "Nice. I fucking help you and you sell me out to him?"

"I didn't know. I still don't know. I didn't know you lived here. I don't know anything."

She rolls her eyes and flashes the fire at me again. "He can sniff us out. Our energy clusters around where we live."

He crosses his arms impatiently.

She puts her hands on either side of me. I want to fight her and struggle but warmth seeps into me. I shiver and let the warmth creep in under my skin. It's the best I've felt all day.

"I don't know what she is, but it's not Succubus. It's her way of feeding, yes, but whatever her powers are, they're locked away. I wouldn't mess with this one, Wyatt. You Van Helsings get too cocky. Let her go back to school."

He smirks. "How long did you know what I was?"

She laughs. "Please. I spotted you from the minute we met. That's why I had my guards up. If I help you, you leave me alone?"

He nods once. She drags me into the house with Wyatt following.

Her house is cute and clean. She points to a couch. I sit down. She kneels and lights some candles. She puts her hands into the fire and makes a ball. She puts the fire up to my face. The heat of is intense.

"Take her hand."

He takes my hand and she looks at me. "You sure want this?"

I shake my head. "What?" I'm almost biting my lip from the pain of his hand over mine.

"If I handfast you in magic, it's like being married in the magical world. It'll stop the pain when he touches you and stop you from feeling sick all the time. But you'll be together. Like together— together."

I think for a second, but the burning is getting to be too much. I nod quickly. I am tired of being tired and feeling sick. I want to be with him anyway. If I'm really honest.

She places the ball of fire over our two hands. She lets it go and it falls onto our hands. I scream in pain. Wyatt winces. The fire rips through my hand. I see our skin melt and our hands are one for a second. The skin retreats and forms two hands again. The fire licks and burns. As the flames die, so does the pain.

My cheeks are wet with tears. I look at her. "What was that?"

She laughs. "I now pronounce you man and wife. Good luck, kid." She looks at him and drops her gaze. "I have to ask you to leave. If anyone saw you here…"

He lifts me by my hand. "Of course. Thank you."

I stutter, "H-h-husband and w-w-wife?" I cradle my burnt hand. "I thought you were kidding. Like we could date or something?"

She ignores my simpering. "You're gonna have to run."

"Where? Where should I go? My house burned down." I almost sniffle again but I don't. There must be a quota for how much one person is allowed to cry in a week.

"You can come with me." He looks at me and squeezes my hand. I want to belong with him. His touch is cured. No pain in my stomach, no burning or sparks. His touch feels like I always wished it would. The dirty feeling in my stomach is gone. His grin makes my stomach flutter, but it's in a normal boy-girl way.

He looks at her. "You're free. Free to do magic and be who you are. I can't guarantee it will be that way, if you decide to practice like your ancestors. Keep the guard up. Apparently, something wanted her hid away. Not sure if that means it's coming here or Plattsburg, but either way, I would be careful."

She nods and walks us to the door. "I know."

He ignores her and walks out. He gets into the car. I walk out onto her porch and shake my head. "You know? You know what's searching for me?"

She nods once. "I know, but I can't help you. Find the Earth Witches, Rayne. They'll help you. I can't."

I look down. "Well, uhm... thanks. I guess."

She lifts my chin and gives me a severe look. "Don't thank me yet. He has no magic over you, but that doesn't mean he will let you live. Keep your eyes open. He and his kind don't ever do anything without a reason. And usually, that reason has something to do with killing one of us. Don't trust him or anyone like him."

I want to stay with her. For whatever reason, I like her. I pause and watch him. "Can I ask you a question?"

"Sure."

I look back at her and marvel at the fiery eyes. "How did you know what I was? How did you see me when he couldn't."

She crosses her arms and smirks. "The Van Helsings think they're so powerful, but the witches of the earth have learned to block them. You had a powerful spell around you, protecting you from things like him. I could see it—it and the dead things that hang off of it. They told me about the dream. They said to say that and you would believe. They wanted you out of the restaurant."

"Dead things? You mean the whispering dead?"

She looks around. "Yup. Slow things down one day and have a chat with them. Let them take you home. Good luck with him though. He's a piece of work."

My frown is fixed when I look at him. My feelings for him are still at war with each other. "Can I get a magical divorce?"

She laughs and closes the door. "Good luck."

I walk to the car and try not to think about what she said, or didn't say.

Chapter Nine

We don't go back to school. I don't know why. I don't want to know why. My constant stomachache is gone. My feelings of intense and unnatural love for Wyatt have to go with it.

It was like we crossed a state line and all of a sudden, I looked over and was disgusted. The memory of his hand whipping across my cheek makes me feel a new kind of sickness. It's as if a veil has been lifted and I see him for what he is, just a boy.

He looks more relaxed.

I can't relax. My fingers dig into my palms. I'm pretty sure I've drawn blood with my nails.

The scenery flies past us. I've lost track of where we are.

I want Willow. I want yesterday. I would take the stomachache back if it could be yesterday. Yesterday, when I was getting dressed and crying over the phone, with the woman I believed to be my mother. I want that back, more than I want anything. I want to be free of the life I took in the grass. The debt of the dead man feels heavy, as it should.

He smiles at me. I just watch him.

We've been driving for six hours. My back is aching and my legs are cramped. He's only stopped for gas once.

"When we get there, let me do the talking, okay?" Talking to whom?

I want my cell phone. I want to phone the police and confess and tell them the dead man was my doing. I want to snuggle on my bed and have Michelle stroke my head, while Mona Photoshop's pictures of us. I want so many things. Yet, all I do is stare out the window and watch as countryside I have never seen before flies by me at an unnatural sped.

The car swerves when he tries to hold my hand. My natural fear of him has started to sink in. Somehow now, I see the things I should have seen all along. I see the way his eyes look through me and the brutal strength in his voice and hands. He could choke the life out of me and I don't think I could stop him. My natural fear doesn't have common sense. She is just a bitch who hates the man next to me, as much as she wants him. I don't know where I fit into that scenario.

He slows the car for the first time in what feels like ages. The engine of the Lexus purrs as he makes a turn onto a dirt road. He drives slowly up the gravel driveway. It winds in a thin forest until it comes to a huge white mansion. I've never seen anything like it before. It's stunning. It looks like the White House.

"Where are we?"

"Falmouth."

I frown. "On the Cape? We've been driving for the whole day. It doesn't take this long to get here. Not the way you drive."

He glances at me, no doubt when he catches my tone.

"I was going somewhere else and changed my mind."

I don't know if that is a good thing or a bad thing. I don't know what to think.

He pulls up to where a young girl stands at the front door watching us. She looks about ten. She has a gray hoodie on and skinny jeans. She looks like him. Dark hair and blue eyes. I can see the thing in her face that I saw on his. She is evil like he is. I could stab her in the throat, and she would live. My common-sense bitch wants to stab her in the throat. It's a weird feeling for me, wanting to harm a child.

She scowls at me.

I don't get out of the car.

He climbs out and stretches with the door open. "Hey Maggie."

She points. "What is that?"

He bends and looks at me. "Get out."

I can see what she is. Something in me recognizes the hatred she has for me and meets it with a fresh dose of my own.

I shake my head. "No thanks."

He groans. "Mags, turn it off."

She chews her lip and suddenly her face is sweet and innocent. Instantly all I see is a small girl with long, silky hair and too skinny, skinny jeans.

The way she turns it off freaks me out, more than the weird intense eyes and hatred.

He closes the door and walks to my door. He opens it and takes my hand. The seat belt holds me in the car. He bends to undo it but I swat at him. "No. I don't want to get out. I don't want to."

He grabs my hands and shows me the dry brown blood in the creases, where the hand sanitizer never reached. It's under my nails and on my shirt.

"You need to come in and get cleaned up." He takes my thick book. "And we need to read this."

I look into his blue eyes and press the release on my seatbelt.

He pulls me out of the car.

"I'm Maggie. What are you?"

I shake my head. "I don't know. My name is Rayne."

She tilts her head. "How come you can touch her?"

He frowns at her.

She raises an eyebrow. "Mom is gonna kill you, Wy." She is super shitty and bratty. I almost look up and thank God for making sure I was an only child, but I don't. I might not be an only child. I might just be the only child they gave away.

He grips my hand. "Yup." He pulls me up the huge front steps that have to be twenty feet wide. We walk through the massive double-front door. The foyer is huge. Dark tiles and a grand, sweeping staircase slide up the cream-colored walls. Cherry wood tables and a huge green and beige bench and other finery are everywhere. I think I gasped at one point.

"We had two very different childhoods," I mutter and look around at the grandeur of his house.

He shoots me his boyish charming smile. "This is the summer house."

I nod. "Of course it is."

The foyer is bigger than my house.

He drags me up the stairs to a huge open area. Two huge hallways that have to be eight feet across branch off the massive sitting area at the top of the stairs.

He pulls me down the hall on the right. His steps are so big, I'm jogging to keep up. He is always dragging me and pulling me. I'm tired of his leading and not knowing where I'm going. I remind myself that I'm a fugitive. Bitchy common sense reminds me that he is the reason I'm a fugitive.

He opens double doors to a massive room that is four times the size of my dorm room. A king-sized, four-poster bed and dark, cherry wood furniture fills one corner of the room. It's the biggest bed I've ever seen. It's the size of a Hummer.

I get nervous seeing it.

He spins me and kisses me. I push him off. "What are you doing?"

"Kissing you. I've been wanting to do it all day." He speaks like he's entitled.

I shake my head and wipe my lips. "Don't. I don't know anything, and it's making me feel weird. I just want to have a shower and then read the book. I want answers, Wyatt. I killed a man and my mom vanished and you burned my house down."

His dark eyelashes and dark-blue eyes have me captive. He leans down slowly and presses his deliciously-soft lips into mine. He pushes back my hair and shakes his head. He smiles. It's cocky and it makes my skin crawl, in a good way. Damn him.

"Wanna get clean and consummate our marriage?"

I kick him in the shin and push him off.

He steps back and turns grabbing the door handle and walks out. He speaks softly just as they shut, "Shower fast, Rayne."

I hear a lock click. I dash at the doors and turn the handles. Nothing. I am locked in. My brain works as the devil's advocate and whispers, 'maybe the others are locked out' and my heart tries to agree. I still don't know why it's defending him. Bitchy common sense is quiet. I think she likes the kisses.

Chapter Ten

The bathroom is ridiculous, the bed is soft and lush, and the clothes on the bureau are my size. I don't know what kind of magic is at work. How did he get the clothes here without me knowing? Did he plan to abduct me all along?

I look out the window and clutch the book. My wet hair dripping on the dark hardwood floor is the only noise I hear. The jeans and t-shirt are not only my size, but they're clean and smell like Bounce. Like him.

I watch the waves crash into the rocks in the distance. The ocean view is amazing. The sea is gray and stormy. I imagine my eyes look similar. I know I feel stormy.

My fingers tremble and my stomach feels like it's gnawing on my spine.

I am lost. I look out at the ocean and have the faintest feeling that I could run and jump in and swim away. Like I know that there would be something at the bottom of the sea, waiting for me. A whole world waiting for me to wake up.

The door opens. I don't turn. I'm angry and confused. I'm afraid of my response if I turn. I'm afraid of him. My natural responses that were hidden before are there.

"Ready?" he says.

"For what?"

His warm hands are around me and pulling me into him. He

smells my neck and plants soft kisses that resemble a whisper along my nape.

"To read about what you are." he mutters into my ear.

I turn and push him off of me. "You can't love something like me. I just want to make sure you remember that."

His cocky grin decides to join the conversation. "Sex doesn't need love."

"You've proven that. I'm still not letting you paw me after saying that."

His eyes turn dangerous. "We are married, Rayne."

"I think your plan there backfired. Your charms don't work on me anymore. I don't feel like I did before."

"I don't see why we can't have a mutual agreement that benefits us both."

I gasp, disgusted, "What? Oh my God, you're disgusting."

He leans against the huge Queen Anne chair next to him. "Don't be such a prude. I saw you with the guys at school and not at school."

"I think I'm done. I think I need to go back to Burlington and confess now."

He chuckles. "What will you tell them? You'll end up raging and killing everyone in the room when they cuff you. Your instincts are sharp. Trust me. Things like you are amazing at survival."

I step back. "Things? Really? Things? You talk like I know what you're talking about. I hate that. I don't know what you mean in any of this. I don't know what anything is. It's like you're scared to tell me, and you've given me nothing to go on."

He licks his lips. "We need to figure you out. I don't know either."

I bend and pick up the book that fell when he attacked me with kisses and mauling. He grabs my hand and drags me from the room. "We need to go to my basement. My uncle is down there.

He'll know what's what with you."

We walk down the stairs and I have the slightest urge to push him down them. He glances back at me and gives me a look. His eyes see everything. I know they do. Every thought. They turn and shine like before. It's not a good thing. He's reading me with them.

We cross the foyer and walk into a room with a buffet. He reaches inside, turns a piece of crystal, and the buffet pushes in.

Another secret passage? Is the whole world crazy? Or have I been blind to all the possibilities out there?

We walk slowly down a winding set of stairs similar to Willow's. Only nicer.

It opens at the bottom into a massive area with huge shelves and what looks like a wrestling or boxing ring. There are small lamps lit everywhere. The room is lit, but my eyes are doing their thing again.

A man is reading at a table. He has a small lamp attached to his head and glasses. He looks like he's going caving but he's wearing a sweater, and he looks too feeble and old to cave.

He is writing furiously and reading.

Books are opened across a long table. Debris covers the table, papers and books and feathers and pencils and pens and pots of ink.

It looks like nothing I've ever seen. The whole room does. Swords line the far wall. The basement must be as big as the whole mansion. The whole basement is finished, as it was upstairs. Dark furniture and finery are in every corner, but with a medieval feeling to them.

The swords, wooden stakes, and pole arms lining the wall are freaky. I wonder which of the things on the wall would be used to kill me. I feel weak enough that his huge hands could wrap around my throat and end me with very little effort on his part.

He looks at me with confusion.

Is he reading my mind?

He looks back at the man I assume is his uncle, and clears his throat.

The headlamp lifts, and he smiles under the bright light.

He smiles until he sees me and then he jumps back off his chair. He moves fast for an old man in an old sweater with a dirty-looking mustache.

He looks like Mr. Noodle from Sesame Street. The headlamp actually suits the bizarre sweater.

He looks at me and for a moment, I think I see a look of recognition. Then a holy-shit look takes over. He tugs at the collar of his sweater and gulps. "What have you done, Wyatt?"

Wyatt takes a step forward with his hands out. "It's not what you think."

His uncle pulls a rag from the pocket in his brown cords and wipes his face. He's sweating from the heat of the headlamp.

"That is, she's..." He frowns. "What is she?"

Wyatt shakes his head. "I don't know." He turns and takes my hand, pulling me to a chair. "We were hoping you'd be able to tell us."

His dark-brown eyes flash at our hands. They widen. "What have you done?"

Wyatt swallows hard. "I saved her."

Confusion covers his face. "Why?"

"I had to."

His uncle's face crumples. He collapses in the chair and pulls the headlamp off, throwing it on the wooden table. It scratches the shiny, dark wood. I wince. I don't know what that means, but it's clearly bad.

"She needs to leave. She needs to leave now. Take her to the Earth Witches."

"Sir, I don't know why you hate me, but I need your help. I killed a man, and my mother isn't my mother, and I don't know what's wrong with me. Please just tell me what's in the book."

He looks at me and smiles weakly. "Where are your parents?"

I shake my head. "No clue."

He looks at the book, "Where did that come from?"

"My mother. She wasn't my mother though. I just never knew. I thought she was."

He pulls out a chair and I sit in it. Gingerly, I place the book in front of him.

He looks at Wyatt and scowls. "You can't stay here. I'll help as much as I can, but you can't stay here. They'll be home tomorrow. You have to leave when I help you. You can't come back." He stands and looks at Wyatt. "I need to make a call."

Wyatt nods and sits. We sit there in silence as Fitz leaves the room. He returns after a few moments, flushed and preoccupied.

"Sorry for the interruption." Wyatt looks at me. "Start from the beginning. Leave nothing out."

I nod. I tell him everything. I don't leave out anything. Not the dreams or the eyes glowing or the way I was raised. I tell him everything, including the way it felt to kill the man in the grass.

With every word I speak, his face becomes more and more distracted. He starts to sweat again and wipe nervously. He looks at Wyatt and presses his lips together. He closes his eyes and sighs. He opens the book and rifles through it. He turns the book so I can see what page it is on. I can't read the words, but I see a drawing of a girl. She looks like me, but she is on a cross with blood dripping from her hands and feet. She looks like Jesus. She is dead. A man holds a sword at her throat.

He runs a finger along the line under the picture. "She that is born dead will wake dead every morning and die again as the sun sets. She will be sacrificed five times for the good of the world before her soul may rest."

"My dreams." I whisper.

He nods. "You are it."

"What is it?"

He gulps and looks at Wyatt, who is white as a sheet.

"Every time you die, a small piece of the evil left on earth dies with you. It's replaced with love. You take the evil with you to the underworld. You're the Sin Eater."

A huge laugh bursts from my lips. It makes me sound like I should be a huge burly man. The laugh is huge, bigger than I am. But I can't help myself. I laugh until I cry, and I cry harder than I laugh.

Chapter Eleven

"They were the fallen. The Angels fell in defiance of God. They imbalanced the world and brought evil and corruption. Falling made them human, so to speak. Human in appearance but not in nature. Lucifer, your father, fell in love with an Angel and instead of ending the romance, he chose to fall. He was considered the highest of the Angels, but when he fell, the role went to Metatron, your uncle."

I frown at Wyatt's uncle. "Was he in the Transformers movie?"

He pauses and chooses to ignore me. "Your mother and father were, or rather are, Angels. Archangels."

I arch an eyebrow. "I went to Sunday school with Michael... uh, Michelle. I know that the Angels were asexual."

He shakes his head, chuckling. "Why? Because the Romans thought it to be true? No, the Angel men were beautiful, so handsome it was said, that they would put any human woman to shame. The Romans found it impossible to ignore their beauty. This is what made them asexual. Being aroused by a man makes you a homosexual in their eyes. They decided the Archangels were asexual to explain their attraction." He rolls his eyes. I can see he thinks this is ridiculous. I unfortunately find all of this ridiculous.

He sighs and continues, "At any rate, your mother and father allowed their lust and love to corrupt the world. Your mother was Lillith, and your father was Lucifer. They were the first two to walk the earth." He sees the skeptical look on my face and sighs. "You have to remember this prophecy has been in the making since the beginning of time."

I raise an eyebrow. "I believe in science."

He laughs. "Regardless, it's the prophecy of your birth. Lucifer and Lillith have a story that goes something like this. Boy meets girl, boy loves girl, girl loves boy, boy convinces girl to give him her forbidden fruit. Their lovemaking was the catalyst for darkness and evil. Lillith became pregnant the moment his seed spilled into her womb. You were birthed then for the first time. You were an abomination. The first abomination in the eyes of the other Angels and God, after your parents little indiscretion, of course. The evil they created corrupted you. God did something to you when you were in the womb. You were born dead. God took the soul of the child you should have been out of you and replaced it with the soul of death. You were born dead. Soulless, so to speak."

I frown and look at Wyatt. He is stoic. I'm glad I don't have any uncles who say things like seed spilled in wombs. Gross.

Fitz continued, "You lived, regardless of that fact you woke from death as the sun rose and fell back into the arms of death every night. You grew sickly around the age of eighteen, nineteen. Your hollow soul started to fill up with the evil your parents had made."

I feel my face twisting. "That's sick. God did that on purpose. To a child?"

He shrugs. "He was angry with them. You got sicker and sicker. Lillith went back to the garden God created for man and begged God to cure you. He refused. He said they could die for their child. If they died, she would live and be healthy. They refused him. He said that they could walk the earth as man and wife, but they must sacrifice the child they had grown to love and cherish. Otherwise the child would die and cleanse the earth of their sin." I don't like where this story is going. It's like I've come to a cult, and they are just getting ready to start serving the Kool-Aid.

"Your mother was against it, but your father was a survivalist. He sacrificed you. Your mother left him. She never saw him for a long time. Maybe never again. I know it was said that she wandered the earth alone. I know at some point, you were born again and when you died, your death brought the age of Enlightenment. You were sacrificed. I don't know who gave birth to you, and I don't know how you became what you are. I know your title is Sin Eater. You feed on negativity, pain and suffering."

"Crazy." It's what I say when I'm lost in the conversation, and I have never been more lost.

He raises an eyebrow. "You realize this is all starting, right?"

I shake my head. "I am only nineteen. I technically still have two years of sin eating to do. I mean, according to legend."

He shakes his head. "I don't know much about your kind. The Earth Witches are your guardians. You must seek them out."

"Who wrote this fantastical story?"

He looks at me like he's examining me. "The Angel Metatron. Your uncle."

Wyatt, who has sat still and listened intently, leans over and asks, "How do we find him?"

His uncle frowns. "You don't. He would have to fall and touch the earth."

"How can she get to heaven to see him, since she is a child of Angels?"

He slices an old gnarled finger along his wrinkled throat.

I cringe. I look at Wyatt, who shakes his head.

"She is Nephilim. She is a child of the Angels, well in soul anyway. She will be reborn and sacrificed until they have paid their debt."

Wyatt argues. "Her father wants that, but Lillith doesn't sound like she's keen on it. What if we find Lillith?"

"No one has seen her since the Garden of Eden turned to dust. Well, it's not documented anyway."

I am completely lost. "What about Adam and Eve?"

"They came right after your parents. Metatron is the keeper of records. He ensured the story went a little differently when it made its way into the bible and lore. Of course, there was also the whole debauchery of the ancient texts in Constantinople."

I shake my head. "Hold up. No more facts. I'm lost and confused. So I suck people dry of their bad, but they die? The guy on the grass died."

He shakes his head. "I only know what's in the book. You're a Sin Eater. It all makes sense and fits."

I want to throw the book across the table. "Sense? To who? This is fucking stupid. I'm not getting answers. These aren't answers. This is a joke. This creepy old mansion needs a bald dude in a wheelchair and other kids like me." I stand up and pace. "I touched the man and breathed him in. I tasted his soul in my mouth. I sucked him dry, and it felt like an orgasm, believe it or not. I can't even make myself feel bad about the experience. I'm trying so hard to feel sickening amounts of guilt and it's hard. Honestly, eating him was the first thing I've ever done that felt natural." My eyes dart to Wyatt. "Beyond hating him."

"That is natural. We are your enemy. Your parents are the creators of the things we kill. The fallen Angels made the things we hunt."

I cross my arms. "What made you?"

He laughs and points upward.

I shake my head and look at them both. "You can both go to hell. I want to go back and turn myself in. I want you to drive me back."

Wyatt's dark-blue eyes narrow. He thinks for a minute and looks back at his uncle. "We handfasted. What does that mean for her?"

He rubs his eyes and shakes his head. "I don't know, Wy. She's dead inside already. She was born dead. She's dead every morning. She is a vessel of death. That's what the prophecy tells us. What do you want me to tell you? She isn't human. She..."

"I WANT TO GO BACK! I AM RIGHT HERE! I CAN HEAR YOU! I WANT TO GO BACK!" I feel like pulling my hair out.

His uncle looks at me and then up at the roof. Thunder fills the house. Panic crosses his face and he looks at Wyatt, "Get her out of here. Now."

I hear a scream. Wyatt looks at the TV monitor on the wall that I missed somehow. It shows Maggie holding a sword and screaming. She charges nothing but fights with it. I see swirls of black and her face knock back when she takes a hit. She isn't even as big as the sword she holds.

He pulls my hand toward the wrestling mat.

"She's in trouble. She's only little. We need to help her."

He laughs. "She'll be fine, Rayne. It's you who is in trouble. We need you out of here now."

He drags me to the back of the room.

"Find Lillith and you'll find the answers. Take her to the Earth Witches." his uncle shouts at him. Wyatt pulls me into a corner of the room. A wall shoots across when he hits a button. It's lightning fast. It would cut you in half if you weren't fast enough getting into the corner. Suddenly the floor drops out. It jerks to a stop, and we are in a bat cave of sorts. It's like nothing I've ever seen before. The ocean water splashes softly and laps against the rocks. He pulls my hand down several stone steps to a speedboat in the water. The water has carved away a massive cavern.

"Did they film Batman here?"

"No." He starts the boat and I sit down.

"Why couldn't we see what she was fighting?"

"Vampires. They move too fast for video to catch." He revs the boat's engine slightly. He drives out as a wave comes in and is starting its way out of the cave.

I don't understand why vampires would be coming for me. I don't understand how they exist. I don't understand anything. I hold tight to the seat and try not to vomit. I have never been on a boat before.

We hop along the waves out to sea. I am shaking with fear and nerves. The cold wind makes me feel worse.

He drives us for a long time. We see nothing. I don't even know how he knows where he's going. He looks back at me, but I point to the front of the boat. He drives too fast and too jerky, and it's just like being in a car with him.

I throw up once from the rocky seas and the skipping we seem to be constantly doing. I imagined boats would glide in the water, not hop the surface like jumping waves.

When we slow down, it's misty. I can't see anything but the mist in the air. Everything turns white like the froth on the sea. The thick cold air smells like salt. I'm pretty sure I can taste salt. In the mist I think I see something moving. I squint and gasp when I see it. It's a decrepit, old black house with a frightening, haunted gothic look.

This must be where the vampires live.

Something evil lives inside. No house with love and kindness inside looks like that.

He docks the boat at the end of a long pier. He shuts the boat down and ties it up. I'm wobbly and woozy, and when he takes my hand I throw up over the edge of the boat again. He moans and holds my long hair. He rubs my back.

"You throw up a lot."

We climb off the boat, which for him looks graceful. For me, it consists of rolling over the edge and lying on the wooden pier for a minute. Everything moves like I'm still on the boat. I lean over the edge of the pier and throw up again. I don't have anything in there, so it burns.

He lifts me up and carries me in his arms. He smiles his boyish grin that I instantly distrust. "Please don't throw up on me again."

I wipe my mouth and try to breathe away from him.

"I'm so sorry. I have never thrown up in my life until I met you."

He looks worried. "I hope it's not me still."

I look back at the boat with contempt. "I'm pretty sure it was the boat." I don't add the part about his driving.

He carries me through the wrought-iron gate and the weedy courtyard. The house is enormous. Ridiculously colossal.

"Is this an inn?"

He smiles. "This is home."

"Your family is weird."

His grin increases. "Not my home. This is Willow's home."

I frown. "My home that you burned to the ground was Willow's home."

He shakes his head. "Earth Witches live here. I want answers. There is no way she raised you and knows nothing."

He walks up to the front door and places me down. He flexes his huge hands and knocks on the massive black door.

"I kind of imagined Earth Witches would live in a faerie land, with flowers everywhere and colors. This is like the Wicked Witch's house."

The door creaks open. A stunning redhead answers. She smiles bright-red lips at us. Her eyes glow green like Willow's. Her skin is pale white and her long, green dress looks like it came over on the Mayflower.

"We've been expecting you, Van Helsing." She has an accent.

"Were you one of the brides in Dracula?" I ask.

She wrinkles her nose at me and looks confused. She opens the door. He leads and she looks at him like he is a piece of meat. I feel sorry for her. I don't miss feeling that way about him. I'm enjoying the odd contempt and disgust I have when I think about him.

The house is exactly the way I would imagine a bunch of witches would live. Cats, dust, cobwebs, dimly lit, and an actual straw broom in the corner by the front door.

The foyer looks like an old fashioned brothel. There are huge velvety couches everywhere and tall floor lamps. Women mill about in old-fashioned, floor length dresses, with bright-green eyes and beautiful faces. I feel homely. It's like hanging with Michelle and Mona.

I hug my arms around me.

He looks around at them and grins. "Ladies."

Some smile coyly and others outright lick their lips. They all seem to feel the way about him that I used to.

The redhead looks at me and points to the huge, red-velvet couch to my right. "Have a seat."

I shake my head and creep up behind him. She watches me and laughs.

I smell something familiar and look to the right. Willow stands amongst them. She looks hurt, no, pained. I run to her. I can't fight it. I run to her and wrap my arms around her. She hugs me and kisses my forehead.

"I'm so sorry, Rayne."

I shake my head and burrow into her chest.

She isn't in jeans and a t-shirt. She's in an old black-velvet dress with her strawberry-blonde hair in a bun. I wince when I see the knitting needle.

She feels me tremble and hugs me harder. "I wish I could have told you. I wish I'd just made you stay home."

I start to cry. "I killed a man, Willow. I killed a man, and I don't know what's wrong with me."

She pulls my face back. "Nothing is wrong with you, baby girl. You're perfect. It's the five devils that are coming for you. It's them that will ruin you and make you evil."

I frown.

"Willow, you're getting ahead of yourself." The redhead smiles at me.

I cling to Willow and let her comfort me. If she stabs the knitting needle into me, I know it will be with love. I know it will be her freeing me.

Wyatt struts around like a cock in a hen house. "We need answers."

Willow sighs. "He's in love with her."

I look back at him and watch his eyes. They never leave me. He can see the question on my face. His face gives away nothing but the discomfort of being with Willow.

"I don't love her. I saved her. That's all. Don't try to read something into it, witch."

He glares at her. He hates her. I don't blame him. The stabbing in the neck had to have scared the shit out of him. It scared me and I wasn't even the one getting stabbed.

The redhead laughs and crosses her arms. "He can't love her, Willow. That's like a dog falling in love with its food dish." The others laugh and watch his face. They lick their lips and want him. I can see it.

He shakes his head. "I handfasted with her to save her. She was sick and getting worse." I have to admit, I didn't want him to love me, but his words sting nonetheless. His dark-blue eyes sparkle, and he grins at a woman across the room with curly blonde hair.

"She shouldn't have been with you. She wasn't sick. She was hungry, and you know the effect you have on us if we aren't careful." Willow speaks softly and strokes my head. She is my mother. I don't care about the rest.

Willow ignores them and looks at me. "The five devils will bring you the pain and sin of the world and fill you up. They can get to you in the last years of your life. Once they come, the change starts. I figured with all the different species at a college, you'd be fine. I put protection charms all over you. Plus, I put the spell on your dorm. No evil or anger or pain would find you in there. It wouldn't be able to see you. You slept there every night, right?"

I feel panic. The man in the chair.

"She slept at my place twice."

Her face lifts. Her bright eyes smolder. "You never left her side, did you?"

He shakes his head.

I look at her and then at him. "The man in the chair. The man with the sweater. I heard the water running. He was there watching me sleep."

Willow's face is devastated. "I told you no sex. No sleepovers. No sex. No meat. I told you to do the poses. I did them for nineteen years, Rayne. I was teaching you."

Wyatt takes a step forward. "It's my fault. I took a shower. I made her sick. She would have gone back to her room, but I made her sick. She took mini sips from me in the bar."

The witches make a face. I can tell they know the pain I've been in.

"The sickness is the evil. Is he the only one you've seen?"

I nod. "Yeah. I haven't seen any others, but I've slept at Michelle's, in her dorm."

"I protected her dorm. I figured you would sleep there. Her father told me she was going and about the surgery and changes. The only thing I never figured on was a Van Helsing."

The redhead laughs. "Not one that would fall in love with the Sin Eater." There were those words again, love and Sin Eater.

117

"I told you, I'm not in love with her." He crosses his arms and looks indifferent. I believe him, but they don't seem convinced.

The redhead laughs again and crosses her arms. "Me thinks the Slayer doth protest too much." She looks like she is toying with him.

He looks angry but then puts his fake charming face on. "I've never been much of a one-lady sort of man." The blonde with the curls giggles. I almost throw up, but I know my guts are empty.

The redhead looks severe for the smallest of moments. "She can't stay here." Her eyes dart at Wyatt. She fears him. They all desire and fear him.

I sigh.

Willow squeezes my hand. "I know that, Glory, but she needs a moment of explanation. I owe her that. I owe her what I know." I get marginally excited.

"What am I? What is a Sin Eater? How was I born dead? How was I born at all?"

Willow's eyes sparkle. She is getting emotional. She looks at the others and then she takes my hand. She pulls me to the back of the room and through a hallway. It's long and dark and black. My eyes do the thing they do and I can see the doorways that line the hallway. Every door is closed. She pulls me to a huge black door, and when she opens it, I am stunned.

She pulls me into a white light. My eyes hurt it's so bright. I shield my face and let her pull me along.

The bright light turns out to be a garden with huge lights and really high ceilings with skylights. The garden is warm in a way that gets into my bones and warms my soul. Pretty flowers and strange plants are growing in huge rows. The green house is the biggest I've ever seen. Vines climb the walls. Bees and bugs flit about doing their work. I can see Willow being happy in a place like this.

"What is this place?"

She smiles and looks proud. "This is our garden."

Chapter Twelve

He's quiet and continuously gripping the steering wheel of the boat. His fingers seem to be a part of whatever conversation is going on in his head.

I don't feel sick. I feel glorious. It's remarkable. Everything is alive and moving in a constant harmonious pattern. Even his erratic driving is not noticeable.

He looks back at me and rolls his eyes. "Whatever she gave you is obviously helping."

I scowl. "She never gave me anything."

He grins. "You never ate anything while you were in the garden?" His tone is patronizing.

I am about to answer but I recall flower petals. They were rose colored and sweet. She put them in my hand, and I ate them like candy.

"What was it?" His grin widens. "They're Fae; you shouldn't eat things they give you. Ever. Alice in Wonderland didn't come from nowhere."

I frown and look over the edge of the boat at the choppy waves. I want to roll my eyes at the Alice in Wonderland comment, but I have a terrible feeling that he isn't kidding. He doesn't really kid like normal people.

I cross my arms and watch the water. We drive up to the rocky cavern, and he parks the boat where it had been when we left. The huge cave is awesome. I can imagine how amazing his childhood was.

I look around and wait for something dark and creepy to attack. The weird elevator makes a creaky noise and then drops to the floor.

Instead of vampires, a woman in a cardigan steps off. She's probably Willow's age but with more city miles. Her forehead wrinkles when she sees us.

Wyatt's back stiffens.

She crosses her arms and refuses to make eye contact with me, no matter how much I smile.

"I had to see for myself." Her words are sharp and pointy, and I'm certain Wyatt's ears are bleeding.

"Hello Mother. This is Rayne. My very own Sin Eater, something I've always wanted." His words are dry and sarcastic.

She meets his gaze and smiles softly. "Your sister had to defend the house. They came looking for her. We learned a few things while we've been waiting for you."

He steps off the boat but keeps his body between hers and mine.

She is wearing tan slacks and a cream-colored cardigan. I'm having a hard time straightening my back and being uppity around her. She doesn't scare me. Not until she meets my gaze.

Then she scares me in ways that make me feel like I have never felt fear before.

Her face changes the way Wyatt's does. Her eyes glower at me and sort through my varying sins. I swear she can see everything. She makes a face, and I'm scared she's looking at my lust for him.

Her mouth sneers, and her forehead gets dark. She is sinister looking. It's almost like a wind comes from behind her and blows her raven-black hair. Okay, it could be that I'm still high from the pink flowers.

"Rayne." I snap out of it and look at Wyatt. I am trembling. "She wants to kill me."

He nods. "She ate the flowers at the Earth Witches' place. Did Fitz tell you everything?"

She is giving me a strange look. "Yes. He said she was raised by an Earth Witch and warned about you by a Fire Witch. Since when do they work together to protect a Sin Eater?"

He looks at me, and I can't help but feel lost, as usual. "I don't know. Using us as the common enemy, maybe. Fitz was the one who said the Earth Witches were the guardians of the Sin Eater. The Earth and Fire Witches are better at playing nice than the others."

She shrugs and he offers me a hand off the boat.

I don't take it. I don't trust him. I climb off and inch closer to the elevator, without going too close to her. I steal a glance at her and notice her face looks normal.

I watch her, waiting for her to turn it back on. "What are you?" I ask.

She looks at me and raises an eyebrow.

"My mom is one of us."

I think for a second. "But if your last name is Van Helsing, and your mom is a Van Helsing...how deep is the gene pool?"

His mother's face instantly turns, and she growls at me.

I put my hands up. "Sorry, I talk when I'm nervous."

He grabs my hand and pulls me behind him. He presses the button and the wall slides out and we start moving up. She doesn't stop clenching her jaw or giving me the death stare.

The wall shoots open, and she storms off the elevator. He looks back at me. "You're rude, Rayne. Really rude."

He drags me off the elevator, and I notice his sister sitting in a chair next to their uncle.

The uncle looks at me, then Wyatt. He shakes his head.

Wyatt ignores the obvious warning and pulls me up the stairs.

Of course, what does he care; it isn't his neck out on the line. It's mine.

I try to tug my hand from his but his grip isn't relenting.

He drags me across the foyer and up the second set of stairs. I start to struggle, but he flips me over his shoulders and carries me to the room.

"Put me down."

He doesn't speak. He places me in the room that I showered and changed in, and he closes the door. I hear a key clanking in the lock.

"Try to rest, Rayne." His voice is muffled from the other side.

I put my hand against the door and slump onto the floor. Tears don't fall. I'm not willing to be weak anymore. I'm not willing to let him be more important than me.

I feel myself fading from the lack of food and water. I'm exhausted and scared.

'Don't be sad.'

I look around the room. No one is there with me.

"Whose here?" I whisper.

'If I show myself to you, you must stay calm. Swear it'

I nod. "I swear." I continue to hunt the darkening room. The whisper is different than the dead who whisper to me.

I see a sparkle of light. It's faint, and I can only see it if I focus hard. It gets brighter. My eyes do the thing they do, and suddenly I can see her. She is a beautiful girl in a long, flowing white dress. She is distorted and ephemeral in her movements. She is there, and then she isn't. She sparkles with life or light that is beyond what I live and breathe. Her long, red hair is shiny and sparkles with the same dusting of Faerie magic as the rest of her.

"Are you a Faerie?"

She smiles but her movements seem delayed and imprecise. Her giggle fills the air but her mouth has long since stopped the giggle. She puts a finger to her lips and floats to me. Her gown flows around her and moves with the air, or maybe her disposition. It is as much a part of her as my skin is of me. I have a hard time seeing where it stops and she starts. She is horror-movie creepy, but I feel no fear.

"I am your mother's friend."

"What are you?" I whisper.

She floats around me and never seems to be able to sit still.

"I have no time, Rayne. The evil in the house prevents me from being here completely. If they come, they will catch my essence and destroy it. You must get away. You must run from them."

"How can I? I'm dangerous, and I don't know enough about myself. I killed a man. Willow told me about needing the sins of bad humans to survive, but she only told me what she knew. She was told by my mother to keep me safe and help me control it. She was to keep me from hurting myself or anyone else. She knew I would collect the debt of the world. That's what she called it."

Her light fades, but her voice is strong, "JUST RUN, RAYNE! FIND LILLITH! FIND THE LIGHT OF THE WORLD, AND FIND YOUR FREEDOM!"

Where her entrance was jerky and inconstant, her departure is swift and frightening. She is sucked backwards rapidly as she screams, and then she is gone, and I am alone. Alone in the dark. I now see this is the theme of my life. I've always been alone in the dark in some way or another. I blink and look at the wall she got sucked out of. I wait for the delayed terror I should be feeling.

I am not shocked or afraid. Everything else that's happened in the past couple of days has either stripped common sense from me or weathered my sensitivity. My responses are not what they used to be. I stand and look around the room. I miss my old self.

I lift one of the windows and feel the instant cold wind attack. It's a blustery day on the ocean, and the wind finds the open window without delay.

I push the screen, and it falls out onto the shingled roof. It scrapes its way down the shingles and falls down onto the grass below. Every scrape and sound is magnified by the wind and the fact that I am trying to sneak out.

I close the window and sit on the bed. Surely he will come after a noise like that one.

I sit and wait. My hands fidget. I love fidgeting. Pretty woman or no pretty woman, fidgeting rocks.

I tap my foot and count to one hundred. He doesn't come. I count to two hundred and nothing. I am standing up to peek out the window when I hear the key. I sit back down and look out a different window.

"You hungry?" I turn to see a tray of food.

I want to eat it, but I saw Flowers in the Attic. I look for cookies with sugar dusted on them but it's a huge bowl of soup. It looks like tomato. I can smell the basil in it. My mouth is watering. I could drool like a dog. Not just any dog either. Like a bullmastiff.

He places it on the bureau. There are huge fluffy white rolls and butter, and an assortment of squares.

"Would you prefer to eat downstairs with us?" he asks.

I shake my head and walk to the tray. I lift the spoon and smell it. It's amazing. They must have a professional cook to go with their mansion.

I hold the spoon up to him.

He frowns and opens his mouth. He swallows the soup. I butter a roll and offer him a bite. He takes a bite and chews it. I might as well have offered him cardboard to eat by the look on his face.

I pour a cup of the tea in the teapot and pass him the china mug. He sips from it and passes it back.

"You may go." My words are soft.

He looks broken in some way. I've insulted his mother and her food, and for that I must suffer through the heartbroken look on his face. Lucky for me, I don't believe he has a heart.

He remains where he is. Watching me.

I feel the treacherous look upon my face as I speak, "You cannot love something like me, remember?"

He winces; it's subtle, and only because my eyes are doing their thing can I see it.

I butter the rest of the bun and the other side. Hunger pains are nearly crippling me.

He runs a single finger down my arm. I shiver from it. He leans in and kisses my cheek. I turn and let him have me. He kisses and pulls, wrapping himself around me. He encompasses me completely. I feel the strangest feeling. It's not like with other guys. When I kiss them, I feel something filling me. With him, I feel like my body is trying to pull, but he is an empty hole. So I pull, but the wind just whistles through him.

His fingers are greedy and his lips needy. He is sucking and pulling and tracing and my body is going crazy. He is stirring everything up but he can't fulfill the feelings I am having. I'm getting nothing from him.

He pulls me back and looks at me. "Stop it." He is smiling, but I can see he's annoyed.

I shake my head. "What?"

He grumbles, "Stop trying to eat me. I can't kiss you and hold the control. I can't do both. You have to do some too."

I push him away. "I can't do this. I'm sorry. I'm just starved. I shouldn't have kissed you. I don't want that."

He flinches again and walks to the door.

He stands at the door and looks at me. "How many times do I have to apologize?"

I shake my head. "I think it will always be one more time, and even that will never be enough."

He nods once and walks from the room. He turns the key and suddenly my food feels like prison food. While he was here, it was a meal. Now it is survival. I try not to enjoy it too much, but I am past the point of hungry and it tastes remarkable.

Chapter Thirteen

I don't slide down a lot of drainpipes. Rebellious teenager has never been my thing. I never snuck out. I never did anything, until I asked to go to college. My idea of rebellious was eating fudge cookies and sometimes whole chocolate bars. I was a binge eater, not a rebel. Willow was strict and I've always been a chocoholic.

I roll my eyes at myself, muttering and sliding down the drainpipe. My fingers bite into the metal that crinkles and tries to announce my escape. I've crawled along the roof to the far side of the house where the garage is. I totally assumed that there weren't many windows here and that I could jump down without them seeing.

Dangling from the drainpipe is an experience all its own. I make it half-way down the first story and jump. My legs and feet sting from the landing. I think about the swords and pole arms, and my skin tingles.

I run. I'm not much of a runner but I run anyway. Just like when I was fleeing from the restaurant, I am wheezing and huffing after a short amount of time. I manage to run though.

"Rayne?" His voice has never struck panic in me the way it does now. My feet dig in and my lungs expand in a hope to escape. My legs burn but I run. My instincts tell me to run to the sea. I veer to the left and push past the branches and bushes.

"RAYNE!" I can hear the panic in his voice. I can feel it.

I know he's fast. I know he's trained his whole life to chase 'things' like me. I push myself and run hard. I can hear him in the trees. I can hear him right on my tail. I can see the water. I dig in for the last bit of energy and my legs push harder. I make the beach and crash onto the rocks. Everything aches. I get up and run for the sandy spot on the beach. I run into the waves and dive into the water. I swim. Swimming in shoes and clothes is a bad plan. I look back and watch him. He doesn't enter the water. He runs a hand through his hair and looks for an idea. I can see him thinking. I bob in the waves and watch. He false starts several times and makes it look like he'll come in the water, but he doesn't. He pulls his phone from his pocket.

He flashes his cocky grin at me and I swim out.

He points as he hangs up the phone and shouts at me, "Be right there, baby."

I fight against the waves and make my way out into the sea. The salt water is in my mouth and making me gag, but I push on. A light comes from below. My heart races seeing it. I start to swim back to shore, but it looks like the girl in the room. I pause and wait. Of course, the moment I decide it could be something good, my bitchy common-sense side snarks at me. 'What if Sirens are real and she lured me out so she could kill me?' The voice in my head is telling me to panic.

I hear a boat. I look up to see a man in Wyatt's boat.

I look at Wyatt. He puts his hands out and screams at me to stay calm, or get in the boat, or a combination of that. I look down at the light and see a woman just like the redhead in my room.

Her hand reaches for me. She smiles and her light makes me feel warm in the freezing-cold ocean water. I look at the boat and decide I need to trust my mother.

I don't know my mother at all, but Willow was her friend and she never hurt me. Willow would never hurt me.

I look at Wyatt on the shore and know he would hurt me again, in a heartbeat.

I reach my hand for her and she pulls me under. I can hear the boat and Wyatt's screams for a second. They die off as she pulls me down fast and silence fills my mind. It's not alone though. The fear I will die at the bottom of the ocean is bouncing around in there as well.

Her ghostly fingers are cold. Cold as the sea. She stops and looks at me. My cheeks are puffed out and I'm starting to struggle with the loss of air.

'Breathe, Rayne.'

I shake my head. She nods. She has the same beautiful face as the other girl, but blonde hair that floats all around us. It is so light that it feels like it's lighting up the dark ocean, but I think it's my eyes.

I start to choke and feel faint. She smiles at me and laughs. 'Breathe'.

I shake my head and grip my throat. I'm clawing at my chest, which feels like it's about to explode.

Just as the light is leaving my eyes and my vision has become pinholes, my mouth opens and a wondrous feeling fills me. I breathe. The water is air. I don't know how, but it feels miraculous.

She giggles and holds her long, slim fingers up to her face. 'Angels can breathe on every corner of the earth'.

I inhale the water, but it feels more like I have something that pulls the air from the water. I don't feel liquid entering my body. I still taste the salt though. It makes me shiver.

She pulls me along the shore, and when we get to a spot where I can see lights on the shore, she brings me to the surface.

'Find the light of the earth, Rayne. Find it and find your freedom'

I nod and swim to shore. My teeth are chattering and my body is aching. I'm not in very good shape for the child of Angels. The floating, creepy lady in white waves a hand at me and is gone again. I pull my soaked and bedraggled body to shore. I crawl on all fours and when I stand, I am exhausted. I can feel the heat tingling in my body. I know I need to do what Willow told me to do when we were in the garden. I just don't know where to find a really bad man to suck dry.

I am covered in sand and seawater. I can hear traffic and see the lights of Newport Bridge. I know where I am. I've been here before. Willow brought me and we stayed with hippie friends. Yeah, hippies… I was a gullible kid.

My hair feels like a clump. The rat's nest is so bad that I can't drag my fingers through and pick it at all. I walk along the seawall of Newport and pass the light blue inn I stayed at with Willow. We slept there one night. The people were kind, and I got to see dolphins. It was my first time. They came into the bay and right up to the blue house. Willow cried.

I am alone. I want to cry, but I'm tired of the taste of salt.

I walk to a small white house that looks like my old house and sneak across the street quickly. I slip into the backyard and walk cautiously to the backdoor. I try the door and sigh when it opens. It's dark, and I'm praying the dark windows mean no one is home. I open the door and look around.

"Hello?" I call out but try not to be too loud. "Hello. Your house is on fire."

No dogs and no people. I close the back door quickly and strip naked. I ball up my clothes and shoes and dump them into the garbage in the kitchen. The house smells like cleaner. Old people's house for sure. I tiptoe and try not to make any mess.

I open the fridge and devour the ham sandwich I find. I drink a huge glass of milk and stuff two huge raisin pumpkin muffins down my throat. Eating has completely become about survival. I rifle through the drawers and cupboards. I find a stash of money taped to the lid of a cookie jar. I steal their power bill from the counter and slice it open. I stuff the money inside. I'll get someone to mail them the money I stole. I'll need their address when I repay them.

I climb the hardwood stairs, assuming the bedrooms are upstairs. For once I am completely grateful my eyes see what they see. I function like normal in the dark.

I climb into the shower and rinse the sand and salt off. With the shower curtain and bathroom door open, I shampoo and condition quickly. That way, I can see if a car pulls into the driveway and lights the front of the house up.

The soap smells like roses and old ladies. I love it. I love old people. Always have. Kids, not so much, but old people—yes.

I climb out and grab a towel from the cupboard. I towel off quickly. I ball my towel and place it in the hamper in the master bedroom. I dry the floor with my hair towel and fire it into the hamper too. I fish through the closet and find men's jogging pants and a thick t-shirt and a sweater. I pull it all on. I am finally feeling warm again. I take a coat that is at the back of the closet. I hope it's something he doesn't wear. I put on triple socks and some old shoes he has in there. Old loafers. I feel like a homeless person. I look like a homeless person.

I slip down the stairs and out into the night, before they come home to find not-so-goldilocks cross-dressing in their bedroom.

I'm better at this than I would have imagined. For the cozy life I've led, I'm not doing too badly.

I walk along the seawall and realize the starvation is still there. I'm starving for something that ham and cheese on white bread can't cure. I rub my hands together and feel something I've never felt before. I feel something calling me. It pulls right. I turn up a street away from the bridge and the water. I cross the street and turn down another street. I stop feeling it. I look around for whatever it was that was calling me.

Nothing is there. I hear a car's tires driving on the wet pavement. I feel a strange feeling, excitement and fear mixing in my belly. I duck into a bush just in time to see the silver white Lexus driving slowly. I don't see his face. I don't need to. Seeing the fancy sports car in the small town is enough.

I wait and sneak into the yard of the house I'm hiding in. I creep in the backyard to the next house over. It has no lights on. I slip into the car in the driveway and look around in the dark for the keys. I don't find any. I get out and look around the car. A small box is hidden on the back of the car. It's tucked up in a lip. I slide if open and take the key. I get in and start the small car. It smells like smoke and mildew. It rattles and clunks down the road, but at least I can get over the bridges and then ditch it.

I drive over the Newport Bridge and then cross the Jamestown Bridge. The car clangs along until I reach the Warwick exit. I pull over and leave a twenty-dollar bill in the ashtray and close it. I lock the car and put the key back. She might not have given birth to me, but I am Willow's daughter. She taught me about karma.

I leave the car and walk toward Warwick until I can smell the ocean. I think I know where the house is. I don't think they'll let me stay, but I am hoping to at least get some answers.

I know I'm close when I smell something I've smelled before. It makes my heart race and my stomach churn. I can't fight the feelings. My body turns away from the sidewalk and pulls me to the scent that's floating on the wind. I'm like Toucan Sam. I follow it to a garage with the door open. I walk in. I am on autopilot. A man is bent over the hood of a car whistling.

He sees me and at first he scowls. He's about to be rude to me. I can see it in his dark-brown eyes. Instead he smiles, like he's lost. He's about fifty and covered in freckles and grease. His dark-brown hair is matted to his head on one side from the gear dope. He walks toward me like I am the almighty savior. My brain is panicking, but my body has taken over. It has a need.

My hands reach for him. My lips brush against his, and I can smell grease and spaghetti. He kisses me passionately. I pull back and hover over his face. I inhale him. The spaghetti is gone, replaced with lust and the sweetness of his soul in my mouth. I feel naughty tingles down low in my belly as I drag the last of him away. His body crumples onto the cold concrete. I twitch and step away. I lean against the tool-covered wall of his shop. As I'm twitching and fighting my knees buckling, an older lady comes into the garage through another door on the other side of the car. She is holding a grocery bag. She sees me and frowns. She can't see his dead body. It's behind the car. "Who are you?"

I stutter, "H-h-h-he needed help."

She looks confused. "Son, you better get out of here. He's not going to be happy if he sees you snooping around in this garage. He gets mean when he finds people doing things he doesn't want them to do."

I nod and turn away.

"Just a sec, kid. Come to the front door." She leaves the bag on the floor and walks back into the house.

My legs gain their strength as the pleasure and sensations die down. I walk to the front of the house. She opens the door and passes me a sandwich.

"Try to find somewhere warm. You poor thing."

The sandwich feels like a warm, beating heart in my fingers. I fight back the tears. I am a sick monster.

I turn and walk and lose the battle. Tears flood my eyes and soak my cheeks. I stumble out into the night, gripping the sandwich she made me. I don't know how to fix the karma I now have for what I took from her.

Chapter Fourteen

I evidently don't remember the way to the witches' house. I want to call Willow and get her to come and get me, but I know the other witches won't let me stay there. Maybe Willow will leave with me. I feel just lonely and selfish enough to ask her for it. I know it'll be the end of her, but I'm scared this is the end of me.

I stumble down onto the beach behind a quiet house. I sit on the rocks and sand, digging my fingers into the beach.

The cool night air is lost on me. Feeding from him has warmed me up, everywhere except my heart.

The water laps at the dock near me. The waves drag slowly up and down the pebbled shore. The noises get to be relaxing. I dig my fingers into the sand, deep. I feel something remarkable. The sand has a pulse. At first I think it's mine, but it's too slow. The earth pulses around my fingers. The earth is alive. I close my eyes and let the pulse start to beat through my body.

I look around the bay I'm sitting in and at the houses and properties. I'm sad for many other things I haven't even touched on. Probably because I haven't given up on them yet. My dream to get my PhD from Yale and to be a linguist and work for the UN. Then maybe get married one day and buy a big fancy house and have some kids. I can still imagine Willow as a grandma. Feeding them carob bark and seltzers made from fruit juice.

I have been building a life and desires for things I won't ever have. Or can I? Can I have the things I want? Can I go back to the school and only eat when I truly have to? Can I live the way Willow taught me and only eat when truly necessary? Can I just say no to the sins of the world?

I rub the sand and let the pulse work its way through me.

I can do it. I can have a normal life. I can at least try.

I stand and walk to Warwick. I find a payphone and call Mona collect.

"Oh my God—what are you doing? Where have you been?" She answers in a panic.

"Mona, I need a favor. Can you text a message to Wyatt from my cell?"

"Where are you?" she demands.

"Home. I forgot my phone."

She is silent and then speaks in a low tone, "Rayne, Willow has been texting and calling non-stop."

I cringe. "She isn't at home. She's at a friend's on the sea."

She speaks as if she ignores me, "She said if I was to hear from you, I should give you a message."

Butterflies fill my stomach. "What message?"

"Stay away from the campus. She said you're not safe and no matter what you think, you need to find the light. What does that mean?"

I lean against the payphone booth. "Not sure." I sigh. Where the hell am I supposed to go? "I need help and I don't know where else to go or what to do."

"Where are you for real?" Of course, she would know I'm lying.

"Warwick," I admit, defeated and exhausted.

"I'll be there in a few hours. Where should I meet you?" She sounds determined.

I want to protest and be a good friend and keep her out of my problems, but I don't. I'm a selfish asshole. "Aqua Vista Marina. I will be sitting at the end of the shortest pier."

"It'll take me probably four or five hours. Are you okay?"

I nod as silent tears slither down my cheeks. "Yup."

Her breath in the phone and her existence are the only things keeping me from losing my mind completely.

"See you soon."

"Bye. Thank you so much."

"You'd do the same for me."

I would. I know that, but it doesn't make the trespass I am committing on her kindness any less harsh. I am asking her to enter into something dangerous.

When the phone disconnects, I feel the sharp cold of the morning air. Dawn is coming. I walk along the beach and wait.

I waste my time at a diner. I have coffee and breakfast, and when I get bored, I go to a second-hand store and buy new clothes. I get new underwear and a bandeau still in the package. The rest of the clothes stink like second-hand clothes always do, but it's better than wearing the stolen old-man clothes. I pull my long hair into a ponytail and walk down to the pier.

I'm huddled with a hot cup of cocoa when I hear the squeals.

I glance up and smile before I realize what I'm looking at.

Michelle and Mona are climbing out of a gorgeous white-silver SUV. I will bet money it's a Lexus.

Fuck.

Wyatt gets out of the driver's seat and looks furious. I drop my cocoa into the ocean. I stand and walk backwards.

"Why did you call him?"

Mona sees the panic on my face and meets my eyes with her own. She shakes her head with a twitch.

Michelle struts up to me. I can't help but notice the glittery high-tops and skinny jeans.

"He wanted to come and help, Rayne."

He smiles. It's cocky, and it makes my blood boil.

"Get in the car, Rayne." His dead eyes are colder than I've ever seen them. They don't match the smile crossing his lips.

Mona runs to me. Michelle and Mona hug me.

Michelle pulls me back. "What the eff are you wearing? You smell homeless!"

My lip trembles and I shudder. "I am homeless." Tears stream down my cheeks.

Their eyes fill with tears and they hug me.

"Honey, don't cry. You're making me cry."

"Rayne, don't cry. We'll go get Willow, and you'll feel better."

I pull back and sniffle. "She isn't my mom. Not my real mom. She is my guardian. She doesn't want me to live with her anymore, and dickface over there burned my house to the ground anyway. I have nowhere to go."

Mona looks at Wyatt and then me. "He said you needed us. He said you would say stuff like that. You're just tired, Rayne."

Michelle looks at me. "A lot of freshmen crack the first year, sweetie. It's a lot of pressure. You've always had such a sheltered life. The stress is probably more than you can take right now."

I stop sniffling and watch them both patronize me.

"You just need a few days of rest. You've been so down since we started school. We won't let you hurt yourself."

"No, we love you, Rayne. Willow loves you. Everyone gets a little down now and then. It's so obvious with all the sleeping and stuff, I'm sorry we missed the cries for help."

I push away and look at him. "You told them I was fucking crazy?

You're an asshole."

Michelle looks back at him. "He told us about how he was trying to help you, and you kept pushing him away. His heart is broken, Rayne."

Mona smiles softly. "He only ever wanted to help you. That's why he tried to stop you from hooking up and tried to be there for you."

The world feels like it is closing in on me. I walk past them both to the SUV. I walk slowly and watch his eyes. "So, you've loved me all along?"

He gives a nod and watches Michelle and Mona.

"Why did you slap the shit out of me on the grass?"

He shakes his head. "She is hallucinating. I never hit her. I wouldn't ever hurt her."

I look back at them. "You saw him manhandle me at the bar, and Mona, you threw a beer at him for Christ's sake."

"I was trying to save you from another meaningless one-night stand." His voice has a hint of humor.

I laugh. It's bitter and full of spite.

I look at Mona and Michelle and raise an eyebrow. "You want proof? Fine." I break into a run. Wyatt is chasing me. I can hear his feet on the boardwalk. I run hard to the end of the pier and jump in. He follows me into the water this time. One of the Water-Angel things is there instantly. She glows and her pretty face turns to anger and pain. She screams at him and grabs him.

His eyes fill with fear as she drags him down. Her screams make my ears feel like they're bleeding. I dive under. I see her. I swim, but she is faster. He is struggling and fighting her. He does something with his hands and sends her back. She is angry and frothing up the sea. She swirls around him, choking him with the white strands of her dress. He never stops fighting her. He pulls something from his back pocket, and in the struggle, he gets his arms free. His hands come up the way Willow's did with the knitting needle. He stabs into her eyes where the light shines.

She screams as she dies. I can see the lights coming. I swim to him and grab his arm. I pull but he fights. He's trying to take something. I pull him and look back. Panic fills me. He grabs my face and sucks the air from my lungs. He grins at me. He's using me as his own oxygen mask. I point. He turns and sees the line of white lights.

He mouths, 'fuck'.

I nod. He swims fast and hard for the shore. When I look back, I can see them. They're everywhere. His feet hit the rocks before mine. He drags me from the sea.

He runs to the car. "GET IN THE CAR!"

Mona and Michelle are standing on the pier watching in disbelief as a horde of white-garbed women climb from the sea. When the air hits them, they move in the same odd way that the one in my room moved.

Michelle screams, and Mona drags her to the car the same way Wyatt is dragging me.

"You killed her," I sputter. He pushes me into the SUV and starts it. Mona and Michelle barely make it into the car when he pulls away. He speeds through town.

He clenches his jaw. "You're an idiot."

I look at my stunned and sobbing friends. "Yeah, well—you're an asshole. You lied to them to get them to talk me into coming with you? What the hell?"

He pounds the steering wheel. "You ran. You ran, and I didn't know how to get you back. God damm. I was trying to keep you safe."

"Prisoner. You were keeping me prisoner!"

He seethes, spitting in my face when he yells, "YOU WERE SAFE!"

"You're crazy. She isn't crazy, you are. You're a son of a bitch. You had us convinced we were the worst friends, that we let her get depressed and become a danger to herself." Michelle leans forward and slaps him on the top of the head. "You son of a bitch. You god dammed son of a bitch."

He swats at her. "Stop. Just stop."

Mona looks at me. "I'm sorry."

I shiver from anger and the cold water. "No, I'm sorry. I've dragged you into something, and I'm sorry for it."

Michelle wipes her eyes and shakes her head. "What were those?"

"Nixie," Wyatt whispers.

The three of us mouth the word and look confused.

"Water Sprites. Water Witches. They have incredible power in the water. Very hard to kill. Unless, you happen to have a silver dagger. Their essence is a healer for people."

He speaks as if the woman in my room is nothing but a good source of Faerie dust.

"You killed her."

He frowns. "She was trying to kill me."

I raise an eyebrow. "She was trying to save me."

He rolls his eyes. "Yeah, same thing I guess."

"So Water Sprites are real?" Mona looks like she is about to laugh.

I nod. "You would beg for death if I told you about the things that are real. That's how I felt anyway."

Wyatt cranks the heat when he sees how much I'm shivering.

"So, those things looked pretty angry back there. That was some scary shit. Watching them crawl out of the water like an army made of chiffon. They seemed like they hated you."

Wyatt nods. "Nothing new there. Everything hates me." His eyes flicker at me. I envy them their true hate. On some level, I still really like him. It's a dirty level where my inner whore lives. I don't like to let her have opinions or sway over what the common-sense bitch and me are doing.

He continues coldly, "They can sense the death of their sisters for miles. They can smell the death of other sisters on me."

Through my chattering teeth, I grimace. "You've killed them before?"

He gives me a blank stare. "When I've needed to."

"Were they attacking you?"

"No, I needed the essence."

I knew the answer. I just wanted to hear him say it. It fuels the fire I need to hate him properly. Even then, when I don't think I can.

"They helped me escape you. Why would they do that? They seem to have my best interest at heart."

He shakes his head. "I don't know. The fact they're helping you is weird. Fire Witches, Earth Witches and now the Nixie. It's unprecedented."

"So they're the Water Witches?" I ask, still shaking.

He nods.

I want to ask him a million questions, but I don't want to traumatize Mona and Michelle.

He glances at me again. "You saved me."

I realize I did and shrug it off.

"Thanks."

I sneer. "It was an accident. I panicked. They looked scary swimming like that at us in a wall of lights."

He chuckles. "That they did."

I shudder. "It's probably going to haunt my dreams forever."

Mona passes me my phone. I take it and see the texts and flashing lights.

She makes a face. "Willow has been sending messages non-stop. She phones and texts every half an hour."

I look at the messages and frown. "She never wrote these."

I glance back at Mona. She frowns. "What do you mean?"

"Someone must have her phone. She never calls me Rayne, unless she is really upset or really angry. And she never calls herself Mom."

I look up at Wyatt. He bites his lip.

"Did you do this?"

He shakes his head. "No, but they might have her phone."

"Who are they?"

He looks at me and laughs. "Who isn't right now? Everyone seems either willing to help you or hurt you, for whatever reason."

I think for a second. "How do I know that they don't have her?"

He laughs a rich full-belly laugh. "The only reason we weren't struck dead upon entering their yard is because they were expecting us. I came unarmed and you were with me. You think for a second that they couldn't have killed us instantly?"

I frown. "You said they couldn't kill you."

He looks over at me and frowns. "Her…one singular witch? She cannot kill me, but they…is another story. I can't fight them all off, and you don't seem to have any ability at all."

"I can eat evil with my mouth. Very special talent, in fact."

He rolls his eyes. "Yeah, well thus far, it's proven pathetic. You ate a guy on the grass."

I gulp. He raises an eyebrow. "Who else?"

I look down. "A man in a garage. I'm ashamed."

Had a cricket been in the backseat you could have picked out the notes he played.

I look back to see their ghostly white faces covered in horrified expressions. My eyes widen instantly. "I didn't eat them like chewed and swallowed."

They look at each other and try to smile. Michelle tucks her hair behind her ear and laughs. "Of course not." She giggles nervously and looks at Mona.

I'm not certain of the course of action I should be taking. I close my eyes and try to remember how Willow put it in the green house.

"I'm something called a Sin Eater. I eat evil. Right now, there is too much evil on the earth. When I've eaten enough evil and put the earth back in balance, I am to be sacrificed and I take the evil to hell with my soul. I have been born three times, the same soul every time. When the balance tips and the world is smothered in darkness, it's time for me to be born again. It happened once in the beginning when the earth was young. Once in the dark ages. Once now. When I'm born I live roughly twenty-one years. In that time, I live like a normal person until the last two years. In those last two years, I fill with the sickness of the earth. Black Angels, Angels of death, bring me the evil of the world. They put it in me. It makes me sick. Then I have to be crucified and burned on the cross and beheaded, I think." I glance at Wyatt.

He smiles and nods. "Weirdest conversation ever."

I laugh at him. "Hardly. Your uncle actually said the words 'seed spilling' and 'womb' in one sentence."

He rolls his eyes. "Oh my God, he was telling the story from the bible."

I sneer. "Anyway, then my soul returns to hell and I take the evil with me."

Their eyes dart between Wyatt and I. Neither believes what they are being told. I don't blame them.

"Willow was my guardian. They don't know exactly how I'm born, but I'm born without life. I'm born dead."

Mona raises an eyebrow. "Like a stillborn?"

I nod. "Sorta. I guess. I still don't have a full explanation on it. But when I sleep, I am with the dead. I'm a vessel for death. That's all I know."

Michelle nods. "I have tried waking you tons of times. It never works."

"You can't wake me. I'm dead every morning until I wake. I wake when the dead let me come back. Apparently, they take me somewhere. Like my dreams aren't dreams, but something else."

Wyatt puts a hand on mine and squeezes. I like the feel of him. Regardless of everything else, he seems to be one of the few people I can count on. Even if his evil family has every intention of hurting me.

Mona watches him and glares, "And him? Where does he fit into this trip down the rabbit's hole?"

I laugh, and the corners of Wyatt's mouth lift.

He clears his throat. "I'm a Van Helsing. My family has been battling the things her family made, since the beginning of time."

I grin. "Yes, Van Helsing from Dracula."

Michelle laughs. "This is the shit. You guys need to write this down and make a novel. Maybe not for kids though. The white ladies in the water are too scary. The movie version would have them peeing their pants. Damn near peed mine."

"So, you are here to kill her?"

He shrugs and looks at Mona in the rearview. "Haven't decided on that yet."

I watch his dark-blue eyes and wait for him to smile, but he doesn't. I guess he isn't kidding. Great. I pull my hand away.

"Asshole."

Chapter Fifteen

Three of us in a king sized bed is too many. I'm cramped and uncomfortable. I hate being in the middle. I climb out of the bed and walk to the door.

I turn the handle, but it's locked. I close my eyes and calm my mind.

"Are you here?" I ask to no one. No one anyone else could see or hear. I haven't properly talked to them in a long time. I remember being a kid and that they could do stuff like lift things and play dolls with me.

The air whispers and sparkles with energy.

I smile when I hear their whispers.

"Can you unlock the door, please?"

I hear the whispers, like children's giggles from a distance.

"Please. I won't block you out anymore."

The lock clicks. I turn the handle slowly and wander out into the night.

They touch me and beg me to wait. They don't like the house either.

I slip down the stairs, making no more noise than a feather would. I almost float across the floor, I am so fast and quiet. I open the buffet and turn the piece of silver.

The latch clicks. It's the most noise I've made yet.

I push the wall and creep down the winding stairs.

The headlamp is the only thing I see when I reach the bottom.

He is bent over his books and alone in the dark.

I creep to him. He looks up as I stand next to him. He jumps and shines his headlamp in my eyes.

"You scared me!" he whispers sharply.

I growl. "I need answers, Fitz. Willow recently told me about you and her. The great love of her life."

I sit on the chair next to him and smirk.

He looks sad. He pulls off the headlamp and places it facing upward on the table to light up the area we are in.

The rest of the room is dark until my eyes adjust.

He leans in and looks at my face. "Your eyes."

I nod. "They can see, no matter where I am. I can see in the dark and in the ocean. When they do this, I can see really far too. Like nothing can hide from me."

He looks grim. "Except your heart."

"What?" I frown.

He sighs. "You aren't supposed to love, Rayne. You shouldn't be able to love him the way you do. It isn't natural."

I have guarded the secret so close, I never even let myself see it. Not fully. "Please don't tell him."

He frowns. "I would never. I thought at first that it was the way we attract all of the things you are. But I see that you don't feel that way about the rest of us. Things like you can't help but want us. All of us. But you are different. Your heart belongs to him."

My skin shivers. "I try so hard to hate him. He has been nothing but cruel to me."

He nods toward the wall of swords and wooden stakes. "He was trained to despise all that you are. He dislikes all of you, naturally. It goes against his nature to even be kind to you."

I shake my head. "He's been kind to the others. I've seen it. There was a witch, and he never hurt her."

He smiles and I can see regret everywhere. "He is biding his time, my dear."

"But he promised her..."

"He lied." Panic rises in me. I have to warn her. I watch his eyes. I might not get a chance to warn her. I wish someone had warned me.

"You hate me, don't you?"

He nods once as his eyes dart around the room. "I don't mean to. I know what you are is not your fault, but I don't have the ability to be kind to you, not without plotting your death. You shouldn't have come back here. The Nixie tried to warn you."

The air sparkles and my skin twitches. "You will betray me then? You will make sure they get me? That's why the Nixies came. They came to warn me about you and the rest of your family. Not him. It never was him I was in danger of. But the rest of you, you'll kill me. You'll betray Willow, even though you once found yourself in the same predicament as me?"

His eyes fill with tears. He whispers, "I'm sorry," just as there is a rush of hands and darkness. I feel instant pain and burning everywhere. I scream, but it's cut short as I pass out.

I wake to pain. Writhing pain, it's everywhere. I scream. Tears instantly spring from my eyes. The air doesn't sparkle with the dead, but I can feel them. They took me when I slept.

I am in chains, hanging so my toes just touch the ground. I'm stripped to the bandeau and granny panties I bought in Warwick. My arms and shoulders are in pain, ridiculous amounts of pain.

"HELP ME!" I cry out, but by the echo and the draft, I can tell I am somewhere old. The walls look like a dungeon, an ancient dungeon. My wrists burn from the shackles.

I cry out again and again, but no one answers me.

"Wyatt," I sob. My dark hair is matted around my face and neck. The tears have been flowing long enough to soak my neck. I can feel them trickling down my stomach and in between my breasts.

Fear grips me as I realize what is happening. His family wants me to be filled with the sin and evil. They want me to take it to hell with me. They will keep me here until the five devils come and fill me up. They know far more than they have let on.

I hang and suffer, not knowing know how long it's been. I see the light of the morning moving across the stone and brick floor. It starts its journey back as it crests the house I'm in and moves toward nightfall. My hands are burning, and I'm certain one of my shoulders has dislocated. The pain almost knocked me out, but I managed to stay awake. Hanging from a dislocated shoulder is excruciating.

I can feel craziness lurking behind my regular thoughts. I hear a noise as the sun sets. A voice. A man, maybe. I try to keep my eyes open. But the problem with sleeping with the dead every night is simple—when I need to sleep, I sleep. No matter what, I sleep. Like the dead. With the dead.

I wake to a stabbing pain in my stomach. My feet lift and push me up. I think both shoulders are dislocated now. The pain doesn't register with me for a minute. When it does, a scream tries to leave my throat, but it's so dry there is nothing. Air wheezes through the wind tunnel. My feet both touch the ground now. I have stretched out my arms by sleeping with dislocated shoulders.

My eyes clear, and I see the face of the person stabbing me. Pain and betrayal take everything away from me. Every moment of love and kindness I have ever felt are all replaced by the agony being inflicted upon me.

"What are you doing?" I whisper harshly. My cracked lips bleed when I stretch them by speaking.

She trembles and sobs as she pushes an old sword into my stomach. "It's crazy the amount of pain you are capable of living through. I should know this. Look at me. I went through it all to be this. To be this perfect." She is sobbing and ranting. She looks demented.

My cries come as wheezes, and my eyes burn as they attempt to cry. No moisture is left in me. My tears are dust, and my eyelid gets stuck on my eye. It stings.

"Why?" I croak.

She shakes the sword with her sobs. It wiggles in the cut. "To be this. To be what I am. I'm a real girl. Not a fake girl. When Mona guessed, I knew the doctors hadn't done a good enough job. I went back. They couldn't take any more of my Adam's apple. There were other issues." She cries out and looks at the ceiling. "I WAS NEVER GOING TO BE WHOLE, RAYNE! NEVER! I WOULD ALWAYS BE FRANKENBARBIE!" She collapses on the ground and sobs. She stops crying and whispers, "A man came to me. He asked for simple things. Your location, your cell phone, where you slept, things like that. Simple things. He wasn't going to hurt you." Tears stream down her cheeks.

I sob dusty tears and feel my body dying. I don't know if I can die early. I don't know anything about myself.

"I just wanted to be real."

I shake my head and feel my legs buckling. "You were real. You were real to me."

She cries harder. "I wasn't real. I was never going to be real. I was always going to be half done. I couldn't have babies. It wasn't fair to be born in a body that wasn't mine. It was never right."

She is a sobbing mess.

I close my eyes and smile. "You have no idea." My voice cracks and breaks.

She drops the sword. It makes a loud clang when it lands on the floor next to her. I can't help but think about the way I acted when I saw her transformed. I wince. No wonder she hates me. I just kept saying the wrong things. I never meant any of it. It doesn't matter now.

She turns and faces the stairs. "I CAN'T DO THIS ANYMORE! I CAN'T!"

She looks at me and shakes her blonde head. Her eyes are dead. She whispers, "My debt is paid." She walks to the window where the cold stormy ocean air is coming in. She stands on the ledge.

"Noooooo!" I scream, but it is barely louder than a whisper.

She looks back at me. The wind blows her hair. "Forgive me." A tear slides down her cheek.

I nod. "Anything. I forgive you. Please don't jump." I feel my throat tear. I taste my own blood. It wets my throat.

She looks down and shakes. "He's going to kill me. He wants you dead, but he can't come here himself. He wants you dead. It's you or me."

I look at the sword on the ground, where she was crying. "Kill me then."

She sits on the ledge. I feel a small measure of relief.

"Kill me. My wrists and shoulders are dislocated. My body is completely dehydrated. I'm dying anyway. Kill me. I think my arms are broken. I know my heart is."

She shakes her head. "I can't. I can't hurt you anymore. I just didn't want to die, Rayne. I tried to kill myself but I couldn't." She trembles in a heap. "I couldn't."

I hear voices.

"Hide. If they see you, they'll kill you. They want the opposite of whoever is trying to kill me. They want me alive."

She winces and climbs off the edge. She picks up the sword and takes it out of the room. I don't know where she is hiding but the voices get closer. I hope she's safe. It's an ironic feeling.

Wyatt's mom walks into the room. She is dressed as a schoolteacher again. Homicidal schoolteacher, maybe.

She looks at me and snarls.

A man is behind her. When he rounds the corner, I gasp. The man in the sweater.

His smile doesn't reach his dull-gray eyes.

He looks exhausted and unkempt.

She crosses her arms.

He walks to me and runs his fingers against my arms. His touch rots my belly. I would squirm, but I have nothing left.

He looks down on me and smirks. He leans in and kisses me. His kiss is stiff, and I feel like it defiles me. He parts my lips with his and before I'm ready, wind is forced down my throat. I can't get my breath or exhale. He does it rough and violently. He forces it on me. His fingers grip into my arms. I feel them puncture my skin as they knead me. I suck him dry. Instead of his life force, I take the evil. He gives me a nibble of a kiss and steps back. He is shiny and clean and beautiful. His clothes look amazing, and his face is young and handsome.

He smiles at me and walks from the room. He says nothing. Wyatt's mother watches me for a moment and then turns to leave. I feel full. I feel gross and dirty and full in a way that makes me feel sick. Like I've swallowed a slug and I can't imagine anything else in my belly with it. The evil sits in there. Rotting me. I can feel it. I'm instantly sick. I would throw up, but I'm dehydrated so nothing is inside of me.

I don't understand how I'm not dead yet.

The pain ripping through me is new. The rot of the world is writhing inside of me. It's stretching my insides and getting cozy. I gag and heave as it slithers around in there.

My legs buckle and a scream rips from my throat when my shoulders stretch again.

'Rayne…Rayne…Rayne…'

My eyes flutter, but I can't get my feet to stand and take the pressure and weight off my wrists and shoulders.

"Help me." I croak.

Mona runs into the room. Her eyes widen and she looks back. "Up here. Hurry."

She runs to me. Her hands shake and tremble. "Rayne. Oh my God—what did they do? WYATT, HELP!"

She is sobbing. Her glassy eyes are full of horror and fear.

I can barely open my eyes. In the sliver of light, I can see him. Everything moves in slow motion. He lifts me and shouts at Mona. She panics and starts shaking. She is sobbing and panicking. He's yelling. My ears are full of the sounds, but my brain doesn't comprehend them.

 She ends up holding me up while he rips the shackles from the wall. He looks savage and crazed again. When I feel the weight leave my arms and his arms close around me like a cocoon, I let myself close my eyes.

Everything is in flashes.

I feel the cold water and the dead weight of my broken arms.

I see him spitting out the seawater and swimming out into the black water.

I'm shivering and convulsing.

I feel close to death.

He kisses my cheek and swims.

His face lights, up and he steels himself against whatever he sees.

I turn my head to see the angry face of a Nixie.

She is about to attack him when she sees me.

Her anger fades and crystals fall from her eyes made of light. She cries the most beautiful tears. They hit the water and make something like a phosphorescent light.

She reaches a pale hand for me.

She cries out when she touches me.

Other lights come to the surface.

I can see them everywhere.

Seawater slips into my mouth.

I swallow and gag.

My eyes close and when I open them, the ocean is lit up by the lights of the Nixie. They are everywhere, bobbing in the waves. Some are crying. Others look panicked.

The one with the red hair swims forward. She looks at me and him and then lifts her face into the air.

I feel him shifting.

I see the bright glint of the steel in his hands. It's the same small blade he used on the last one. He drives it into her neck. She jerks and shakes and bleeds light into the water. It spills everywhere. It's like phosphorescent dancing on the water, but it's her blood. I see the whisper of something float in the air. It's the purest light I've ever seen. He takes the blade and lifts my hand to the surface of the water. He slices my hand. I barely register the pain. My hands are black and bloated anyway. The blood that seeps out is black and gross looking, like tar.

He puts the dagger out into the light. It coats the blade and sparkles with light and life. He stabs it into the cut on my hand, and I feel the scream rip from me again. I feel everything shift. My shoulders pop back in and my wrists snap and crackle. My ribs and stomach convulse again.

The next Nixie swims up. She bares her throat.

I am helpless still. I scream and cry out but they ignore me.

I beg them to stop. Everyone ignores me.

Tears well in Wyatt's eyes as he cuts the essence out of each one.

It takes seven of them before my blood runs red again.

Chapter Sixteen

They are now my sisters. I can feel them watching me from the water.

I look in the backseat of the SUV at Michelle. I reach for her hand. She watches me and ignores my touch.

I squeeze and smile. "I will forgive you anything."

She looks broken. "You can't. You have to stop. You need to be smarter than that. I am a terrible person."

Wyatt looks annoyed. "Lucifer is the king of manipulation. He is a master. He made you weak. Apparently, he does it better than anyone." He isn't defending what she did. No one will.

He looks at me. I smile. He frowns. "I haven't ever met him, but that's what Fitz says."

The name is a razor blade on my skin. I shiver and wince.

He looks at me and then down. "Sorry."

I shake my head to dismiss it, but I can't. Physically, I cannot let it go. I can let go of Michelle's betrayal, because she was used. My own father used her pain and suffering against her. Wyatt's uncle and mother tortured me on purpose. They didn't need to. I was no threat to them.

The drive to the old church is long and I'm antsy. My legs twitch and I tap on everything I touch.

I glance at Wyatt under my lashes. "You saved me."

He laughs. "It was an accident. I panicked."

I blush and smile. It's the first real smile I've felt in ages. I laugh, and it feels like I'm whole again for the moment.

He brushes our moment off. "So, this priest knows about the light of the world?"

I shrug. "Not sure about that, but Willow says he for sure knows how to kill the five devils. She's been researching a ton since we left her place. They all have."

Wyatt sighs. "I spoke to my mom today."

I almost get whiplash from how fast my head turns. My skin crawls, and I feel every pain she inflicted upon my flesh.

"She said to say she was sorry and that it wasn't personal."

I watch his face for his reaction to the words. He shoots a glance at me, but then looks back at the road.

Mona leans into the front seat. "Are you kidding?"

He shakes his head.

Mona looks at me and strokes my arm. I lean into the affection.

I glance at Michelle. She is twisting up inside. She looks ready to crack.

"She can say whatever she wants. I have no intention of forgiving her."

Wyatt looks at me. "You are awfully choosy about who you forgive." He hasn't forgiven Michelle. To him, his mother was trained to do what she did. She had every reason. Not to mention, her son handfasted with a Sin Eater. To him, Michelle chose what she did to me for selfish reasons, and she is the one who is guilty. His mother was doing her chosen purpose in life. Her job.

I want to punch him in the head sometimes.

"Yeah, well, when you watch seven women die to save you, plain old you. One of you, for seven of them. You may then be as choosy as you like." My voice is calm, but my insides are freaking out.

Mona looks at Michelle and scowls. She hasn't gotten past it either. We are taking Michelle back to school after the church. I think it's a mistake. I feel like I need her. Not to mention, she knows what my dad looks like. I need to know why he wants me dead, before I eat all the sin.

Wyatt pulls into a motel and hops out of the SUV.

I look at Michelle and Mona. "Thanks for coming."

Mona looks annoyed and Michelle scowls.

I sigh. "Can we just get past this? Get it out, Mona. You're pissed. Michelle, you're embarrassed. Just say it."

Mona looks at Michelle and slaps her hard across the cheek. Michelle lowers her head and sobs quietly.

"You are a bitch. You betrayed her. For what…a uterus?"

Michelle ugly cries. I lean across the back seat and hug her.

"You aren't a bitch." I look at Mona. "She isn't a bitch. You don't know what it's like to be something you can't love and understand."

Mona processes it and crosses her arms.

Michelle looks at her. Mona reaches over and hugs her. "I liked you better before. Now you look plastic."

Michelle snorts. "You're a dick."

I look at them both and dive in for a hug. It's not one hundred percent better, but it feels like it might be, one day.

He gets back in the SUV and looks at us funny.

He hands them a key and me a key, and drives to the far side of the motel. He gets out of the SUV and stretches. I climb out and open the door with the number matching my key. He is right behind me. I look back at him. "What are you doing?"

He presses himself against my back. "Sharing a room. Open the door." I don't even get to say goodnight to my friends. When I open the door, he pushes me in and locks it. He slides a chair against the door and makes certain all the windows are locked. I stand watching him.

"You can't share a room with me."

He looks back at me and grins. "Scared to be alone with me?" He's cocky and I hate him sometimes, well, really dislike him. My ability to hate him is diminishing. Which is annoying.

He jumps onto the one bed and grabs the remote. He turns on the TV and starts flicking. I look at the door and wonder how far I can make it if I push the chair and make a run for it?

He watches me with one eye and football with the other.

"Don't even think about it."

I sit on the chair in the entryway, and ignore the closed door, the man I love, and the way my belly feels warm and nervous.

A knock at the door startles my thoughts.

I look at the door and wait for something.

"Yes?" he shouts at the door.

"Wyatt, where is Rayne?" Mona is outside.

"Go away, Mona." He doesn't trust Michelle.

I stand and walk to the window facing the parking lot. I tap the double-paned glass.

She comes to the window and frowns. "Open the door."

I shake my head and point to Wyatt. I put a mock gun up to my head and pull the trigger and roll my eyes.

She laughs.

She puts her face up to the window. "Michelle needs you."

I frown and put my face up to the cold glass of the window. I shout back, "Why?"

She looks at Wyatt and shouts really loud with a shitty grin on her face. "She got her period."

My eyes are huge. I can feel the strain of them being so wide.

Wyatt moans, "Gross, what the hell? Keep that shit to yourself. Jesus."

I slide the chair away from the door. "I gotta go. She's going to be freaking out."

He waves a hand at me. "Gross."

I open the door and run out. Mona grabs my hand and pulls me to her room. Inside she slams the door and looks at Michelle.

Michelle is on the bed with the guiltiest look on her face. "He knows."

I look at them both and frown. "Who knows what? About your period?"

"Where the light of the world is."

I am confused. "So no period?"

Michelle tilts her head. I shrug. "I don't know."

She shakes her head at me. "Anyway, I heard them talking at their house when I was sneaking around trying to find you. He's using you to take it. I never put two and two together, until you said something in the truck just then."

I don't trust her. I never realized it, until now. Pitting her and Wyatt against each other is a no-brainer for me. It's him every time. It's always going to be him. I love him. My brain plays the devil's advocate and whispers, 'Even if he doesn't love you? Can't love something like you?'

I watch her face. "Where is it?"

She looks at Mona for support. Mona nods slightly, "It's inside of someone. It's kept in a person. You have to suck it out. You know—the way you feed."

"But who?"

She swallows hard. "Your mother."

I sit on the bed and watch her face. She is in turmoil.

"Where did they say she was?"

She shakes her head violently. "They never said. I swear. I know you don't trust me and I'm sorry for that. I'll always be sorry for it."

"You are my friend. You don't owe me anything, Michelle. You'll always be my friend." I don't say that I trust her. I don't lie.

"How do you know he knows?"

She sighs and stares straight ahead. "I was walking around the rooms, trying to find where they had hidden you. He was at the table with them, the one in the basement. Anyway, the uncle said he needed the Light of the World to do something. He never said what, just that he needed it. Then his mom said, 'well, it's inside of Lillith. It always has been. All she ever had to do was kill her mother and she would have lived, forever.' Then the dad says, 'well, take her to her mother and get her to kill her.'"

I feel sick. It sounds too elaborate for her to be lying to me. But I can tell she is holding something back. "What else?"

She presses her lips together. "Then Wyatt said that if he killed you as the light left your mother, he could take it."

He plans on killing me. I doubted his love from the beginning, but I have never doubted his care for me. He can't explain it, even to himself, but I know he cares.

"He could be leading them on and not planning on hurting me."

Mona rolls her eyes. "No, you're thinking with the va-jay-jay. If he were on your side, he would have told you how to find it. He would have told you how to kill your mother. He would help you. Not plot against you. Besides, he took you back to their house and let them torture you."

I want to scowl at her and rage and tell her how wrong she is. I want to run back to the room and lay on the bed with him. I want to let him have me. I want so many things. Mostly, I want Michelle to be lying to me. I think of the many ways in which this could be her laying a trap.

None are as convincing as him being on his parents' side. Screw him.

I smirk at her. "I can play this game with him. Meet me at the truck in like half an hour."

Michelle looks worried and Mona looks excited.

I leave and walk back to the room. My insides are burning in pain. I open the door and close it softly.

He glances at me. "She okay?"

I shake my head. "No it's bad. Blood clots and other stuff."

He gags. "Oh my God."

"She is like peeing blood and cramping on the toilet. It's pretty typical stuff."

He looks green. "Oh wow. I don't need to know this shit."

I smile inside. I climb on the bed beside him and snuggle into him. He wraps an arm around me and kisses my forehead. He doesn't pay attention to it. He watches football for a second.

I start tracing the pattern on his shirt. I trace it and think about taking his clothes off. I notice him adjusting his position. I lift his shirt and trace the pattern of the writing on his side. The words feel magical. They are obviously a part of what he is. There is no denying it. The heat coming off them is intense. I lean forward and kiss the words.

"What do these say?"

He is lying back and enjoying my attention.

He lifts his head. "What?"

I blush. "The words?"

He looks confused and shakes his head. "I don't know. I've just always had them. They're in Latin."

I raise my eyebrows in surprise. "You have a tattoo and you don't know what it is?"

He looks back at the TV and shakes his head again. "My whole family has them. Probably something about the vow they made to God to vanquish evil." He grins like it's a joke.

I'm not convinced.

He pulls me back into him. I continue to trace the letters delicately.

He looks down at me. I can see fire in his eyes. He bends and presses his lips onto my cheek.

I pull away. "No."

He looks angry. "You can trace my tats, but I can't kiss your cheek?"

I shake my head and pull his shirt back down. His abs flex and he turns on his side. He kisses my neck and whispers, "I think you want me, Rayne. As much as I want you."

I grin and let him start something I have no intention of finishing. His hands slide up and down my body, making nerves stand on end. He cups my ass and pulls me up. He rolls and I'm on top of him.

I let him have it. I suck as hard as I can. We're kissing but really it's a battle of strength. He is blocking and kissing and I'm sucking and kissing. He's better at it than I am. He becomes the wind tunnel again.

I feel him grind against me. He's turned on.

I grind back, teasing him more. He moans and cups my ass and presses me into him. I sit up like I'm riding him and grin.

He shakes his head. "You can push it too far, Rayne." His eyes sparkle.

I move like I want to get off, but he holds me there. His fingers dig into my legs.

"You are killing me."

I want to retort, believe me. I have comebacks for this moment. I've been plotting them since we met. Instead I smile sweetly, like I'm clueless.

He growls and sits up. His lips meet mine with a crash. His passion explodes and I suck. I pull from him. It's not sweet. It's sour and gross. I pull away and cough. He frowns. "Oh my God, Rayne…you have to learn how not to do that when we kiss."

I cough and grip my belly. I roll on the bed and moan.

He rubs my back. "Are you okay?"

I shake my head.

He lies with me and snuggles me.

"I'm sorry. I don't mean to hurt you."

I nod and tremble. He hugs me, but I can feel him pressing himself against me. He can't stop himself.

He readjusts himself and looks at me. "You mind if I go take a cold shower? I can't snuggle you like this."

I shake my head and curl up. I close my eyes.

He kisses my cheek and walks to the bathroom. He closes the door and when I hear the shower, I open one eye.

I wait until I can tell the water is hitting his body and leap from the bed. I take his keys and wallet and run out the door.

They're already sitting at the curb.

I click the lock and we all jump in.

I start the SUV and throw it into reverse. I am driving out of the parking lot when I see him running out in a towel.

Chapter Seventeen

The priest is a friendly man. He has chubby cheeks and a kind disposition, but I still don't trust him.

His eyes are hiding something. I don't know what, but there is something missing from the conversation.

"So, which one of you ladies is the Sin Eater?"

Mona raises her eyebrows at him and nods. He sighs. "You have a very long, hard path ahead of you, my dear. Essentially, you need to destroy the five devils and then your parents. It will reset the evil, and the balance will be restored."

Michelle sits in the corner quietly.

He glances at her and frowns. "I can't help but notice the evil inside of you. Your energy is a mess." He sounds like Willow. "You are at a desperate point in your life, my dear."

She nods and swallows. "I have sinned, Father. Greater than any sin possible. I betrayed someone. Someone I loved like a sister." She looks at me, and I shake my head subtly.

He takes her hands and shakes his head. "No, my child. Anyone who repents for his or her sins can be absolved. Anyone."

She looks down and whispers, "I don't think that includes me. I made a deal with the devil. A deal that he still expects payment for."

He rings a bell on his desk. A nun walks in.

"I think this young lady would like a tour of the Cathedral. Perhaps even some tea. On the ladies' side." He leads Michelle to the nun's hand. She takes her and leaves the room with a slight nod. Michelle is sobbing again.

He closes the door.

"She has Lucifer himself within her. We cannot speak in front of her. I'm surprised she hasn't betrayed either of you yet. He holds her soul." A grave look crosses his face.

I look at Mona and nod slightly.

Mona looks at him and nods. "She has betrayed us already. We forgave her for her betrayal, but now we kind of think she's lying every time she opens her mouth."

He nods slowly. "I see."

He pours a cup of tea and offers it to me and Mona. I take it, but wait for him to pour a cup for himself. When he does and takes a sip, I drink a sip of mine.

He watches me and smiles. "So, the five devils are not hard to get. Simply use her as bait. Starve her and they will feel her need. They will come. When they open their mouths to give her the sin, you cut their heads off. It must be their heads. Instant death is the only way to ensure the sin goes with them to hell. If they suffer or bleed out, the sin seeps back into the air and then back into the earth."

I frown and look at Mona. "Starve her?"

He nods. "A little torture maybe, too. She needs to be suffering and starving. They feel the need. They will come, one at a time. She cannot take more than one feed a month, if that. Three months is better, four is the best."

I watch Mona's face. "Can we track them?"

He nods. "Yes. They typically live in the worst places on earth. The epicenters of sin. Hell on earth, if you will."

"How do we find Lillith and Lucifer?" I ask.

He shakes his head. "If I knew that, I would already have ended this myself."

I put my tea down and bite my lip. "What happened last time? In the dark ages?"

He shakes his head again. "I don't know, but I know the Sin Eater died. Not the devils."

I stand and hold my hand out. "Thanks. You've been a lot of help."

He frowns. "Surely you can't be ready to leave already?" He fusses with the teapot.

I watch his face and look at Mona. "Tie him up." He looks panicked.

She already has a huge urn in her hands. She smashes it over his head and rips the phone cord out of the wall and the back of the phone. She ties him up.

"How did you know?" I ask Mona.

She shakes her head. "His eyes. He kept looking at the clock. I guarantee Wyatt is going to be here any second."

I look over at the door. "Great."

While she ties him up, I rifle through the drawers.

She rubs her belly. "I'm starving."

I nod. "Me too. This is such bullshit. Honestly. We should be at school right now. Having fun and getting drunk."

She laughs and runs her fingers through her long brown hair. "No kidding."

I feel nervous and sick about leaving the room we're in. I'm terrified he is standing in the hall or holding Michelle as bait.

When I look at Mona, her eyes tell me she feels the same way. She walks to the door handle and looks back at me. I nod and together we stroll out casually. I turn the lock on the inside and close the door. I am instantly scanning the massive cathedral. I don't see him or Michelle. Just people praying.

Walking through the pews and seeing Jesus staring at me makes me feel considerably worse about knocking out the priest.

"Where do you think they took her?"

I shake my head and look around. The church is actually a cathedral. It's several times the size of the churches I never went to back home. Willow has a thing with churches. Obviously, finding out she is a witch makes that more clear. She always came up with some story about the priest or minister. I always believed her. Even now I cannot doubt her.

But now I see that the burnings and hangings and torture of the witches pretty much guaranteed I would never be allowed to go.

I walk in front of Mona and climb a set of stairs I had seen from the corner. The red carpet and weird smells creep me out. It's overly warm in decoration and temperature. Part of the sales package, no doubt.

I can't help but notice the carving of Jesus in the hall when we reach the top of the stairs. He looks exactly like the girl in the book.

My skin shivers. It remembers what it felt like to hang by my arms.

We walk around the balcony, but I don't see Michelle or Wyatt.

I mutter, looking over my back, "I'm getting worried."

Mona nods. "What if they took her and are torturing her. He sensed the devil in her. What if the nun did too?"

I don't want to imagine what a church would do to a girl who used to be a boy and sold her soul to the devil. It's pretty much everything they hate, all wrapped in a pretty Barbie-esque package.

I look out the balcony window to my right and see a garden. It's in fall bloom. Leaves of every color are everywhere.

"There's the garden."

We turn to go down the stairs but my stomach twists.

"So, did Wyatt know where they were keeping me?"

Mona shakes her head. "No. I don't think so. He said he could..." Her eyes widen. "Shit." The color is gone from her cheeks. "He said he could sense you. The handfasting."

I wince. I knew it. I should have known it.

"Warwick." The word tastes bad in my mouth.

She looks confused. "What?"

I sigh. "When I was in Warwick, he knew I was there. Somehow. The Nixie swam me far from him. Like a two-hour swim. There was no way he could have known that I was there and yet, I was walking down the road and felt this twisting feeling in my stomach. I ran and hid, just as he drove by me."

She looks at my hand resting on my belly. "You feel that now?"

I bite my lip. "I do."

"Shit."

I nod.

We look around and creep up to the wall where the overlook is for the balcony. My stomach lurches when she points discretely. "There."

He is trying the handle on the priest's door. He is not alone. There is a man and another girl with him.

"Shit," I whisper. He turns and looks around. I pull her away from the wall. We are both shivering.

"He wanted to save me, right? He didn't want me chained to the wall? It was genuine?" I whisper into her clenched body.

She nods. "I believed he was devastated. His mother and everyone wouldn't talk to him. He was screaming and saying that it wasn't time. They told him it was for the best. I have no idea what it meant, but I know he was outraged."

I pull her back from the wall and we duck and run. There is another stairwell. We creep down the stairs.

I run. I don't know where to run, but I do. Mona pulls out her phone and starts texting.

"Really?" I almost shout, but contain myself. I'm trying every door handle we pass but they're all locked. Damned untrusting religious people.

"Michelle says leave. She sent me a text saying she's staying. She wants to stay and find herself."

I roll my eyes. "Shit. They're going to take her and torture her."

Mona frowns. "I sent her a message that he's here. She said she's going to the women's-only section now. It's strictly forbidden for him to enter."

I laugh. It's funny. "Hopefully God doesn't remember who she is, or was."

The only door that opens for us leads down into the dark. The stairs are old and decrepit. We slip in and I look out into the hall as I close the door. I turn the latch on the door.

"I can't see," she whispers and reaches back for me. I slip past her and hold her hands. I can see clearly.

"You don't want to. It's friggin' creepy in here."

I feel her tense. That was probably the wrong thing to say.

The stairs bring us to a large cement room.

"It's like an unfinished basement. Nothing down here," I whisper into the silence. I see a door in the corner. I pull her along. She walks like she's impaired, tripping over nothing.

Her hands are trembling.

"It's okay, dude. There is nothing down here. I'm not kidding. It's just us and a concrete room."

"Okay. You can see for real, right?"

"For real. There is a door over here. Just a sec." I let go, but she holds my shoulder with a grip that feels like it's ripping my skin open.

I turn the old-fashioned door handle.

I push my weight into the thick wood.

The door scrapes along the old floor.

Her fingers dig into my skin.

"Easy. That hurts."

"Sorry." She is shaking brutally.

The door opens into a tiny tunnel. It's skinny and looks as I imagine the Underground Railroad would have. I pull her through the narrow opening. "It's small, but it seems like it's a tunnel. It must lead somewhere."

I close the door behind us. My stomach twinge is worsening.

"He's following us, I think. Or he's directly above us."

She grips my hand. I can feel sweat on her palm. I want to pull my hand away, but I too would be shitting my pants if it were her leading and me following.

I wipe old cobwebs out of the way. "No one comes down here. The cobwebs are older than us."

"You're really bad at this shit, dude. Try telling me cheery shit."

I laugh quietly and pull her through the thin tunnel. The walls are made of old bricks and crumbling mortar.

"We are going to die in here," she whispers.

I squeeze her hand. "Stop being a baby. This leads somewhere. It has to. No one digs out this much dirt without a reason.

The tunnel twists and turns without any actual corners, just meandering like a river would. Finally, after what feels like hours, I see light ahead.

"Look."

"I can't see anything, dick."

I laugh. "Light up ahead. You'll see it in a minute."

The light floods the tunnel. I don't feel good about the end of the tunnel. I feel sick with nerves.

She stops gripping me, like she is going to peel the skin off of me, as we get closer to the light.

"What is that?" she asks.

I can see it clearly. "A grate."

She is looking around, horrified. "Is this what it looked like the whole way?"

I laugh again. "No, this is worse."

The cobwebs are thick and new, and I am freaking out inside. I lean back and strike at them with my foot, kicking and flailing.

"This is like one of those horror shows."

I pause. "Just a sec." I close my eyes and take a breath. "Can you hear me?"

"Yeah?" I shush her and swat at her.

"Can you hear me? Is he near?" The air isn't sparkling or whispering. I strain but still can't hear them.

"Shit." I look back. "I can hear the dead, if I listen hard enough. They can't come on holy land though. We're still at the church."

She grimaces. "The graveyard. I guarantee it." She looks up and starts to panic. "They're right above us. The dead. I bet they are."

I grab her shoulders. "Calm down. The dead aren't so bad. Trust me. It's the living who suck."

We get up close to the door. It looks like a grate, but it has hinges. It has a latch on our side. I open the latch and push. The door doesn't move. I push harder, but nothing.

Mona pulls a tube from her pocket and starts squeezing it onto the hinges with a huge grin, "Lip gloss."

She rubs the hinges with her fingers, spreading the gloss everywhere.

She slams into the door and rocks it back and forth. The metal makes a screaming noise when she pulls in.

I frown. "Pull, not push."

She pulls the door. The metal doesn't scream again, thanks to the lip gloss.

We step out into the light of day. She squints, but my eyes don't need to.

We have stepped out into the graveyard, literally from a hobbit hole in the side of the hill.

I pull the grate shut and look around. The grounds are stunning. Colorful trees and headstones line the leave-covered grass.

I look behind, up to the cathedral. "Wow, I have no idea how to get to the parking lot."

It looks gothic and cool from this distance.

I look at the stream to the right of us that leads into the forest. "We're going that way."

She looks at me and shakes her head. "I hate you right now."

I glance at her ballet flats and nod. "It's cool. I get it. I hate me most days."

We crunch along the trees and rocks. The church gets farther and farther away.

She breaks the silence after a few moments. "I don't really hate you. I just wish you were normal."

I look back and smile. "I know. Me too."

My stomach still feels him. He isn't close, but I know he's coming. Tracking me like a bloodhound.

"So you can feel him?"

I nod. "Yeah. I guess so."

She nudges me. "This sucks. You okay?"

I shake my head. "No. No, I don't think I'll ever be okay. My brain says this is all fake, for sure. None of this is real. My body believes, but that's from the torture. My heart knows it's real, but wants to go back to the old way. I know my parents were evil and broke the rules, but I don't understand why God hates me so much. I don't even believe in God, and yet he is ruining my life."

Her words come out like she's talking to herself. "It's heavy. I want to say I don't believe, but I do. God help me, but I do. The stuff the priest said made sense though. The torture was for a reason."

I furrow my brow. "That doesn't take away from the fact that it happened."

She shakes her head defensively. "I'm not saying that. At all. I know it happened. I can't get the image of you in that room out of my mind. It's burned there. Scarred in my brain."

I look at her. We match. Immense amounts of pity cover both our faces. "I'm sorry. I'm sorry I dragged you into this."

She ups the ante and lets a tear slip from her eyes. "No. No one should have to go through something like this alone, Rayne. We are the loser-nerd girls who will go unnoticed and not be the pass-around girl in the frat. We joined that shit together. I'm in till the end."

I feel tears in my eyes, but I laugh. We pick up the pace and run the rest of the way out of the huge park we are in.

Chapter Eighteen

The warmth of the restaurant and the coffee in my hand isn't enough to remove the feeling of the huge spider I found roaming in my hoodie. Terror and anxiety are still crawling around on my skin where it was.

My skin is crawling, and I can't shake the heebie-jeebies. Mona's screaming face is about the only thing that has gotten me through it.

I shove the last of the Subway sandwich into my mouth. I'm so hungry. I could kill everyone in here and still be hungry. Well, except for Mona.

I glance at her and point at her face. "You have dirt on your eyebrows and forehead."

She scowls. "Dude. How long has it been like that?" She wipes with the napkin, but it doesn't come off.

I smile. "Still there."

"Gross. Graveyard dirt." She stands and walks away. Her perfect little outfit is ruined from the day's adventures. Running in a park and slithering through a tunnel. I shiver again and remember the way the horrid, black beast crept out of my shirt, its eight legs tickling me. I almost gag, but I take a deep breath and smell the bread, and the guy sitting behind me.

We stole a car in downtown Boston and drove here—New Hampshire.

If I ever speak to Wyatt again, I will have to get him to give the owners of the car some money. Just like I did with the last people I stole from. I had him mail the old people from Newport one thousand dollars. He owed me that, at the least.

I probably owed them more. The ham sandwich and the shower had to have been worth a million dollars. Not to mention, the three hundred dollars I found taped to the lid of the cookie jar.

Mona comes out of the bathroom looking remarkably better. Her outfit has been cleaned up and her hair is straight and smooth. The dirt is gone.

"You made good use of the bathroom." I laugh.

She smiles. "I can't stand looking like that. It's a good thing you don't mind. I have a feeling this is all about to get more interesting."

I raise an eyebrow at her, "Why?"

Her eyes dart to the window. A tall man with dark hair and a charming smile is looking at us through the glass. I jump when I see him.

"Who is that?" I ask.

She shrugs. "Not sure. He came into the bathroom when I was there and asked if I had somewhere to stay for the night. I told him to fuck off, obviously. He smiled that exact smile, and then said if the Van Helsings catch you, I bet they'll clean that mouth of yours up. Then he was gone. I actually thought I might have daydreamed it, but there he is." She sighs and covers her eyes for a minute.

I get up from the table and feel my palms instantly sweat. "He came in the bathroom? Who is he? Why are you so calm? That's creepy." He looks familiar.

She gives me an incredulous look. "How should I know? He told me that I should stay really calm. So I did."

I frown. "That doesn't even make any sense. Great. He could be my dad."

She nods. "I thought that too."

I give her a skeptical look. "Well, doesn't that make you want to freak out?"

She smiles at me with glossy lips. "Yup."

I turn and watch him, just as he watches us. No one makes a move. My stomach tingle starts. I groan, "Great."

"Wyatt?" she whispers.

"Yup," I whisper back.

She looks around and sighs. "Take a chance with the stranger?"

I look around. "There is probably a back entrance. We could run."

The man outside the window laughs as if he is in on the conversation.

She shakes her head. "He vanished in the bathroom. Vanished. I don't think running is a good option."

I am weak and exhausted. I need to eat, but I want the devils to come for me. If I get hungry enough, they will sense me and then we can kill them.

I look into the dark eyes of the stranger outside the window. His eyes meet mine and he nods. "Trust me."

The air sparkles and I feel the dead agree. They want me to go with him.

I take the first step, but it feels forced. I push myself to take another and another until I am at the door. I push on it and shiver when the cold air hits my face.

"The Sin Eater at Subway, imagine." His voice is deep and sexy. His movements are confident and relaxed. I know him. It's stuck in my brain.

"Are you my father?" I ask, star struck.

He looks lost. "What? Lucifer? No. That's an odd question."

My movements feel jerky and tense.

His eyes dart to Mona. "Do you always bring food with you?"

Horror crosses my face. I gasp and take a step back and bump into her.

His eyes widen and his hands lift. "I'm sorry. I never meant to offend you. Is she your lover?"

I look back at her and laugh.

He smiles along, but is clearly confused.

I feel the horrified look on my face. "She is my friend."

He tries to swallow his confusion down but he can't. "You have friends, friends who are human? Without, well you know."

I look at Mona and cock an eyebrow. "Yeah. I'm a human too. Well I was, like two months ago."

He looks completely lost. "I don't understand."

I laugh. "Welcome to my world. Who are you? Or should I ask, what are you?"

He chuckles and points to a long black car that resembles a hearse. "I'm a friend of your mother's. At least, I was once."

The feeling in my stomach is getting worse but I'm terrified. "Are you my father? Tell me the truth."

His face grows cold. "No. No, your father is a bad man. I am indifferent to humans, as they are fodder for most of us, but I am not like your father. His intentions have always been focused on revenge and suffering." He sniffs the air. "I suggest we move this conversation to a safer place."

He walks to the car and opens the door to the backseat. Mona is gripping my shirt. I look across the parking lot to the car speeding toward us. My heart nearly stops. I run to the backseat of the car and jump in.

I shout, "It's him!"

The man climbs in the backseat and the car starts. I can't see into the front to see the driver. The dark glass all around the car prevented us from seeing him outside and in. He drives like a pro. He backs up and spins the car in a half circle. When the white car pulls into the parking lot, our black car speeds past it. Through the tinted glass, I can see Wyatt and the woman and man from the church.

Our driver speeds away, skidding and peeling out at every possible moment.

We are flung about and smashed into the windows.

The man on the seat across from us sits perfectly still. The movements of the car don't move him.

We drive this way until the car hits a bumpy area. Then we drive slowly. I look out into the night at the forest around us.

"Where are we going?" I ask.

He smiles. "My home. The Van Helsings will not come there."

I frown. "You don't know Wyatt very well, do you?"

He shakes his head. "The youngest of the sons? No, I do not. They fear my lands. Have since we left the old country. They lost a lot of family at my hands. I don't believe they will want to run the chance of that happening again."

His dark eyes flicker to Mona constantly.

He shakes his head. "I'm sorry. It's just remarkable how much you look like the girl from that show."

I snort. "You watch Gossip Girl?"

He shrugs. "I like TV. That show in particular offers some very tantalizing young flesh."

Mona leans into me. "Gross."

My stomach turns.

He laughs. "I mean you no harm. I wish for you to succeed this time, Sin Eater." His dark eyes glimmer.

I back away from the pull. "Rayne."

His face breaks into a smile. "Willow has spoken of you."

I scowl. "You know my mo… Willow?"

He smiles. "Of course. I know all there is to know. I am Constantine Basarab, fourth count of the House of Basarab."

He is charming, and when he says his name, he has an accent. It's thick and sexy, and Mona leans forward slightly.

"What are you, Constantine?"

He flashes a smile like I have never seen. Two large fangs hang, where his canines should be.

I scream. Mona screams.

He laughs and the car comes to a stop.

Mona is gripping me.

He closes his mouth and muffles the rich chuckles, he let burst from him.

A small man opens the door. He moves quickly. Every movement comes across as a twitch or jerk. But it's because he moves so quickly.

Constantine points to the door. "Ladies first." We grip each other and scramble from the car.

He climbs out and stretches his long legs. He seems bigger, taller. Or I'm just so terrified, I have made him larger in my mind's eye.

He takes my hand in his and kisses the top. "It is my pleasure to make your acquaintance, Madam Sin Eater." His eyes sparkle. He takes Mona's hand and kisses it. "Madam."

We are charmed. We can't fight the charms he has. Mona is worse than I am. His touch has calmed us both. She takes a step toward him. "It's my pleasure to meet you. Not yours."

I've never seen her be forward before. I pull her back and scowl. "Stop what you're doing." I sigh and roll my eyes. "Can we just go inside, before Wyatt shows up and shit goes downhill, like it tends to do when he's around?"

He watches her for a moment and then breaks his stare. He glances at the driver. "Put the car away, Tom. We won't be needing it."

The driver moves quickly.

Mona doesn't notice the driver. She is blushing and tempting Constantine. He is fighting the urge to eat her. I know that feeling.

"Can you go out in the daytime?" I ask.

He looks at me and smirks. "Of course. Thinking about fleeing already? Am I such a poor host that I'm already driving you to that?"

I shake my head. "No, just curious. You know, like Buffy the Vampire Slayer and shit."

He rolls his eyes. "I will say, that show was better than some." He holds a hand out. Instantly, both of us are even more mesmerized. His house is like a villa on the sea, but shaped like a German castle. It has peaked roofs and a smooth finish, like stone.

My mouth hangs open. "This is where you live?"

He smiles and nods, and seems humble suddenly. "It's just a house, Rayne."

Mona walks forward like she is in a dream. "It's beautiful. So beautiful. Like a magical castle."

We are at a circular driveway in front of a huge, front entryway. His house makes Wyatt's seem plain and tiny. The huge square pillars out front are two feet in diameter. Windows are lit, giving it a warm look. The house is amazing. Amazing.

The doors are the size of a wall in a regular house. A thin woman in a maid's uniform opens the door and greets us with a smile, "Good evening." Her face drops when she sees me. She looks shocked and confused. I know I look terrible. He's dressed so refined, and I look homeless.

We walk in and get lost immediately. The foyer is marble with statues and a staircase that belongs in a southern plantation. Plants, a fountain, ceilings high enough to be four stories, and a pianoforte all fill the room.

"What does the rest look like if this is just the front door?" Mona spins. "Who has a piano in their foyer? That's weird."

He seems annoyed. "You Americans. All so impressed by grandeur and size. It's just a house. And I like to hear the piano all over the house. This is the best spot, acoustically."

Mona blushes again, but I can't help but look around more.

"Would you like something to eat?" he asks politely.

I shake my head but avert my eyes. "No thanks, we just had those subs."

"That's not what I was offering, Sin Eater," he says with a smile.

My head jerks. "What?"

He smiles and holds a hand out. "I keep a selection of things you might be interested in down in the basement."

I feel sick and intrigued. "You keep people hostage?"

He nods. "Come, I'll show you."

Mona takes his hand. She is entranced again. I am frozen in my spot. I want to eat one of the hostages. I can't deny it, but at the same time, I want to be disgusted. It's gross that they are held downstairs, as cattle for the master.

I follow them and tell myself it's to keep Mona safe. Not to eat a hostage.

The hallway we are in turns a corner and suddenly an industrial theme becomes noticeable. We enter a doorway and descend down a wide set of stairs. The floor is rubber and the walls are steel.

It doesn't feel luxurious like upstairs.

Mona walks, watching his eyes the entire time. He has her spellbound.

"You can't hurt her," I whisper it, certain he can hear me.

He looks back. "I swear on my own grave, I would never. I couldn't imagine her skin marred. She is pure."

I point at him. "You have to take the spell off."

He shakes his head. "I can't. I'm not putting one on her. It's her response to me. She has to be the one to change it."

He opens a wide metal door. When we enter, he closes it and locks it with a key.

It looks like a horse barn. Stalls with bars line the huge hallway.

I shudder. "It looks like a prison."

He pauses and tilts his head, looking around. "It's meant to."

His eyes are dark and dangerous, unpredictable. His face is handsome and calm. He towers over Mona and me. He puts a large hand up to the first room and holds the bars. "Come out, come out, wherever you are." He almost sings the words.

I peer into the dark. I can't see anything until my eyes do their thing. Then I see her, it, maybe her. She is my size but a bit thinner. She has a white nightgown on. Her long blonde hair is stringy, and she is filthy. She stands in the corner of her cell, watching the moon from a small barred window.

I take a step closer to the bars. As my face almost makes contact, she turns and screams. I jump back.

Constantine laughs.

She is at the bars raging and screaming.

Mona clutches him, like she did me before.

"Easy girl. Easy." She reaches a white scrawny hand through the bars at him. He touches her and the trembling stops.

She closes her dark eyes as tears stream down her filthy cheeks.

"She drowned her children, on purpose of course. She didn't want anyone to know, so she lied to everyone and said she had moved them to small farmhouse outside of the city. She collected the child welfare for them, but they were dead. No one knew." He strokes the palm of her hand, tickling it. His voice becomes a soft whisper, "No one but me."

My skin crawls. "How-how do you know?"

Her eyes dart at me. Her edgy behavior is back when she hears my voice. I watch the homicidal look in her eyes and decide she is an it, not a she.

"I can read things about people, Rayne. That's how I found you." I know him, and it's driving me insane.

I look back at the woman. Her evil is great. I can sense it, like Willow told me I would be able to.

He moves away from the bars and walks to the next stall. "This was once a teacher. He likes young people, more than most teachers. A girl tried to tell her parents what he had done to her. They never believed her. She had been promiscuous before. He knew that. He has a gift for picking them. The ones no one will believe."

The thing in the stall grunts. He looks at me with hatred and a hollowness I would expect to see on death row.

"He is new. He is not trained and broken properly yet." I look at the expression Constantine has and shiver. He is an evil man. I can sense his evil too. If I let myself, I can taste the blood the way he does. I can feel the life he steals flowing into my mouth. I know I will like it.

"We are the same," I mutter.

He looks at me and frowns. "You are innocent. Never let them tell you different. None of this is your fault." A sick and filthy grin crosses his delicious lips. "I, however, have enjoyed many aspects of my life." His tongue flicks from his mouth and wets his lips.

I am horrified at my attraction to him.

Sexually, I am dysfunctional. I am only attracted to danger and pain. I should have stayed at the convent with Michelle.

Mona's eyes are closed.

He sees my expression and speaks softly, "I don't want her to see them. I want her to remain unchanged and unspoiled. I have her believing she is in an armchair watching Casablanca. She deserves that. I just can't let her alone in the house. She is pure."

He looks around as if the house is listening to us.

He holds a hand out. "Every stall has someone in it that has committed horrific crimes and gotten away with them. Feel free to enjoy the company of one. Just pull the lever at the end of the hall for the one you want. Tom will watch for when you want out of here."

I nod and he leaves. I never realized he would leave me alone here with criminals. Nerves start to fill me as he closes the metal door and I am alone in the hallway.

Every noise they make gets under my skin. My fingers tense. I look around. My heart beat speeds up.

I can hear them breathing. I can hear the sick thoughts they have. The teacher watches me from the bed in his cell. He watches me and thinks something I can't let my brain comprehend. My blood boils. I feel something coming alive inside of me. My skin vibrates. I look at the metal door and the wall where the levers are. I walk to it, letting the boiling anger and disgust inside of me fill up. I pull the second lever. The stall door slides into the wall.

The thing that used to be a man, before he let his darkness overtake him, steps from the cell. He is much larger than I thought. My nerves come back. They push away the bravery I have mustered.

He smiles and tilts his head. "You're a very pretty girl. What's your name?"

My mouth twitches. His thick fingers ball into fists and then straighten out again. I can hear the knuckles cracking.

I shiver and watch his shadow on the floor. The air whispers and sparkles. The dead want me to run. They fear him. When the dead fear you, something is wrong inside of you.

He looks at my chest and licks his lips. I try to focus on the feelings I have inside of me. The feelings of disgust. I can't make them bigger than the fear.

He lunges suddenly and pins me against the metal wall. I start to cry. His warm skin is making heat everywhere. It's angry heat. He licks my neck and pins my arms against the wall. His legs hold mine. He has done this before. He anticipates my moves and counters before I even have a chance.

I feel a sob rise in my throat. I'm still panicking. He doesn't kiss my mouth. He must know not to. His face buries itself in my neck. He spins me and throws me to the floor. He pounces. I try to scramble away but I can't. My head slams into the floor and he is on top of me.

I see stars, but then I see something else. I see a color. It builds at the back of my eyes and becomes everything I see.

I see red. Raw, red anger and hatred.

It's his, not mine.

My eyes do their thing. I inhale him even from the floor. I can drink from him without seeing him. I can taste him in the air. I drink and feel his essence inside of me. I can taste his evil. It's sweet and delicious. He weakens for a moment. Apparently, it's all I need. I turn and wrestle him off of me. I pin him to the floor. I'm sitting on him the way I did Wyatt. Pelvis to pelvis. I lean forward until our faces almost touch and take the biggest breath I can. As I am doing it, I hear a click.

I suck him until I feel fingers biting into my skin.

I look up to see the angry child killer looking at me with contempt and hatred. She wraps her dirty fingers around my throat. My mind is panicking but my body ignores it. It reacts on its own. I push her and pin her in the air. I suck from her until the next click.

I am lost in a sea, no, a buffet of tastes and pleasure. The clicks are coming two at a time but I don't fight them. I dance with them. I twirl and suck, choke and suck, and devour them one after the other. I choke one while eating another.

Something is happening and my body is giving in to the moment. Every bad thought and dirty moment is filled with the sweetness they stole from someone else.

My leg kicks at a tall man. I pin his face to the wall with my foot and drink from the man trying to grab at me and scratch me.

I drink from the man I choked with my foot like a ninja. I pull away and feel like I could run straight up a skyscraper. I am invincible. I am on fire in a good way. My stomach rumbles low; it feels hot and naughty. I look around the room for my next bite, but there is no one. The floor is littered with bodies. Their faces are distended in awkward positions. Like they died crying out.

They did.

I look at the cells. Every stall door has been opened. There is no one left. I walk to the hall and let the food I've had be enough. When my finger grazes the cold metal of the door, I feel it. Reality slams into me.

I look back, horrified at what I have done. Remorse, self-loathing, and regret battle around inside of me.

My jaw trembles. I have murdered a dozen people like it was nothing. The moves of my death dance fill my mind. I sucked them and never thought another thought.

I have never had such a conflict inside of me. Not even when loving Wyatt whilst hating him.

He speaks, awestruck, "You are more impressive than I remember."

I look at Constantine, who is beside me. The metal door is closed and yet he is here like he never left.

"Why did it taste so good now? When the devil used me to cleanse, it tasted so bad." I speak but don't recognize the voice.

"He forced it on you. Plus, it's so much all at once. Nothing tastes good when it's shoved down your throat. Here you ate like you should. Naturally." He sounds as if he's advocating a healthy life style of sorts, not murder.

I look back. "You opened all the doors."

He nods. "I needed to see if you were ready."

My hands react. I have no control over my body. I pin him against the wall and look up at him. "What did you do to me?"

He smiles. "I freed you."

My fingers stop biting at the soft dress shirt. He wraps his arms around me and holds me to him. "We'll succeed this time, Rayne. I promise."

My eyes shut but fill with images.

I'm standing on the cliffs. It's raining and dark and the sea is everywhere. The salt clings to me. I'm wearing a long dress. I'm me. My dark hair clings to my face. I hold a sword and a dagger. A man comes at me, and I fight. My body twitches as I watch the images. It wants to move along with what I see. Like how I twitch watching dancing, like I should be dancing too.

I kill the man and he falls off the cliff. I'm standing on an outcropping of rocks, jagged rocks.

Another man comes at me. I spin and butt the hilt of the sword in his face. His nose bleeds. We fight and I slice the dagger across his cheek. I grab his face and lick the blood from his cheek. I press my lips against his and suck him dry. He drops to the ground in a heap. I kick him off the cliffs and watch as Constantine walks along the rocks. He laughs and grabs my face. He kisses me and I remember it all.

I look up at him. He bends his face, pressing his lips into mine.

"You came back to me," he whispers.

His lips are feverish. I let him devour me. I swear I can feel the rain upon us and the sword in my hand.

He pulls away and cries out. He grips my forearms. "What have you done? Have you handfasted?"

I tremble. "He tricked me. Wyatt tricked me."

He looks at the white ceiling and screams.

Chapter Nineteen

She moans in her sleep and it bothers me. Not because she is making noises, but because she is dreaming about him.

If I could have normal dreams and normal sleeps, I would bet we would both be dreaming about him.

Asshole.

He pushed me hard enough to make me remember him. Unfortunately, my memories are not whole. I remember the feeling of a sword in my hand and the feeling of killing something without guilt. I knew what I was and had no issues with it. What I don't remember is a much larger list than what I do. Constantine is the center of my confusion. I loved him. I know it. When I look at him, I feel it. But I also fear him and sense a betrayal.

I can't sleep. It's never actually happened to me before. I don't seem to be resting with the dead. I can't help but wonder if it's him or if I overate. They didn't fill me up. It wasn't the same as the devil who fed me. He made me feel full and sick. This is more like I am full of energy.

I get up from the bed and leave the room. I wander down the wide hallway and glance at the paintings. I walk like my feet know the way. Suddenly the air is sparkling and the dead are calling me. They want me to lie with them, there in the hallway. Weirdos.

My feet walk through the mazes of hallways and corridors until I come to a dark door. It's closed. I reach out and brush my fingers against it. I've seen it before. I act before I can think and stop myself. I reach for the handle and turn it slowly. I slip inside of the door and close it quickly.

My back is pressed against the door. My heart is attempting to beat out of my chest. The door makes me nervous. The room makes it worse. So many things feel like they're trying to come back to me all at once.

I look around in the dark. My eyes have been doing their thing all night.

The room is jam-packed with old trunks, boxes and chairs. Dust lingers in the air. I recognize one trunk instantly. I cross the room silently. I kneel at it and run my fingers along the carvings in the oak. A tear slips from my eye. I trace the old fashioned design. I remember it.

I remember my maid filling it with my things. Her face is hidden from me, but I know I loved her like a mother. So many pieces of my memory are still blocked.

I know I was about to leave for the Americas the next week. I remember so many things upon seeing it.

Constantine was there.

He was with me constantly.

He laughed and told me the lies I needed to hear. He rescued me the first time it happened. The first time I changed. I was in a heap down a long dark alley. I sat there sobbing in a torn gown with a dead man in my arms.

Constantine kissed my fingers and carried me away. He saved me from myself and the hatred I began to feel as I began to understand what I really was. He trained me with the swords and daggers. He taught me to fight using what I was. He loved me and kissed me, and together we plotted the demise of the seven devils. My parents and the five.

"What are you doing in here, Ellie?" I turn hearing my name from

191

before.

The moonlight coming in the window glints off his eyes. Seeing him standing in a corner the way he is brings it back. The memories flood. The emotions take over. I barely recall who I am now.

The last of the memories filters in slowly, taking its time. It burns me slow and deliberately. Ellie wants me to remember exactly how it felt when Constantine drove a sword in my side and let the Van Helsings take me.

He sees the recognition on my face.

I leap at the wall, but he's gone before I get the chance to rip his throat from him. I slam into the wall chipping my nail on the corner.

The memories merge. The story fills in.

I have the answers I have been seeking.

I turn and walk from the room. I don't slip through the halls. I stomp and pound my way to our room. Feelings as old as time crush against me.

The monster in me wants to feed and let the pain of others wash away my own, but the girl with the broken heart takes over. I drag my fingers along the wall, knocking the paintings to the floor. I swipe my arms across the desk at the top of the stairs, knocking everything to the floor. I am angry and broken. Wyatt and Constantine. In every life, I have been broken by love. Fitz was right. I never should have fallen in love.

No matter where I run, or what I do, or who I eat, the heartbreak is there.

I am broken.

Tears blind me.

Mona is in the hallway looking alone, small, and frightened. She is scared of me. Finally.

I look at her and drop my gaze in shame. If she knew of the things I'd done, she would run away. She would scream and run and never look back, and I would be completely alone. I deserve to be alone.

She does the thing she always does. She wraps her arms around me and lets me mentally collapse.

"We need to get out of here now," I whisper into her hair. "He's evil. Like Wyatt."

She nods and holds me. She doesn't ask, not yet.

She asks in the car we steal. Of course, I take the nicest of them. It's small and red and the inside smells too new and clean. It's fast. I don't think I can control it. Even with my newfound strengths. I stroke the steering wheel and grin. I know he loves it. He always liked the fastest of things. Horses and hounds and women. I flinch at the memories I now have. Him in the arms of women. Women he would always tell me were food. After the sword stabbed me in the side and I was dragged to the tower to be tortured and starved for the devils, I knew. I knew he was a liar and a bastard and they were more than food. They were conquests. No different than I was.

I steal a look at her. She is fidgeting. Michelle would freak.

She looks at me and watches my face. "What happened?"

I need to get rid of her. She is in danger with me.

"I remember the last time I lived," I whisper.

She looks confused. "In the dark ages?"

I shake my head. "This is my fourth time being born I think. They were all wrong. Besides the first time, I was born in the Dark Ages and the Middle Ages. The last time was the late fifteen hundreds. I was a girl named Ellie. I had a mother and father and they were very rich. They bought a plantation in the New World. I was to take a ship to meet up with them. Traveling with my fiancé and my maids."

She grimaces. "Fiancé?"

The burn behind my eyes threatens me. I focus on the dark road. "Constantine. He was a Romanian Prince." I feel a smile cross my lips. I can't fight it. "We met at a dinner party in the winter. We went on a sleigh ride."

She laughs. "All vampires must be Romanian Princes."

I roll my eyes. "Anyway, he was to marry me when we arrived in the New World. I was upset about it. I didn't want to go. I wanted my wedding in England with my friends. I was in a shop buying some supplies to take with us when I smelled something. It was the best smell in the whole world. I ended up in an alley killing a man. They never told me what I was. My parents never even knew. I was in a heap, sobbing, when Constantine found me. He saved me and showed his true nature to me. He, of course, knew what I was. His plan was to help me kill the devils. The seven devils. The five Sin Eaters and my real parents. He brought me to America. He married me, and we lived in an amazing house, where his house now is. We plotted, and then one day, he betrayed me. He let the Van Helsings take me. I was tortured and starved in the same tower you found me in. I died in that room. Crucified and rotting from the evil of the world."

Her face looks how my heart feels. "Gross. You for real remember this shit?"

I nod, and sniffle. A lone tear slips down my cheek.

She sighs. "What the hell do we do now?"

I shake my head and wipe my eye. "Not we. Me. I can't bring you into this. I remember how to fight and how to kill the devils. I remember who I am. It's too dangerous."

She laughs. "I'm coming. Before you say no, hear me out. Firstly, I can guarantee either the Van Helsings or Constantine will come for me and use me as bait against you. It always happens that way in the movies. You drop me at school, and in the middle of the night they come for me, and dangle me like bait for you to come rescue. Bad idea." I nod. I can't argue with that.

She points, slightly savagely. "Secondly, after everything we've been through, I am completely certain I won't last like, a day. I will be pulling my hair out and squirming in my seat. School is like a distant memory. This life rocks. As scary as this shit is, and believe me it's scary, it's also exciting."

I laugh.

She tilts her head. "Thirdly, you're not as smart as I am. You may like languages and all that shit, but I am actually smarter than you. You need me. Everyone needs someone. Even if I have to sit in the car all the time, you need someone."

She sits back and that is that. She is coming. Mostly because I don't want her to be bait.

She grins. "Constantine is hot. You have the two hottest guys I've ever seen, in my life, trying to kill you and sleep with you."

I sigh. "Yeah. I wish it was just a battle over who to pick for sleeping with, and not for who gets to murder me, slowly."

We look at each other and both shout, "Constantine." And laugh.

We drive to Mona's parents' house in New Haven, Connecticut. I am stunned when we drive into the town. My heart leaps a little bit. It's my dream life. My dream town. Her mom and step-dad are wealthy, obviously. Her house is on a circle street next to the country club. It's stunning and breaks my heart. I don't mean to be envious, but I have always wanted it. Always. The plan was to get my Linguistics degree from Vermont, with honors, and then get into Yale to get my PhD. New Haven is a painful place for me. Her mom is a specialist, and her step dad is a professor at Yale.

I know she too had dreams of attending there for her PhD. Instead, we will be failing out of Vermont, more than likely due to lack of attendance.

Her mother greets us coldly, and I instantly understand the headband and perfection. It wasn't a choice, it was the expectation.

Her mother is perfect. She doesn't look a day over thirty and her stepdad has an obvious roving eye. I'm uncomfortable around him. He licks his lips and hugs both of us for too long.

"Darling, it's fabulous to see you of course, but what about classes?" I hold my glass of red wine and look around. The room is portentous. It matches them. Their life suddenly doesn't seem as appealing. My home with Willow always felt like a home. This feels like a museum. Their life is obviously minus love. Love is what makes a home from a house. Willow and I lacked so many other things, but love was never one of them.

"So, linguistics?" she asks though her teeth.

I nod. "Yes. I suppose Mona's father will be my professor next year." I leave out the part where I might not be alive then. And that Mona might not be either.

She smiles like she wants to cut me. "I suppose he will. How interesting." It doesn't sound interesting the way she says it. It sounds like I'm offering poison, instead of conversation.

Richard watches me like a predator. His evil is so thick, I can feel the low burn in my belly every time I make eye contact with him.

He watches me. I know exactly what he will taste like. I know why he is a professor in a university. He is a bad man. The dead whisper things about him. Not good things.

Her mother takes her into the kitchen to get another bottle of wine, and also to lecture her for cutting classes, no doubt.

Richard's eyes sparkle when we are alone. He sits back and spreads his legs. He looks like he's daring me to look between his legs. Testing me. "So, is that a roadster I saw you pull up in?"

"I have no idea." I shrug. "My boyfriend's car."

He cocks an eyebrow. "It must haul. Is it the twelve cylinder one?"

I laugh. "I wouldn't know. It drives very fast and uses a ton a gas."

He laughs. "I think I did see it was. Wow, that's an impressive car for someone so young. What does his family do?"

I shake my head. "Blood-sucking leeches, I think. Fanged and evil."

He smiles and tilts his head. "Must be acquisitions and mergers or something like that. Investment lawyers."

It makes me laugh that he assumes I was talking about lawyers.

I drink from my near-empty glass and take the opportunity to lean over to Richard and smile. "I know your secret, Dick. I know what makes you tick. I know what you are." His dark-blue eyes flare. He attempts a sneer, but I suck him from the one-foot distance. It's just enough of a suck to weaken his spirit.

Mona walks into the room with a new bottle of wine and a frustrated face, hidden behind the plastic smile that matches her mother's. Richard gets his own plastic smile, and we play pretend for the evening. Richard seems to be in a daze for the rest of the night.

I sleep like the dead with Mona by my side. In case Richard gets any funny ideas.

Before we leave, Mona steals bags of shit from the house. Extras of soap and conditioner and shampoo. We each pack an ass-ton of clothes and coats. Unfortunately, the car doesn't have a large trunk. But what it has, we stuff with warm clothes, kitchen knives, food, water, Gatorade, toiletries and boots and runners.

Her mother walks us to the car. She looks different in the light of the day. "Cold up there, is it?"

Mona nods. "More expensive, too. Everything costs more. It's cheaper for me to steal it from here."

Her mom rubs her arms. It's the first motherly act I've seen yet. "You take care of yourself, okay? You're looking thinner and more tired than I've seen in a while."

Mona kisses her cheek and hugs her. "I will."

Richard watches us from the front window. I wave to him. He just watches.

I smile sweetly. "Thank you, Dr. Watts."

She blushes. "Felicia. I told you. Take care of my girl for me, Rayne." She says my name like it tastes bad.

I nod. "I will. Thanks for dinner and the bed."

"No, thank you for bringing her for a visit. It was nice. See you in a few weeks for Christmas, darling. Hopefully not sooner."

Mona just smiles. She has no intention of coming back for Christmas. We have devils to kill.

We get into the car.

She gives me the death stare. "What did you do to Richard? He seemed weird last night."

I frown. "Who, Dick? We got on famously."

She rolls her eyes. "He didn't perve on you, did he?"

I laugh. "He didn't get the chance." The car leaps forward when I press the gas.

She looks around the crowded car. "You know if we had been smart, we would have taken the SUV and left him this stupid car."

I smile. "I know, right? This damn thing is ridiculous. I don't understand the need for something so impractical. It guzzles gas and holds nothing. Not practical for questing."

She glances at me. "So, let's just say you succeeded and killed them all, and can live a normal life—what do you think you'll do?"

I shake my head. "I don't know." When I look at her, I see the panic and worry. Her mom got to her.

"You want to go back to school?" I ask.

She swallows hard. "Can we do classes and do the demon killing part time?"

I am relieved. "I want that too, but I'm terrified of the way things have turned out. I have Constantine and Wyatt trying to kill me or abduct me, and my father to contend with. Every minute on campus, I will be looking behind my back. I'll be a sitting target."

She shakes her head. "We can do this. I know we can. I just don't want you to succeed and then we have to start college all over again."

I agree. "I know. I still want my life. Maybe not linguistics, but I want something more than working at Target and stressing over what I will be. I can't keep stealing cars, money, and food."

She gives me a hopeful look. "Our future is school."

I agree. I bite my lip. "We need to go get Michelle."

Mona laughs. "I tried calling her and some bitchy nun said Sister Rosaline wasn't allowed to take calls. Then, like an hour later, Michelle sent me a text. Listen, I'll read it to you. She is nuts."

She pulls out her cell phone and reads, "Miss you tons. Kick Rayne in the arse for me. Make sure she doesn't wear rubber boots all winter, for the love of God. Oops—I mean God. So, I'm staying. I think this is my shit. This God business is making me feel whole. I rock the nun outfit. I'm a sexy nun. I'll have my own rich Viscount in no time, and we'll be running in the hills and singing with his four little rugrats. Peace, bitches. Sister Rosaline."

I furrow my brow. "God has no idea what has hit him. His followers will be running for the hills alright."

She snorts.

I shrug. "She's safe."

She laughs. "No one would predict that's where she would hide. I bet Wyatt walked right past her and never had a clue."

"Sister Rosaline. She probably picked it because of the Da Vinci Code. What a weirdo."

We drive the coast back. I put the top down a few times, but it's freezing.

We get close to home, and I find myself taking a detour.

She is asleep. I drive up close to the mansion. The air sparkles and the dead try to convince me it's a bad idea, but I need to. I need to see him. I don't know why. I know he'll sense me, but my car can outrun his car. Hopefully.

From the highway, I can see the slightest glimpse of the house through the trees. The white mansion is lit up. They're having a party. I slow the car down and unroll Mona's window. I can hear the party.

She wakes and looks at me. "Where are we?" She stretches and rubs her eyes.

I point. "Wyatt's parents' house. The epicenter of sin, as far as the Van Helsings are concerned."

She looks at me confusedly. "You have a death wish?"

I nod. "Yup. Think we should go see what that party is all about?"

"No. No, I absolutely do not." She looks horrified.

I look at her, my mind is made up. "I do. I think it's about me. Let's go peek. Just a peek."

She sighs. "No. No, this is a bad idea. We need to go back to school."

I turn onto the gravel road just before the house and drive down it. I turn the headlights off but the running lights still shine. I turn the car off and hope no one saw me.

I climb out and flip the trunk. In the dark, I can see perfectly. Everyone at the house is coming in the front door, dressed to the nines and shaking his mother's hand. There is a man beside her. He must be Wyatt's father. He looks like the man from the boat the day I met the Nixie.

I pull a black coat and some runners out of the trunk. I pull them on and zip up the jacket.

She crosses her arms. "I'll wait here. If there is trouble, I'll honk and drive to get you, okay?"

I nod.

I'm faster without her anyway. My body isn't fit like it was in my memories, but I know I have some push inside of me.

I run through the woods silently. Not as silently as Ellie could, but silent enough. I run past the house, down near the beach. The lights are lit in every room. The mansion shines brightly against the gray seas and cloudy night.

I can watch them and see everything in the windows.

I see the little girl. She walks around looking bored. She seems to stand out amongst the rest. She is in a dress, but she looks like she would kill for her skinny jeans and hoodie. She might kill, just because. She has a dangerous look on her face. I remember it well.

I sneak along the grass and trees, closer to the house. When I get close enough to look up into the whole back of the house, I slide my body against a tree. It's amazing what I instantly know how to do, thanks to Ellie. Looking in the windows is painful for Ellie. Her hatred is thick and her memories are vivid. It's like she, we, remember things but can't see them. Not completely. One thing I remember, without doubt, is Wyatt's mother.

In one of the windows, I see the girl who was with Wyatt at the church and the parking lot of Subway. She is dressed in a hunter-green dress that I can't help but hate. It's too formal and eighties prom. She has long, white gloves on and a martini in her hand. Her pretty blonde hair is in tendrils around her face and tucked up in a bun. Her face is content.

She smiles at a man next to her and removes her glove to show him her ring. It's an engagement ring. Wyatt walks up and kisses her on the cheek. My stomach hurts when I see him. The man shakes his hand, and I realize the fool I have been.

My heart feels like it's fallen out of my chest. My chest is hollow. It feels like it's open and bleeding. I can't get my breath. I remember his arms around me and his lips on mine. The dangerous look he got in his eye when we made out, like he was about to lose control. I have a montage moment and everything hurts.

I spend too long thinking about the things he said, and the way he acted, and how I was convinced that, somewhere deep down, he loved me. Even if he swore he didn't.

I let myself love him.

I let him make a fool out of me, again.

When I look up again, I see him looking out the window. He senses me. I know he does. I slide up against the tree tightly.

The tree hides me, but that doesn't stop his eyes from seeking me out. He feels me, just as I feel him. I see the people next to him try to talk to him. It looks like he brushes them off. He points to the huge balcony out back. He walks out under the guise of getting some night air, no doubt. But really he is looking for me.

The back door opens, just as I assume it will. He walks out onto the terrace alone. He places his drink down and scans the forest. My heart is beating out of my chest.

He turns and walks to the wide staircase. I take it as my chance to run. I bolt into the forest. I run hard for the car. These are the same trees as the last time I ran from him.

I can hear his feet in the trees. I hear something breaking branches. I beeline for the car. My feet dig in and push.

"Rayne!" He's close.

I run hard.

"MONA, START THE CAR!" I feel like the Ikea commercial.

I hear Mona start the car. She is sitting waiting for me with her head out the window. As long as she doesn't put the car in gear, the stupid running lights stay off. I pray she doesn't put it into drive and give her location away.

I feel his hand grab for me. I push harder. He tackles me to the ground and pins me.

"What are you doing?" He holds me on the ground.

I kick at him and push him off me.

He looks stunned. I laugh. He wasn't prepared for me to fight back with any skill.

His face is fierce. "What are you doing here? You want me to take you in?"

I laugh.

He shoves me with his hands and I fly back. Apparently, he's also been holding back. This might get interesting. Ellie has memories of other Van Helsings and their mad skills.

He pushes me again. "You want me to take you in? You want to be chained to the wall again? That's what they'll do to you."

I watch the anger in his eyes. I backhand him before he expects it. "Fuck you."

He wipes the blood away from his lip. He looks at it and raises his eyebrows. "You want this?"

I smile. "I owed you that one, and you fucking know it."

He laughs bitterly. "I told you I was sorry."

I meet his grin with my own, but mine is full of pain. "And I told you, it will always be one more sorry, Wyatt. I can't forgive the things you've done to me."

He glares at me. "And what? I should forgive what you are? I have to forgive what you are?"

I have a flaw. It's annoying.

I cry when I'm angry.

Tears flood my eyes, and I'm bawling like a baby instantly. "You want to know why I'm here? I wanted to see you. Asshole. I wanted to see you. I wanted to see you once, before I put us on opposite teams for good. I know you plan on betraying me and killing me for the light of the world."

He grips his hair. "Rayne, I'm on your side. I don't know how else to tell you this. I've rescued you, paid for you, saved you numerous times. What more do you need?" He points to the house and whispers harshly, "I told them that's what I would do. That wasn't my plan." He looks exasperated.

I see red. "That woman in there is wearing your engagement ring. You're engaged. You're not on my side. You never were." Tears are pouring from my face. I see it softens him. He straightens his dinner jacket and tries to hide the shame on his face.

He winces. "She is like me. You are…you. It won't ever work between us. That doesn't change the fact that I want to help you."

I laugh and cry. "The funny thing is that I actually have a husband. I completely forgot about him. So don't you worry about me. I don't need someone like you on my side anyway."

His eyes burn. "Husband?" He looks hurt. I savor the look. If I could wrap up that look and snack on it later, I would.

"Constantine Basarab. Maybe you've heard of him." I know he has.

His eyes flare. "What?" His look becomes more delicious and pained. I want to roll around and kick my feet when I see it.

I nod and wipe away my tears. "We married a long time ago. Ask your mom about it. She was there. I know what she is and I know what you want. I remember everything." I probably should have held that back, but I've always sucked at poker. "I know you were tricking me and planning on killing me for the light of the world."

I hear voices in the woods behind him.

He takes a step toward me, and I take one back. He smiles his cocky grin. "You didn't think that me and you had a future, did you? Something like you, with someone like me? Yeah, I have a fiancé. Yeah, I used you. We're at war, Rayne. It isn't ever going to be fair between us. Why do you think I handfasted with you? I knew I'd be able to feel you. Track you. That's my job."

My heart is breaking, but I smile bitterly through the pain. "Does she know your job involved making out with me? Does she know you can track me? I don't think she does. I think you never told her that. Because she never noticed you looking out the windows when you felt me just now? She didn't come with you to hunt me down?"

"Come with me." He puts a hand out. "Come gently, and I won't hurt you."

I laugh. "You can't hurt me. You don't matter to me."

The voices get closer. I can hear them calling him.

He pounces for me, but I leap out of the way and somersault. I jump up and run for the car before he's even off the ground. My legs are done, but I force them to work. I run for the road, past the car. Mona sees me and drives to where I'm running. I run along the road. When she drives up and holds the car door open. I jump in. I kneel on the seat and look back at him with the door still open and wave.

He's standing on the road huffing and puffing. Looking sexy in his suit. I climb in and close the door.

I wipe my face. I want to smile and laugh, but I can't. It's all hitting me like an avalanche of emotions.

"You okay? Did he hurt you?" she asks desperately.

I try to shake my head but it betrays me. I ugly cry. I lose all control and become a sobbing monster.

The through the sobs, I get out a sentence. "He's engaged."

She looks confused. "What?"

I shake my head. "Engaged. Called me a thing. A thing. Not worthy of him."

She swings the car around and punches it. I'm thrown against the window. The car skids and straightens out. He leaps out of the way as she swerves for him. She swings the car around again and punches it again. I hear and feel a thump. The car jerks from the hit. She stops the car and jumps out. "A THING? FUCK YOU,

WYATT. YOU'RE THE THING. YOU'RE A SMARMY BASTARD. YOU'RE ENGAGED?" He's on the ground on his back. She is kicking and hitting.

He winces and moans, but she lays the boots to him without pause. I jump out of the car and drag her in. The people coming for him are almost to us. I throw her in the driver's seat again and run around to my side. I'm barely in when she punches the gas again. She drives forward and slams on the brakes. She puts it in reverse. She looks insane. She backs up and hits him with the car again.

"STOP! YOU'RE GOING TO KILL HIM!" I shout.

She grins. "He can't die. He already told me that. Besides, you shouldn't care." She throws it into drive and skids away.

He's lying on the ground looking unconscious, and we leave him there. I feel sick with guilt. I feel sick leaving him. I feel sick because I'm a pathetic loser where boys are concerned.

Chapter Twenty

Mona was right. Classes feel like the dullest thing I've ever done in my life. I find them too easy now. I speak the languages I'm studying. Ellie spoke German, Russian, French, Latin, Romanian, and Spanish. Her memories and mine are merging more every day. I remember how to speak the languages.

I have a hard time sometimes differentiating between her life and mine. She loves and hates Constantine, the same way I love and hate Wyatt. It's like having my heart broken twice.

I leave Spanish and walk down the outdoor corridor. I feel something and glance up. My skin crawls. I know something isn't right. My stomach twinges.

He's here.

I hug my coat and try to walk with the other students. Stay with my herd. Mona and I have rules on how to survive everyday life and Willow's guard holds. I am in my full power, so it still holds. Once I enter the building, nothing intent on harming me can see me or feel me. It's my only saving grace.

I hurry to the building, but I can sense him. I turn. He's leaning against a tree. He isn't smiling. He's always angry when he sees me. I flip him off and turn away. He smiles at that.

"Rayne," he calls me. I pick up my pace. "Rayne, wait up."

His hand is on me, spinning me to face him. I give a threatening suck. I know he knows what it is. Sucking him tastes like dandelions, but it's worth it.

He puts his hands up. "Not here to cause a problem. I just want a truce. For now."

My eyes can't help but notice the lack of a ring on his wedding hand. No wedding yet.

He sees my eyes and looks further annoyed. "How's the husband?"

I smile. "Awesome. Best husband…ever."

He winces.

I cross my arms. I'm ready for him. "He stays at his house, pays my tuition and bills, gives me money, and lets me keep his Mercedes convertible. It's a good gig."

His bitter look lifts. He looks almost hopeful. "You aren't together?"

I shake my head. "No. I barely know him."

He is in pain. He can't hide it.

I like his pain. "It's funny. I am different. I know I am. But I'm still the same person I always was. I'm the one who never lied about who they were, or acted like they were someone else. I never tricked you into liking me. You just liked me on your own, for who I was. Am. Ironic, huh?"

He looks upset. "You have a pretty important job, Rayne. You have to die to save the world. I'd say you're not exactly the same as you were when we met."

I flinch. "And you ARE exactly the same."

His jaw is set. His eyes are full of regret. "You have to die. You know that."

I chuckle. "There is another way. I intend to do everything in my power to make the other way work for me. I know my mother will die for me. I just have to convince my father."

His mouth lifts. "You have to find him first."

His cocky smile pisses me off. "No, I don't. He'll come for me. When he does, I'll be ready."

He is beautiful. I step forward and press my lips against his. I take advantage of the fact that the greens are covered in people and give him my best kiss ever. He doesn't fight. He devours me as always. I slide my fingers up into his hair. I pull slightly. I remember liking the feeling of pulling hair and having mine pulled. I kiss him with the years of experience Ellie has.

I kiss the side of his face and duck my head into his throat. I lick along his jugular and whisper, "Willow was right, wasn't she? The minute she met you, she saw it? You loved me. You still do. But I'm not ever going to be yours, Wyatt. Does that bother you? Other men have had what you have tried so hard to get? I gave it to them without even the slightest bit of thought or effort. Have a nice life, Wyatt, with the wife you let Mommy pick out." I kiss his cheek softly and turn away from him.

He calls after me, "You're right. Rayne, you're right about it. About all of it. Is that what you want to hear? Is that enough for you to stop tormenting the fuck out of me constantly?"

I turn back and smile harshly. His dark-blue eyes break my heart a little bit. "Well, it changes nothing. Being right and not being together is the same as being wrong. What does it matter?" I blow him a kiss. "And no. I like tormenting you. A lot." He laughs bitterly and follows me. I know when I enter the building I vanish to him.

I'm shaking, but I'm free in a sense. I have returned the smack he gave me in the beginning. I have taken back the power he held over me. The power of the knowledge that he loved me all along and that I wasn't alone in it. His mother saw it. His uncle saw it. Willow saw it. I saw it.

I still see it.

But I don't care anymore. I am free of him because I don't care.

My life is complex enough without him tugging at my heartstrings, and then marrying some girl because his family likes her and approves.

Mona is in our room with books everywhere. She scowls at me as I close the door. "I missed so much."

I collapse on the bed. "I know. God. And I have to go out tonight. If I don't do the mini sips at the bar, I get too hungry and end up eating a whole person."

She grimaces but looks back at the books and her laptop.

My phone rings.

I answer, "Willow?"

"Hey, kiddo." She sounds different.

"Hey. How's it going?"

"Good." She is just tired. "I've been doing a bunch of reading and it looks like Constantine is right. He's right about the devils. Beheaded and instantly dead. No suffering. You're staying away from him, right?" She still sounds like my mother.

I sigh. "Yes."

Her tone becomes even more motherly. "Promise? Cause I had a dream the other night and you were drowning in a sea of blood. I think it means you're not eating enough and your body is craving things. Like sexy things. You're not having sex, right? It makes your condition worse."

I laugh. "No. I promise. No sex. No meat. No processed food. It's been vegan and water and healthy." It's true, and I miss everything, except sex. "I saw Wyatt. He's back at school, I think." Mona's nostrils flare, and I'm sure Willow looks exactly the same. I put a hand out and continue, "I think he fears me, a little. He knows I can drink from him and not suffer any pain. I tricked him the one time in the motel room, but now he knows. The handfasting cost him something, just like it did me. I can sense him the way he can me. I can drink from him and kill him if I want to."

She sighs. "Be careful, for Goddess's sake. You don't know that you can kill him."

I nod even though she can't see me. "I know. I'm being careful. How's tracking the devils going?"

She moans. "Not so good. So far, we think the one who came and used you to cleanse is from either Detroit or New Orleans. We think he maybe lives in both regions. The turmoil and corruption there is the best place. He was so accessible to you. He must be stateside. The next ones we believe are in Rio de Janeiro, Karachi, Ciudad Juarez, Caracas, or Capetown. We can't be positive, but we think we're on the right track. Should know more in the next couple weeks. We have witches dispatched to each city and looking into it. Do you forgive me yet?"

I frown. "For what?"

Her voice cracks. "For abandoning you to the Van Helsings and not leaving my coven to be with you?"

I shake my head. "I never was angry with you. I know everything you have done was to help me, in some way."

She sighs in relief. "Oh thank Goddess. I was so worried. I fled when he came to the house with you because I was scared and confused. He loves you, Rayne. Make no mistake. That man loves you. I still believe he has your best interests at heart. I didn't want to stay and lead him to the lair. I knew he could torture me and make me tell him. I didn't want him to know what you were. I fled to protect you. Their touch is especially bad for Earth Witches. I just can't leave you."

I sigh. "Well, I don't believe it. I don't think he wants to help me, Willow. I think he's team Van Helsing."

"I hope you're wrong," she says softly.

I chuckle. "I don't. I don't need complications like boys right now. I need to hunt these devils and end my issues."

"I can't leave my coven, Rayne. I would lose my magic if I did. I would die without it. I would come with you, otherwise." I can hear the guilt in her voice.

I shake my head again, like she can see me. "I don't want that, Willow. Stay there and be safe with the others. They can't get to you there. Wyatt told me that he can only kill a couple of you at a time."

"Yeah well, he hasn't tried messing with us, so that's good. How did Fitz seem? Did he look okay?" Her voice breaks.

I scowl. "Cruel and ruthless. Was that how he looked before?"

She pauses. "He's not really like that, you know that? He's the sweetest man alive."

I can let her believe that. I can keep her from knowing the things they did to me. The way my shoulders slowly dislocated and the way my wrists broke.

"Well, make sure you're being safe. And if I find anything, I'll let you know. We are desperately searching for Lillith's whereabouts. So far it seems like she's vanished off the face of the earth. Nothing is written about her. But I'm not giving up. As soon as one of the witch groups finds the devils, I'll let you know. We will get you flights."

"Thanks Willow. I love you." I almost call her mom.

She sighs. "I love you too. I miss you."

"Me too."

I hang up the phone. Mona is examining me. "You think it was a good idea, right? Coming back here?"

I nod. "I think so, but I feel exposed. I feel like his family could take me anytime. Like the crowds and hordes of kids on campus can't keep me safe."

She smiles. "Maybe that's how they want you to feel."

I shrug. "Maybe. Maybe that's why Wyatt came here. He wanted to make sure I knew I was being watched. Then when the next devil is ready, they will just take me and there isn't anything I can do about it."

Mona shakes her head. "It feels so hopeless. I feel hopeless."

The outcome is inevitable. I look at her and feel the fear and pain in the thing I'm about to ask, "Promise me something."

She nods. "Anything. Except leaving you. I won't do that."

I give her a desperate look. "Kill me before they get a chance to do that to me again. Don't let me live through that. Please."

Her eyes widen but she knows. She remembers what she saw. She knows how bad it was. She stares blankly and nods her head, as if automatically. "I swear."

"You have to swear that you will kill me."

Confusion mixes with the empty pain. "I swear, but how?"

I shake my head. "Not sure. I think we need to visit Michelle and see what's shaking. They should know. That priest knew more than he let on."

Her face brightens. "Okay…sweet. This weekend?"

I nod. "Yup. We can leave tomorrow." I grin. "I'll call my hubby and arrange some cash."

She rolls her eyes. "You're so mean. He likes you, and you're tormenting and extorting him."

"He deserves everything he gets. He fucking betrayed me." The pain and anger and hatred aren't mine, but I feel them, nonetheless.

"Whatevs. I gotta go to class. Be safe. Stay here. If you need something, text me." She leaves.

I look at my phone and smirk. I like talking to Constantine and hearing his voice. I pick it up and leave the room. I should be staying in, but I need some air. His voice makes me warm and the memories make me something else altogether. But it usually involves a cheesy grin and clenching my thighs together.

Walking down the stairs, I smell something. It's familiar and makes my stomach twist. I lean against the wall and watch as two men come up the stairs. The older one looks exactly like the man in the boat, the day I met the Nixie. The other one is the man who was at the church with Wyatt. I press my back against the wall and watch them walk the stairs. The older man has a bouquet of flowers. I panic, even though they can't see me.

I know they're here for me. I turn and run, texting Mona. 'CAR NOW'

I have my phone and my keys. I rack my brain to remember if I left anything in the room that I might need.

I race across the greens to the student parking. The car makes me smile most days. I stole it from a vampire; it's pretty much the coolest thing I've ever done. I don't smile when I see it this time. I panic, pushing the buttons. I can't help but feel them behind me, breathing down my neck the way Wyatt does when he chases me.

I get into the car and wait. The parking lot is packed. My phone vibrates and scares the crap out of me.

'COMING'

My foot is tapping and my palms are sweating. They're coming for me. The other devils must be full. It hasn't been a month.

'They need to starve you' my brain whispers.

I bite my lip and my whole leg shakes from the tapping of my foot. I see her at the same moment I see him. She sees him and runs for the car. I see her mouth open and words leave it.

The guys in the parking lot hear what she's screaming and gather. They grab Wyatt. He struggles but one of them pins his arms. Three of them hold him. He stops fighting. His dark-blue eyes meet mine. He doesn't smile his cocky smile.

He was the bait. I fell for the trap. I kissed him and talked to him. I flaunted the fact I was here.

She's huffing and puffing when she gets into the car. I slam the car in reverse. I watch his eyes as I pull away. He looks relieved. I swear he does. Maybe it's what I want to see.

"Holy fucking shit. What was that all about?" she asks, out of breath.

I point. "They came for me. Wyatt's friend from the church came to our dorm with the old guy from the boat. They came for me."

She's struggling to get her breath. "I'm going to fail this class for sure. My prof looked at me like I was crazy."

I give her a look. "What were you shouting to get those guys to grab Wyatt?"

She grins. "I said he was stalking me. I had a restraining order against him. He beat me up two weeks ago."

I sigh. "He is going to get beat up."

She speaks through bared teeth, "Good. Fucker. I needed to be at that class."

"I'm sorry, Mona. I'm sorry I ever got you into this." I can never apologize enough.

She touches my hand and grips. "No. They were coming to take you back to that tower. I know it. It's time to start starving you again. They don't care about you. They care about their job. You have the same rights as any other human, Rayne. So your parents suck. Lots of people have sucky parents. Yours made a deal that they should have to honor. Not you. You were a baby. They aren't even your parents this time. You're born of that virgin."

I drive to the priest at the cathedral. I know he has answers he isn't telling me about.

I press the Bluetooth button and say, "Willow."

The robot voice says, "Calling Willow." I snicker at Mona who rolls her eyes.

"What? I grew up poor."

Willow answers, "Rayne?"

"Hey, they came for me. I left the dorm. I'm on the road to get the priest, but I don't think he'll tell me anything."

She sighs. "Constantine."

I frown. "You just said..."

She cuts me off. "Forget what I said. He's the only one who can help you. NO SEX, RAYNE!"

I shake my head. "Mom, I'm not gonna have sex. For God's sake. He's like eight hundred or some shit. Give me a little credit."

She laughs a little. "I love you."

"Love you too."

I look at Mona who is holding her mouth. "Don't even think about laughing."

She bursts, "Oh my God...she's the best."

I press the button again. "Constantine." I say.

The robot voice says, "Dialing Constantine."

He picks up on the second ring, and I feel a wave of heat and thigh clenching.

"My love. To what do I owe the honor of this phone call?" He sounds sarcastic.

I laugh. "I need you."

He chuckles. "My favorite words. Give me just the smallest of hints as to why, so I can imagine it's for something only infinitesimally related to being naked."

I look at Mona and roll my eyes. "No, ewww. Meet me at the church I told you about."

His sarcastic tone gets thicker. "You know I can't attend church, my love. Perhaps I can give you what you need in the parking lot, in MY car perhaps."

His tone makes me smile. "You sound bitchy, Constantine."

"You sound less afraid of me than you should be, Rayne. You're extorting money from me, using my pain and guilt. I will eventually get what is rightfully mine in return for all of these favors." He says favors with distaste and annoyance.

I scowl. "I need your help with a priest. How can I get you and him to meet?"

He sighs. "Bring him outside. I'll snag him there."

I don't know how that's going to help. I know he can't walk on holy land, but I don't ask any questions. I drive. I can count on him to help me. I know that.

I nod and look at Mona, who nods. "We'll text you when I get there. There is a garden. We'll meet you there."

"And I will wait on your beckon call, my dears." He hangs up on us.

Mona looks worried. "He sounds pissed, and I can't even blame him for it. He might be evil and shit, but you're being cruel to him."

My anger flashes. "He betrayed me, before. I was tortured and fed the evil of the world and then murdered because he let them take me. Trust me…my attitude toward him is justified."

She glances at me. "Well, what's with the flirting and leading him on?"

I shake my head. "I still love him. Me, from before. Her memories are merging with mine and I remember the way I loved him. I also remember the way my heart broke when they dragged me away and he watched. His dark eyes looked broken, but he never fought them. He could have killed them all."

She crosses her arms. "It still feels wrong to take money from him."

I nod. "I know, but we're broke and I have no one else. Willow is so busy looking for the devils. I don't want to burden her with my worries. I don't want her to leave the coven. She'll die."

Mona looks confused. "I don't get that? She could live with you all those years and not die."

I laugh. "We were with them all the time. I just never knew. We traveled with psychics and stayed with other spiritual people and went to vegan retreats. All witches. She made me take my entire spring break, summer vacay, and Christmas break, to be with them. Not to mention the other holidays and vacation time. God, then there were the ones that stayed with us. No, they were there. Always. I was just gullible and dumb. I watched a lot of movies while they chanted and lit candles and planted shit."

She frowns. "Why did they let you grow up like that? Why did the witches protect you?"

I shake my head again. "I don't know. She hasn't answered that. She says they're friends of my mom's. She's scared of my parents, though. When Wyatt came there, she was ready to die rather than betray my mother or be taken by the Van Helsings. If the Van Helsings caught her now, they would torture her and kill her. Or use her as bait for me. She's safer with the other witches."

"Was she ever going to tell you? It seems like she was going to wait for you to just become what you are."

I shake my head again. "I don't know. She doesn't answer those questions. She says weird things like that's not information for right now. That's only going to complicate things more. Nonsense. I need the answers to all those questions. I'm short on answers. From everyone."

Chapter Twenty-One

Michelle looks like a real girl, in a different sort of way. I see no trace of the boy I used to know. She looks sweet and innocent. She looks like a nun, just a very pretty nun.

"This is a good look for you," I say.

She laughs and has a hard time meeting my eyes. "I feel great. The sisters are amazing, and the church is full of encouraging people and enlightenment. I never stray to the boy's side any more. Got to keep the temptations to a minimum. I've already had a couple issues. I mean no one knows, but Him." She points upward.

Mona laughs. "You had lesbian-nun sex? Does that even count as lesbian?"

Michelle makes a disgusted face. "No-my-God. Oh gross. Dude. Beaver has never been my favorite mammal. No, I had altar-boy sex."

I raise an eyebrow. "Aren't they minors?"

She bites her lip and nods. "Like seventeen and shit. I'm only two years older, but it still felt dirty." Her eyes turn mischievous. "Dirty good."

I laugh. "You are here to cleanse your soul and instead you're tempting altar boys to sin, in a church no less."

She feigns a wounded look and nods. "I'm ashamed." Her pretend shame lasts seconds. "What brings you two here?"

"The priest," Mona says.

"Why?" Michelle looks confused.

I give her a look. "He has answers. We were hoping you'd be able to lure him to the garden for us."

She swallows and nods. "Yeah, probably." She looks guilty just thinking about it. This actually makes her look guilty. Sex with minors in the confessional makes her smirk, and this makes her feel guilty?

"Have you seen my dad?" I ask.

She gulps and trembles. She shakes her head, and I feel sick for bringing it up, but I need answers.

Mona asks, "He can't come here, can he?"

She shakes her head again. "No. Are you guys still mad at me?"

I shake my head and grab her. I pull her in and hold her tightly to me. "I love you. Forever."

She sobs quietly. "I love you too."

"Have they attacked you again?" she asks.

I shake my head. "No, but Wyatt can track me, so you better bring him out. Then we can be on our way. We'll meet you in the garden."

She nods and leaves. We walk to the garden, and I text Constantine.

The stone bench is cold. It's December and the weather is starting to turn. It stays like fall until almost Christmas, and then it gets cold and snowy. The weather here is like a switch activates it.

The bench feels cold through my clothes. The snow is coming.

The door opens and the chubby, pleasant-looking priest exits the church. He looks less pleasant. "You came back? I am surprised, considering you know which side I am on."

I grin. "Well, Father, I'm hoping I can convince you to at least try to see things my way."

He shakes his head. "No. Your friend is a Sin Eater. Without her the world becomes worse than it is now. Famine, War, Pestilence, and Decay. The Revelations can start if the Sin Eater isn't killed with the sin of the world in her."

I frown. "Revelations?"

He nods. "Lucifer will take over the world until the Sin Eater can be born again and raised to try again. If he takes over, the chaos we have lived with becomes much worse. I am sorry, my child, but your friend must die."

I look at Mona and shake my head. "Not if we kill the devils and make them take the sin."

He shakes his head. "Band-Aid situation. The only way is to kill Lucifer, the devils, and Lillith. That isn't going to happen. Lucifer doesn't just die because you get lucky once and shoot him. His head must be separated from his body, same as Lillith. The devils are the same. You are two little girls against all seven of them. Have you ever cut a head off? It's not eas...." Arms reach down from the overhanging roof and snatch him into the air. His screams replace his words.

We jump back. I laugh nervously at Mona, who is white as a sheet. "Well, that was creepy."

She holds her hand to her chest. "Constantine gets points for effort and creativity. I think I peed my pants. That scared the shit out of me."

I look back at the church. "We need to tell them it's me and not you. They're going to go all extremist religious nuts and kill you. It's better if they try to kill me. I don't die as easily as you would. You're feeble."

She laughs. "No, this is good. They have no idea what's what. Let's go meet Constantine."

Michelle doesn't say goodbye.

"She just sent a text saying she is going to be ready to leave soon. She wants us to come before Christmas and get her." Mona looks at her phone.

I nod. "I get that she doesn't want to be attached to the disappearance of the father. Honestly, I don't imagine he's coming back. But she could have at least said goodbye."

Mona laughs.

The priest isn't coming back. I plan on eating him unless Constantine beats me to it.

We drive back to Constantine's house. The driveway and view of the house is painful.

I remember pulling up to our home the first time as man and wife. We were in a carriage. He made me cover my eyes. The house was stunning. I loved the proximity to the sea. I could smell it on the wind. I loved the feel of his fingers on my face and his kisses in my neck.

The house looks different now. It's modern and beautiful. I don't know where our house went and why he built this one instead.

I need to see the house that's here along with the man. Not the house I loved and the man I adored more than anything in the world. Neither of them exists in the real world.

I park in the round driveway and when we walk up to the door this time, I don't knock. I walk in and blow past the maid. "Where is he?"

"The study. This way." She looks distraught.

She walks us to a large dark door. We enter, and I instantly feel my head swoon. The room is exactly as I recall it. Or is it the same room? Confusion sends me spinning.

I look around at everything and blush. The same old mahogany desk and the shelves of books. Hundreds of years old. The hand-painted globe. The hand-drawn map of the new world that's

222

framed in glass and hangs over his desk. The windows are large and bright, but he has the blinds turned to dim the light.

The priest is tied in a leather chair in the corner. One I don't recall. It looks new.

Constantine isn't in the room.

I turn and see smoke moving like fog from another doorway. He materializes and Mona jumps. I've seen it before. He smiles at me, like I am the only person in the whole world. He sees me and his face changes. My heart skips beats and then races. I see the corners of his mouth turn up. He can hear my heartbeat. He knows his effect on me.

He's commanding as always. He looks at the priest. "You want to kill her, do you?" He points to me.

The priest frowns and shakes his head. "No, the Sin Eater." His eyes dart to Mona.

Constantine looks confused. He says nothing. He knows better. He moves on. "Tell us how to find Lillith. No more playing around, Padre."

Constantine offers the two chairs against the massive wall of books. My legs are shaking. The room smells exactly as it would have in his old office. My memory is playing tricks on me.

I sit. Mona watches us all intently.

Constantine sits in his huge leather chair behind the old desk he has ravished me on dozens of times. I bloody well remember that clearly.

I can't focus on the father or Mona. I can recall the feel of his fingers sliding up my skirts, and the way he felt between my legs. I squeeze my thighs together.

Constantine is grinning. He's not even fighting it. He glances at me and shakes his head disapprovingly. He knows what I'm thinking. He can sense my arousal. He brought us here on purpose. He has dozens of rooms, and yet, he chose the one that would make me remember.

I can play that game too. I remove my sweater and hold it in my lap. I'm in a thin pale pink tank top, no bra. The tank has the built in one. It's spaghetti strap and nearly sheer. "My sweater is inside out." I smile.

The priest swallows hard. He works very hard at not paying attention to all my flesh. I raise an eyebrow at Constantine, who has frozen. He is watching my pulse and my neck. It's his favorite.

Mona, who is oblivious to my tank top, leans into the priest and sneers at him. "You need to help us. We will end the hell on earth if we get rid of Lucifer for good. Or we just say frig it and let Lucifer take over."

I glance at Constantine, ignoring the laughing priest, and finger the neck of my tank. I watch his eyes. I tug at my shirt slowly, revealing almost all of my cleavage. I bend forward and pretend to tie my laces on my boots. "My boot's untied too. I'm a mess."

I smolder my eyes at him. He knows I'm begging for him to rip my clothes from my body. I make sure he notices the way I lick my lips and bite the bottom one.

I smirk when his fingernails cut into his desk. I pull my sweater back on.

Mona gives me a weird look.

Constantine takes a breath and glances down at his desk. He makes a face and cusses quietly. He has treasured the desk for hundreds of years. It was virtually unmarked, until now.

I look over at the priest and snarl, "Father, spare us the nonsense and tell us where to look."

The father watches Constantine. "What are you, my son?"

Constantine smiles his fangs at him. "Your worst nightmare. Let's chat, shall we?" His fangs almost make me moan. The feeling of them dragging down my skin and biting in rolls through my mind.

He walks to the father and squats between his legs. He looks into his eyes. "Where is Lillith?"

The priest fights it but relents after a few moments of attempting to close his eyes. "Ireland. The Fae keep her safe."

"How do we get to her?" Constantine asks.

He smiles. "You can't. You are unholy. Only a person with a pure heart can find the Fae."

I glance at him. "How did this happen? How did my father and mother come to this?"

He presses his lips together and looks down. Constantine touches his cheeks and brings his focus back. "Answer the questions she asks you, Father."

His mouth opens and he speaks like he is in a trance. "Our Father cursed them for their betrayal of his love. They made their love more important than his. When they chose to fall and touch the earth, they tainted it with a stain. An evil made from their defiance of God. They had a child and lived happily. The child grew sickly in her late teens. They panicked and came to God for help. He offered them redemption. He said that if they wanted so badly to stay upon the earth, he would forgive them—if they sacrificed their only child. She could carry the sin they created by defying God and take it with her. Lillith disagreed. She ran with the child and refused. The child grew sicker. Lucifer saw this as an opportunity. He went after Lillith and abducted the girl. He was certain they could conceive again. This child was nothing to him, in comparison to his love for Lillith. He took the child and sacrificed her on her twenty-first birthday. Lillith was heartbroken. She was devastated. He found her and convinced her that they could try again. They did. They conceived once more. The child remembered them. She remembered the life she had had with them. Again, they had given birth to the Sin Eater. Lillith was crushed. She refused to love the child. She ran from Lucifer again and entered the sacred garden of the Fae. The earth's people. Not God's creations, but Mother Earth's creations. Lucifer again sacrificed the child." He takes a deep breath and continues with hollow eyes and detachment in his voice. "God created Adam and Eve. Lillith had learned tricks from the Fae. Shape shifting was one of the things she learned. In anger and madness, she snuck into the Garden of Eden and disguised herself as a snake. She tempted Eve with the poisoned apple. Eve ate and cursed God's creations. God was furious. The evil stain became too great for one girl to collect. He allowed five Angels to fall and become the sin gatherers, who would feed the evil they collected to the Sin Eater. They could live upon the earth as immortals, so long as they gathered the sin."

I frown. "Wait, so Lillith birthed me twice. But then in the dark ages and the age of enlightenment, I was born as well?" I don't even think about the fact he thinks Mona is the Sin Eater.

He nods blankly. "A virgin birthed you the other times. Lillith refused to allow Lucifer near her. She refused to allow him to create another Sin Eater. God put the baby in the belly of the virgins. You have been born four times."

"You lied to me." I point.

He nods. "I did. I didn't want you to think this was your last chance as a human. We need you to do the final cleansing of the earth. Not desperately scrambling to save yourself. You're a martyr, child. Don't be so selfish."

I gasp. "Why did God create his son to die for our sins, if he was using me the entire time?" I am angry; it's deep and desperate. I am running out of time.

He shakes his head. His lips press together. He's fighting telling us. His eyes flutter and he passes out.

Constantine looks back at me and frowns. "Well, that was interesting. Much more than we got out of the damned witches."

I sigh. My palms are sweating, and I'm exhausted. I need to feed.

Mona looks deep in thought. "So, this is the last time you can be born? What does that mean?"

Constantine looks dismally at me. "It means we kill them or she dies forever."

"Can you make her a vampire?" Mona asks.

He smiles bitterly. "We tried that last time. Didn't we, love?"

It flashes into my brain. The pain and agony was intense. My brain refuses to let me see it all. "I remember throwing up blood."

He winces. "So much blood. I didn't know people held so much." He stands. "What would you like me to do with him?"

I watch the sleeping priest. "I want that answer, and then I want to eat him."

He nods. "I was afraid you would say that. Even after you depleted my resources here. I will say though, he probably doesn't have many sins. You'll be even hungrier after you eat him. Whereas, I know he has loads of blood in that chubby body. I will be sated. I think we'll have to wrestle for this one." He walks from the room and I sit back.

"You're going to kill him? He's a priest." Mona looks sick.

I nod. I don't want to explain to her that I am seconds away from eating her.

She gets up and leaves.

She doesn't want to face the fact that I am the monster everyone keeps telling her that I am.

I look up at the ceiling. My other lives are coming back. I remember things. I remember my mother. I remember my father walking me up a hill. He held my hand and spoke to me of love and responsibility. I never saw the flash of steal or felt a thing. He ensured I went peacefully, but that changes nothing. He has cut my head off twice. A shiver runs up my spine. I see his face. I look a lot like him.

The priest rolls his head and mutters. His face drains of color. He struggles to lift his head. His lips seem fat and thick.

"My child," he mutters.

I lean in. His hands latch around my throat. "MY CHILD!" His eyes are completely black. He is spitting when he speaks. "You must honor the agreement. You must. YOU MUST!" he screams in my face. I can't breathe. I try to claw at his hands, but the strength in them is unnatural.

He is leaning in breathing his hot breath on my face. "YOU MUST HONOR THE AGREEMENT! SOUL FOR SOUL!"

My eyes are getting dark from the lack of oxygen. I panic and push at him.

I feel something sharp grab at my arm and suddenly the room spins. I land against something hard. Blackness fills my eyes. I hear hissing. The last thing I see is Constantine consuming the priest.

Chapter Twenty-Two

I am surrounded by warmth. It's a familiar feeling. I pull the arms around me tighter. I moan a little and wiggle into the embrace. I hear a chuckle and look up. Constantine is across the small dark room. "You wish it were me, do you?"

I frown and look behind me. A face I do not know lies next to me. His expression is slack.

Constantine mutters like he's giving a tour. "Murdered his mother and her cat. Stole her car and crashed it. Took his clothes off and ran down the road naked. Got taken to a mental hospital. Never got tried for the death of his mother. I really don't feel like it's fair, you know. He should pay for the death of the cat, at the very least. Anyway, he received a clean bill of health two weeks ago. Ten years of intense therapy has determined he is sound as a pound."

I squirm away from the sleeping guy. "Why is he next to me?" I look around. I am in a cell. "Why am I in a cell?"

His eyes gleam. "You let yourself get hungry, my love. That has always been a problem with you. I couldn't let you kill Mona."

Jealousy pangs flutter inside of me. I recall the way they looked at each other when they met. The way he called her pure. It was an insult directed at me.

Something bursts from my mouth, but it's like the words are not my own, "Yes, God forbid anything happens to the love of your life, at the hands of another. I know how you like to be the one to ruin them."

He is beside me in a flash. His face is so close, his words are a part of my breath. "I don't want you to feel guilty for killing her. It would ruin you. Unlike you, I've only had one life, one love." His black eyes scare me for the seconds they remain. Then he is gone and I am full of sadness again. I would never want anything to happen to Mona.

I look back at the young man on the crappy little bed. He is handsome. I reach a finger and trail it along his arm. He is sweet. Probably the sweetest thing I've tasted since the madness in the stalls here last time. My mouth waters when I taste the evil lurking inside of him. His skin is warm and soft. I knead him like a cat and let the suck start. I'm starving. I pull hard and fast. He screams as I pull it from him roughly.

I sigh and shudder. Sweat drips along my face. I squeeze my thighs together and try to catch my breath.

He murdered another woman last week. "So much for therapy," I mutter to myself.

I stand and press on the cell door. It's stuck. I push harder but it's locked. I look at the dead kid on the bed and slump against the bars.

"Constantine, please," I call out. "Let me out. I'm sorry I said that. You know how sometimes I talk out of hunger." It too has always been a problem.

He doesn't come. I watch the shadows move along the floor of the only window down here. The shadow moves with the passing hours. Panic starts to build inside of me. The dead kid stinks. His skin is sweating. He's making a wet mark on the bed. I am in the far corner, plotting my escape. The worst scenario I can imagine is playing around in my mind.

'He has betrayed us again.'

I feel sick at the thought of it.

I fall asleep against the bars. The dead take me.

When I wake, Mona is hugging me and sobbing. I wake calmly as always, but start to panic.

"Mona, what's wrong?"

She is holding me and crying. "I couldn't find you. He wouldn't show me where you were. He said you needed time to cool off. You were a danger to me."

"Did he touch you?" I growl.

She shakes her head. "No. No, of course not. He asked me a million questions about you, Wyatt, and school."

"What did you tell him?" I feel panic forming.

She shakes her head. "I'm not sure."

I put my face in my hands. "Fuck." He's made her tell him everything about me. He's jealous on a bad day. Now he knows I've had sex with other men. Lots of other men.

I look around me. She has dragged me from the cell. The bars are open. I look back at the open door. "There's a dead guy in there. Don't go in there."

She cries harder. "I know. I know I saw him. He stinks."

I can smell him on me. I grimace. "I need a shower. I'm gonna kill Constantine."

She looks horrified.

I get up off the floor and try to stretch my aching body. I climb the stairs and notice the kinks everywhere.

"Son of a bitch. How long was I in there?" I storm up the stairs.

She heaves behind me, trying to get a grip on her tears. "Three days. He's been acting crazed. I didn't know what to do. He wouldn't let me leave and he wouldn't let me call anyone. I felt like Jonathan Harker."

I laugh wearily. At least I'm not the only one who speaks in movie talk.

She leads me to our room. I don't smell him in the house. Our room has a huge walk-in shower. It has showerheads pointing all around. It's like standing out in the rain. Rayne in the rain.

"Try to relax," she whispers and leaves. The trauma of it all is starting to wear on her. Death is a hard thing to take for an innocent person.

I turn on the shower and step in. The hot water is gross at first. The stench of the dead man has permeated my pores, and the steam releases it into the air.

After the third time soaping up, I slip down the side of the tiled wall and let the water pour down on me.

I cover my eyes and wait for the dirty feeling of sleeping next to a dead man to sink in, or just vanish altogether. I don't understand my own detachment from it all. I'm not angry or disturbed or anything. I am grossed out a little at the thought of him lying there, but I am completely detached from it. I fed on him, killed him, and lay next to him. Very serial killer-ish.

I hear footsteps and look up, expecting to see Mona with towels or a drink. Instead Constantine walks into my shower. He's completely naked. I jump up and avert my eyes.

"What the hell are you doing?" I stare into the beige tiles.

He wraps his arms around me and nuzzles into my neck. "I've missed you, my love."

I squirm out of his grip. I try to ignore the massive thing between his legs or the ridiculous fire burning in my face and neck. I think my entire body is on fire.

I shudder from the desire and growl at him. "What are you doing in my shower? This seemed like the right way to approach the fact you betrayed me and let them kill me?"

His eyes burn. He pulls me into him and kisses my cheek softly. "You don't want to discuss this right now." He looks into my eyes. I pull away. I know what his eyes can do. What they can convince me of.

I shove him off. "You left me in a cell, a locked cell, like an animal. I was next to a dead man for three days. Open your mouth and taste him in the air. Then go fuck yourself."

His eyes widen. "Don't speak to me like that, Rayne. I'll only warn you once." The muscles in his fierce body flex from his anger. His dark eyes are wild. "I realize you're young in this body, but I do not tolerate that from anyone. Be a lady, for God's sake. It's bad enough you've soiled your virginity already." My hand flies out and slaps him hard. Instantly, I regret it. I recoil. His dark eyes fill with anger. He grabs my arm and drags me from the shower.

I scream for help, but he laughs and drags my soaking-wet naked body to my bed. He throws me on the bed and tosses a huge blanket at me. He wraps me in the blanket and curls me into a ball. No one comes. My screams go unheard. He pulls a towel around his waist and sits on the edge of the bed, holding the blankets around me.

"Where is Mona? What did you do to her?" I ask, trying desperately to remain calm.

He frowns. "Mona? She's fine. She went back to school for a few days. I told her you would be fine."

I struggle from the blankets that are soaking wet now. I point at him. "Screw you. You told her to go back to school and forget about me. Goddamn, Constantine."

He raises an eyebrow. "I would stay in those blankets, if I were you. Unless you have intentions of us doing things beyond talking."

I wrap the soaking wet blankets around myself and shiver.

"I hate you sometimes," I mutter and climb off the bed. I drag the blankets to the fire across the room. I kneel in front of it.

He laughs. "I have missed you."

I look back at him with contempt. "You are an asshole."

He points. "Last warning, Rayne. I'll turn you over my knee if you keep acting like a child." His smile turns dangerous. "If I recall you liked it. A lot."

I remember it and blush. My skin is in flames. I sputter and turn away from him. I did like it. A lot.

I shake my head. "You left me for dead. You let them kill me."

His voice is in my ear. "You made me do it."

I turn and his lips press against mine. His tongue parts my lips. His arms lift me up into him. His hands separate the skin and the wet blankets. He lays me down on the blanket and kisses me. His towel is pressed against my hipbone. He kneels beneath my legs and I feel something I've never felt before, reluctance. I don't want him. Not that way. The old me wants him. The new me doesn't know him, and I'm way too sober to do this. I push him off and shake my head. "No, please."

He pulls back, confused. "What are these games you're playing with me? Hot and cold and then repeat."

I pull the blankets and try to cover myself. "No games, Constantine. I don't know you. Not in this body. My soul recognizes you, but my heart and body don't."

He bends and kisses my lips. "My sweet wife. I loved you the minute I saw you. I have loved you in this life and the last and the one before that."

His words bring a chill to my spine. "You have known me three times?"

He looks like he might deny it but doesn't. "Yes."

I frown. "How?"

His dark eyes burn. "You were mine then. You are mine now. You'll always be mine."

He gets up and leaves the room. He does that when he's done

answering questions. I hate that. Always have. Apparently, for all three of my last lives. I storm to the closet and find it full of clothes I would wear, in my size.

"This is creepy," I whisper. This is twice now. Wyatt's and here. Only here, it looks like my own closet. I can't help but wonder if Constantine has been spying on me and buying things based on my own purchases. I wouldn't put it past him. At all.

I throw on underwear and a sports bra. Easier to outrun Wyatt if I wear a sports bra and harder for Constantine to get into. I pull on a t-shirt, a sweater and some jeans. I feel like I'm dressing like a homeless person. Technically, I am homeless, so layers are important.

I put on two pairs of socks and a thick jacket. I grab the handle but the door is locked.

"Asshole," I mutter.

I close my eyes and listen. The dead aren't there. "Are you here? Can you help me?" Nothing. He must have some kind of enchantment on my room. Which makes sense. The dead never called to me in my bed when we slept here before. They called to me when I got to the hallway. They wanted me to sleep in the hall with them.

I turn and look at the windows. It wouldn't be the first time, and I have a sinking feeling it won't be the last.

I put the window up and try not to let the frigid air off the ocean scare me off. I climb out onto the window ledge. If he catches me, he can drag me back without any fight.

A huge gust of wind blows past me. I grip the ledge of the house with my nails. The trembling in my hands isn't helping my balance. I slide along the ledge to the roof of the conservatory. Taking breathes and attempting to muster courage, I jump. My fingers desperately try to grip the shingles as I slide down the roof. I'm not sure, but I think I hear myself screaming. Pain is everywhere. My fingers are scraping against the singles and my face is scratching as I slide. I push my legs in, and as I hit the rain gutter, I stop. The metal makes a snapping noise and a groan. I start breathing again. My heart is attempting to pound its way out of my chest. I take a deep breath and wait for my entire body to stop shaking.

The cold wind is stinging my chin. My fingers are bleeding and stinging too. I lay my huffing and puffing face against the cold rough shingles and close my eyes for a moment. I'm not sure how to die, but falling off a roof and landing in some psycho's rock garden seems like a bad plan.

I start the journey across the roof after I've calmed my breathing. I clear my throat and look down. I'm still winded and starting to feel exhausted from the adrenaline rush.

I get to the lowest point where the grass looks lush and a bunch of old bushes sit against the house. His gardens surrounding the conservatory are beautiful.

I don't know how to get off the roof. I slide to the corner where I think the downspout will be. I slide my hands down the roof to the gutter. I grip it and let my legs fall off the back. The metal cuts into my already-sore hands. I swing back and forth for a moment. The windows of the conservatory are empty. He isn't there. I reach for the downspout and kick my legs until they reach it. I shimmy down like at Wyatt's house. When my feet touch the ground, they sting. I turn to run, but standing on the grass with his arms crossed and a huge smile playing with his lips is Constantine.

He claps his hands as I drop to my knees. "That was amazing, my love. Really, I never ever imagined you would grow to be so resourceful. No wonder they put you in a tower."

The first step he takes towards me brings tears to my defeated eyes. I slump over and sob.

He stops and watches me. "Don't cry. Please. It breaks my heart."

I shake my head. "You don't have a heart." I sob

His look is pained. "I know I don't. I gave it to you over seven hundred years ago and I've never asked for it back."

I cry harder. My bitchy brain is chanting 'it's a trick,' but my heart is remembering his tender love.

I smell the ocean in the air. The Nixie are calling me.

I look up at him. He knows my thoughts. He can read my face.

He raises an eyebrow and crosses his arms again. "You really think you can outrun me?"

I shake my head. "I know I can't."

He walks to me and lifts me from the ground. His fingers are soft and gentle where they touch. "I have loved you for all of eternity, Rayne."

I wrap my arms around him and kiss him fervently.

His lips try to keep up, but I am moving fast. I run my hands through his thick dark hair and tug on it slightly. He moans into my mouth. His tongue caresses mine as I suck it. He almost drops me. I wrap my legs around him. He sits down on the grass and lies on his back. I am on top, dry humping him. I kiss and almost get lost in the show. He tastes like every sin I've ever eaten, all mixed into one. He is delicious. But I can't seem to eat him. Something blocks it.

His hands are cupping me and grinding me into him. I struggle from his grip and stand. I make like I'm about to undo my jacket and instead I break into a run. My legs explode with the effort and energy. The Nixie slide from the water in twitching movements. Hundreds of them line the shores. They were waiting for me. I could have heard them singing in the water if I had listened close enough.

I leap from rock to rock and push hard. I see a blonde one first. She twitches and jerks in slow movements towards me. They are the scariest shit I've ever seen on land. Her smile is bright but her eyes flicker behind me. I push harder. I know he's right behind me. I leap for the Nixie. They swarm around me instantly and twirl. I am lost in the cyclone of them until we are in the water again.

They swim me out fast. Constantine can swim fast, but not as fast as Nixie can. I struggle for the surface. When I reach it, I bob amongst the hundreds of glowing heads.

He is on the shore again and laughing, but I can see he's pissed. "Well played, Rayne. Well played."

His dark eyes are red. They always turn red when he feeds. At his feet are three dead Nixie. He licks their colorful blood from his fingers.

He turns and leaves the shoreline.

Ten Nixie have died for me.

Chapter Twenty-Three

Willow hands me the tea. I hate it. It's nettle and Oregon grape. It tastes like cat pee smells. The mug's warmth and the smile I get from her make the taste tolerable.

"The Nixie are your mother's truest people. They are the Fae. True Fae. Creatures of the earth. Water Witches. They are the best bet for finding the sacred garden," the redhead says.

"Why are they helping me, if they know she is going to die when I kill her?" I ask.

The redhead shakes her head. "We don't know. We don't know if they've helped you before or if this is a new development."

I feel exhaustion like I've never felt. "Well, I know this is my last lifetime. This is the last time I will be born. I've been born four other times. This is the fifth. Apparently, Constantine knew me for the last three."

The redhead frowns. "What?"

I nod. "He's known me three times. Says he loved me all three times. Says I'm his."

This news doesn't improve either of their faces. "His?" The redhead, Glory, almost spits the word at me. She looks worried. "How has he tracked you down three times? We had a terrible time finding you. You were three when we finally did."

I'm confused. "What? I was three? Where was I?"

Willow looks distracted. "You were in an orphanage. The nuns said that a young girl who swore up and down that she was a virgin brought you in. She was Catholic and said you would be the Antichrist being reborn."

"Antichrist? Who thinks that about their baby?" I ask, offended.

Willow shrugs. "A fifteen-year-old girl who's never had sex before. God puts you in the place you have the best chance of surviving the twenty-one years. He never gives you to people who will hurt you."

Still confused. "How did you know who I was?"

Glory shrugs. "The Nixie. They came and told us that you had been born again and you were alone in the world. They said you were in an orphanage. We would know you by the light in your eyes. We can see it. We always have been able to. We searched every orphanage until we found you. We were asked by the Nixie to take you into our care. Lillith herself tasked it to us. Willow volunteered and the rest is history."

"Why did you raise me like a normal kid? Why not here where the magic is?" I'm always confused.

Willow smiles and puts her hands over mine. "We can't let you stay here. You weaken our magic. You bring the evil inside of you and the evil looking for you everywhere you go. You taint the very earth you stand upon. This is a sanctuary."

I don't like that answer.

"Have you ever spoken to my mother?" I ask, trying to change the subject.

Glory shakes her head. "No, only the Nixie and other true Fae can get to her."

I watch her eyes when I ask, "How can I find her?" The redhead reveals nothing.

Willow leans in and kisses my forehead. "We don't know. We

know there are four types of witches and each one is a small aspect of her. We are Fae but not true Fae. Earth Witches guard the earth, balance the energy and care for the plants and creatures. We heal things. The Fire Witches are the same as us, part human, and walk upon the earth. The Nixie, the Water Witches, are the only ones who are still true Fae. They have lived separate of the humans and have remained unsoiled. We Earth and Fire Witches have become more human than Fae. We are no longer permitted into the sacred garden. The knowledge of the garden was lost to us ages ago. Humans can't get to the garden, unless they are completely pure of heart."

"I thought that the witches were part of Lillith?" I ask, still watching Glory.

Willow squeezes my hands. "We are. Lillith is an Angel; she isn't human. We got our magic from Lillith. The Water Witches have a bit of Lillith's blessing in them. Mostly they are Fae. True Fae means they have no human in them. The bloodline isn't watered down with non-magic, so to speak."

"What about the Air Witches?"

Willow points to the sky. "Opposite of the Water Witches. Angels. Mixed Fae and Angel. Mostly Angel though. Snooty. We don't get on with them."

The redhead crosses her arms. "The Nixie are the only ones who know anything about the sacred garden, and believe me, they protect the secret with their lives. The Air Witches can't get to the garden because they don't have enough Fae. It's confusing, okay?"

I sigh and rub my temples. "Super confusing. Yikes."

Willow looks at me with her glowing green eyes. "You need to find the witch who handfasted you and get her to take it off. Only a Fire Witch can handfast and only the witch who does it can remove it. Then Wyatt can't track you." Her eyes soften. "I believe he loves you. But better not risk it."

"You need to focus on the task of killing the devils too, Rayne. Until they die, the sin is just filling up and waiting for you to be ready. Take away the human's chance of filling you up." Glory looks spicy.

I nod. "Okay."

I feel the dismissal lurking in the air.

Willow smiles but it's empty. "You can't stay, my sweet girl."

I laugh. "What happened to the labels? You hated labels, and now you call me everything under the sun."

Willow laughs. "You called me Mom. I wasn't your mom. I didn't earn the title. I told you I didn't like labels. It was easier than explaining that you were the human equivalent to an angelic garbage disposal, who would be sacrificed if I wasn't careful."

I watch her eyes. "Who is it you're afraid of? Who is coming for me?"

She flinches. She takes a deep breath and closes her eyes. She looks like she is about to cry. "Your father."

Glory jerks her head around. "What? You spoke to him?"

Willow nods. "I was trying desperately to divert his attentions. He felt the change in her, like we all did. When the Sin Eater awoke in her, he came looking for her. He told me he had to meet with her. It was the way things were done. The way the process worked. She needed to look upon him and know he loved her, and that she was doing the world a great service. She needed to see the martyr she was."

Glory grabs Willow's arms and shakes her. "You spoke to Lucifer, and you kept it secret?"

Willow looks down, ashamed and defeated. "He made me keep it secret."

The redhead looks crazy. She starts to cry. "No, Willow. No. What have you done?"

I'm more confused than before.

Willow looks at me as a single tear slithers down her cheek. Her green eyes glow bright for a moment and then fade. "I saved her." Her lips tremble as she whispers.

The light behind her eyes is gone.

She collapses on the table.

I don't know what is happening. I reach for her but my hands reach into a pile of daisies, instead of her. Tiny daisies. Hundreds of them. Thousands. "What? Willow?" I stammer and reach for the flowers. I grip them and claw through the pile. She isn't there. The daisies fall onto the floor and spill off the table. I scream in a rage and panic. Tears blind me. "What have you done? Is this magic? Where is she?"

I look around but Glory is on the floor sobbing. The daisies are everywhere. Willow is nowhere.

I collapse onto the floor and sob.

Glory is rocking back and forth. I am near screaming.

"W-w-w-what h-h-h-happened?" I ask in sobs.

I hear noises and commotion. I hear other people sobbing. Someone screams and thumps onto the ground next to me.

Daisies are everywhere.

Fingers grab at me and voices fill the air that feels too heavy. "She loved you, Rayne. She loved you so much. You were always her child. In her heart, you were hers." I feel hands touching me. Rubbing my back and trying to hold me. I push them off.

I can't listen to it.

I push myself up and stagger to the front room. I run for the front door. I run out into the dark, black garden and down the pier. I dive off the end of it into the water. The Nixie are there, waiting for me. They hold me, and we cry together.

"Take me to my mother. Please." I whisper into the water.

The brunette woman holding me shakes her head. "We can't, Rayne. You're not ready. You must kill the devils."

I cry into the waves. "Please. Please, I need some help. I need someone."

They hold me and let me cry, and we swim. When I see the lights of a harbor, I know they didn't bring me to her.

I pull myself from the waves and look back at the lights filling the water. I can't see much in the fog. I think I am at Constantine's house again. It's not a harbor. It's where I ran from. They brought me back. The house looks like his. In the fog it does.

They must hate me for the death of Willow and the three other Nixie. They made me come back to him. I stumble up the rocks to the grass.

I collapse on the grass and curl into a ball. I'm freezing. I pray for death. I know I won't be granted it, but praying can't hurt.

I close my eyes and let the dead take me.

Chapter Twenty-Four

She is sitting making me a daisy wreath. It feels morbid, but I let her put the crown of daisies on my head. She smiles. The light in her green eyes is almost blinding now.

"I saw her, Rayne. She thanked me. She thanked me for loving you and being the mother she could never be," she whispers.

Tears roll down my cheeks. "I'm so sorry Willow. I'm sorry my evil killed you."

She shakes her head and wipes my tears. "No, my darling girl. You have done nothing wrong. He knew I would lie to him to protect you. He knew it would corrupt my soul and end my light. I was happy to protect you. When he asked me to give you to him, I lied to him. I never intended for him to take you, ever. I told him to meet me at the house, but I put the charm on the house. He wouldn't have found you inside the house. It was the only way to keep you safe. I lied to him and corrupted my soul. Lying to Lucifer means you take some of his evil. Earth Witches can't have evil inside of them. It spreads like a weed and kills the light. My only regret is leaving you so soon. I wasn't ready to leave you." Her fingers grip mine and for the smallest moment, I feel the light inside of her.

I open my eyes and wake calm as always. My heart is broken, and the pain in my chest takes a second to register. Tears flood my eyes when I register that I am in my room.

His arms wrap around me. He holds me to him and kisses my

cheek. His kisses are soft and sweet. His touch is gentle and compassionate.

"What happened?" he whispers into my ear.

"Willow," I sob. I can't say anything else. She was so beautiful in my dream. I know it wasn't a dream. She came to see me, like the dead do. I sleep with the dead.

My body convulses. It feels like she took the light with her, all the light there was inside of me. It's gone now.

All of the goodness I had was from her. She saved me, every inch of me. I could have grown up evil and angry from being abandoned and instead, I was raised with love and kindness.

"Shhhh. It's okay, Rayne. I won't let anything happen to you." His body forms around mine and for the first time, I notice the stomach twinges I have. I look back.

My body tenses and panic rips through me.

"Wyatt? Where am I?"

Wyatt frowns. "You didn't know you were with me, did you?" The question hurts both of us.

I sniffle and shake my head. How could the Nixie betray me like this?

I don't have the energy or anger to fight him.

"Come here. Lie back down. I swear I won't hurt you," he says, but I don't believe him.

I shake my head and pull farther away.

His dark-blue eyes flicker in the dim light of the lit candles. I don't recognize the room. My brain played tricks on me. It saw my room at Constantine's. I wanted to see it. I should have known I wasn't there though. The dead never take me when I'm in my room at Constantine's. I can't help but wonder if the reason the Nixie brought me here was to make sure I could be with her. Or they really are just angry with me.

"Where are we?"

He sits up and pulls my face to his. He looks deeply into my eyes and kisses my cheeks. "Fitz's house." Chills run up and down my spine.

"Please, let me go. Please," I beg instantly.

He shakes his head. "I can't."

I close my eyes as silent tears drip from them.

He kisses them away. "I can't, because they're looking for you. You're safe here. My uncle felt your mom die. They were handfasted, too."

My eyes open fast. "What?"

He nods. "Fitz and Willow were in love for a long time. They kept it secret. He says that's how Lucifer tricked her into revealing where you were. He used Fitz as bait."

I feel sick.

"No. No."

He smiles and kisses my cheeks again. "We weren't the first ones to handfast, I guess."

I sob, "Wyatt, I killed her."

He holds me tight. "No. Lucifer killed her, Rayne. Fitz felt her light go out. That happens to witches who take on some of the original sin. She lied to him and took his evil. Lying to an Archangel is a sin. Fallen or not. She protected you because she loved you."

I look up into his dark-blue eyes and get lost for a minute.

He bends his face and presses his lips against mine. "I love you too."

I let him kiss me, hold me, and soothe me.

I close my eyes and let him lie us both back down. He holds me, and the dead take me.

When I wake, I am alone in the small dark room. I look at the candles lit and the shabby-chic décor.

"She loved you, child. You saved her as much as she saved you." Fitz looks rough. He's sitting in a corner with a big bottle of something. I watch him take a drink and shake his tear-stained face. "She loved you so much, she sacrificed everything for you." His tone has a hint of bitterness in it.

"I'm sorry," I whisper. I guess he was one of the things sacrificed.

He looks at me and smiles. "No. Never be sorry. She did what was right. She loved you and wanted you safe, and she gave up everything to make you safe. Never be sorry for that. Be grateful."

I nod.

"Be grateful such an amazing creature wanted to help you." He loses it. He bends over and sobs. His sobs are the harsh broken kind. He hides his face from me and shakes with pain.

I climb off the bed and walk to him. I wrap my arms around him and we cry together. Our pain is the same.

He looks up at me. "You have to live, for her. You have to. Her sacrifice can't be for nothing."

"I'll try." I nod.

He kisses the top of my head and hugs me hard.

He gets up from the chair and leaves the room.

I walk back to the bed and try to process it all. I grab the cordless phone next to the bed and dial Mona's number.

"Hello?" She sounds confused.

"Hey, it's me." My voice is lost. It's a hoarse whisper.

"Rayne?" She sounds scared.

"Yup."

She sighs. "Oh my God, where are you?"

I shake my head. "I don't know. I'm with Wyatt somewhere. I don't know where it is. Are you okay?"

"Yeah. They've been here like three times looking for you. Wait what? Wyatt? Oh my Got...they have you?"

I sigh. "No. Wyatt and his uncle seem to be on my side. Fitz and Willow were handfasted."

She snaps. "Shut up. No way. Weird."

I nod and look around the room. "Yeah. I have bad news though."

She doesn't bite right away. She braces herself. I can almost hear her doing it. "Okay."

"Willow... uhm... well, she died. I think it was yesterday." My voice cracks.

She is silent.

"She's gone," I say as if I still don't believe it.

Her voice becomes small. "I'm so sorry, Rayne. How? Want me to meet you?"

I think about it and shake my head. "No, stay there. I have to figure out what's next. I'm pretty lost right now. I'll come for you in the next couple days, okay?"

She sounds down. "Yup. Be safe. Please, for the love of God, be safe."

"I will."

"I love you, Rayne. I'm so sorry about your mo-Willow."

I shake my head and try to swallow my tears. "Say mom. She was my mom."

She starts to cry. "Mom. I'm sorry about your mom."

I sniffle. "Thanks."

"See ya in a couple days."

"Yup." I hang up and lie back.

"Are you okay?" Wyatt asks from the doorway. He almost takes up the entire thing.

I shake my head. "I'm confused and lost."

He walks to my side and sits on the bed, "I know. Me too." I glance at the ring finger on his left hand and feel a pain I have never felt before. There on his hand sits a silver ring.

I feel like I've been stabbed in the heart.

"You got married?" I ask.

He looks at the hand and then tucks it under him. "No, this is the promise that I will marry her. We replace the silver with gold when we do the ceremony."

Relief floods me. He isn't married yet. He's still mine in some twisted fucked-up way.

I look into his dark-blue eyes and get lost. They're like the sea. I can float in them and let myself imagine possibilities without the pain of reality attacking me. He mutters, "You know I love you, and I know you love me, but I don't know how to be what we are and be together."

I watch his eyes and smile. "Me either. Your mom wants me full of sin and then dead. My family is a shit show. I don't even understand how he killed Willow."

He sighs. "The Fae are made up of the Light of the World. The small piece of light is what makes them Fae. The Nixie light we used to heal you is from the light of the world. Those Water Witches are Fae. All the witches are Fae. They are bound by a rule, one rule. A golden rule. 'Do what ye will and harm none.' They are bound by it."

I frown. "This is like following a bread crumb trail, but like the crows ate half the stupid bread crumbs."

He laughs. "Anyway! The light is easily corrupted. A dark deed, a lie to an Angel, murder... not in self-defense, theft; any of those sorts of things can kill the light. When the light is gone, the Fae die. They were made of the light, in the light. When they're murdered, their light may be taken."

I shiver. "Like the Nixie who died to save me."

He nods. "They cleansed you. They removed the sin you ate but at a cost. Sacrifice. Everything with God is sacrifice. Willow sacrificed her light to save you."

"I wish she hadn't." Eleven people have died for me.

He kisses me lightly, like a feather would. "I'm grateful to her. I would die without you."

I kiss him back and try to forget there is a silver ring making promises I don't want him to keep.

His fingers trace along my tank top and shoulders. He makes chills and shivers everywhere. He kisses my shoulder and up into my neck. I push him away. "Please don't."

He pulls back and gives me his grin. "You want this, Rayne. I can feel it."

His fingers knead into my thighs.

I nod. "I do, but I'm scared you'll take away my pain."

He kisses me again and whispers into my lips, "I want to take away your pain."

I shake my head. "I deserve it. I need to feel it. It makes her real."

I feel his defeat. "Okay. Let me hold you?"

I curl into him. He lies back and wraps himself around me. I can feel him pressed into the back of me.

"Will you marry her?" I ask.

He kisses my ear. "You feel like adding to your pain, do you?"

I shake my head. "I want you to tell me no."

He challenges me with his stare. "Tell me you don't love Constantine Basarab, and I will."

I roll over and look at him. "Not the same way I love you. The girl I was before, Ellie, she loves him. Her memories and mine are merging. The things I remember are all hers. I remember bad things about him too. Not just the way she loved him. He betrayed her, me. He gave her to your mother. He stabbed her with a sword and made her weak. I remember it."

He grabs at me. "I would never betray you like that. You must know that."

I shake my head. "You already did. You got engaged to that girl, and you let them take me to the tower. Fitz betrayed me then too."

He shakes his head. "No, my mother lied. She said the first Sin Gatherer wouldn't be full for months. She lied to Fitz and me. And I got engaged because I must. My entire family has arranged marriages. Always has."

I watch his eyes. "Why didn't Fitz ever get married?"

He smiles his huge cocky grin. "Lied and said he was gay."

I laugh. I don't mean to, but it's funny. Lying about being gay to avoid an arranged marriage is genius.

"Does she want to marry you?"

His cocky grin gets bigger. "What girl wouldn't want to marry me, Rayne? Of course she does. She loves me. She thinks she's won the man lottery."

I frown. "Gross. Lucky you're humble, because that could really inflate your ego. Man lottery. That's disgusting."

He laughs.

I don't. "Thanks for that. I needed something to cool me off. That worked. I'm going back to sleep again. I'm exhausted."

He grabs my arms. "Oh, come on. It was a joke. No, she doesn't want to marry me, okay? Happy? No. She is as annoyed and devastated as I am. She's playing pretend very convincingly though. Whereas, I am the shame of my family."

I laugh again. "I could have guessed that easily. Your sister seems like she is your mother's pet though."

He nods. "She is. She is the one who called our mother when Constantine sent the vampires to collect you the first day you came home with me. She is exactly like our mother."

I frown. "You knew those vampires were coming for me, even then? You knew about Constantine then?"

He looks like he might lie or at least attempt it, but he doesn't. He nods and shrugs. "He's always been after you. For the last three lives you've had, he has been with you. Always as a husband. When you said you were with him again, I panicked. I thought you'd gone bad again."

I frown. "How do you know about this?"

He speaks plainly, "Lore."

"What?"

His smile stays on his face but I can see it's forced. "Lore. We have legends and stories about you dating back to the beginning."

I push him away. "You knew this was my last life?"

He nods. "I only found out after you ran away from me. I'd studied you my whole life, but I never knew who you were. We always assumed Lucifer had you kept somewhere. When you got away from me, Fitz fessed up about knowing about you all along. He had helped Willow several times at keeping you safe."

I shake my head. "I don't remember him. Not at all."

He chuckles. "Well besides her stabbing me in the neck, I'd never met her either. They kept each other secret. Very secret."

"What was life like before I came along?" I ask.

He laughs. "Plain. I trained and hung out and had regular girlfriends and planned my life after university. Obviously it's always been the family business for me, but I never imagined it would be this annoying and stressful. You have a gift. Let me tell you. Stressing me out is not easy, and yet you do it with ease."

I blush and snuggle into his embrace. "Why didn't you ever just tell me the things you knew about me?"

"My whole life has been training for the moment you would be reborn and killing the things that go bump in the night. You and I are enemies, Rayne. Natural enemies."

I close my eyes again and sleep. All I ever do is sleep.

Chapter Twenty-Five

"RUN, RAYNE! RUN BACK TO HIM! WAKE UP!"

I open my eyes and look around the room. I heard Willow. I swear I did.

"RUN!"

The voice isn't Willow's, but I can hear it outside of my head. The voice is screaming at me like the Nixie did. I climb from the bed and open the door to the hall.

I open it a crack and look around the empty hallway. I close the door and go back to the bed. I pull on all my layers of clothes Fitz cleaned for me. I pull on my boots and try not to notice the slight dampness from the sea.

"RUN!"

I sigh and look up. "I'm frickin' tired of running, okay?" I whisper to whoever is screaming at me.

I open the door and slip out into the hallway again. The dead are sparkling around me, whispering. I follow their whispers down a long hallway. I open the door they sit in front of and peek inside. No one is there. The room looks like an old-fashioned weapons room.

"LOOK!"

I look around the room. I'm confused and scared.

On the wall, in the far-right corner, is something that breaks my heart and lifts me up instantly. I run to the wall and pull the sword off. It's a Katana. It's my Katana. The silver sword gleams, just as it did the day they took it out of me. I shiver, remembering the feeling of the sword being pulled from my side. Memories flood my mind.

Wyatt's mother, Gretel, was the one who pulled it from my side. The sheath is on a shelf below it. I grab it and sheath the sword. I pull the matching dagger from the wall and hold it. There is a shelf of belts and harnesses. I grab a belt and put it on. My body is twitching and shivering. Excitement and fear are rolling around inside of me like storm clouds.

I slide the dagger into the belt hilt and carry my sword. Weapons line the walls. Daggers, swords, maces, axes, nunchucks, arrows, bows, cleavers, knives, polearms, and spears. Guns with wooden bullets and silver bullets fill an entire shelf.

The room freaks me out. There is no doubt a weapon for every kind of creature. A silver knife for the throat of the Nixie, a wooden bullet for the vampires and a silver spear for a shifter. Leather armor and metal armor fill the far-side of the wall. Special armor is encased in glass. I recognize it somehow.

I want out.

I turn and walk to the door quietly.

I peer out. Nothing moves in the hall.

The dead whisper and sparkle in the air around me. They want me to follow them a different way.

They trickle over to where a huge brick fireplace and chimney are.

"PRESS THE STAR TO SEE THE STARS!"

I sigh and close the door. "You guys are annoying."

I walk to the huge fireplace. I see a small sign that reads, 'Caress a star to see the stars and find eternal love'.

256

I look around for the star but see nothing.

I hear a noise in the hall. The dead cluster their sparkles around a picture across the room.

It's tiny and black and white. I squint to see the picture. It's a man and a woman sitting on a hillside with the moon in front of them. You can only see the backs of the man and the woman. I look closer. It's Fitz and Willow. I'd recognize the daisy chain on her head anywhere.

There is a single star in the sky. It's close to the moon. I look back at the door. It opens as my finger touches the star.

Suddenly I'm freezing. The wind whips around me.

I'm standing on a hillside. I look around. It's the hillside from the picture.

"Who are you?"

I turn to see a woman holding a basket. She's dressed funny. Like in my memory. She wears full-gathered skirts with an apron. In the dim light of the night, I can barely make out her face, until my eyes do their thing. Then I can't help but notice she looks familiar.

"Who are you?" she asks again. I take a step forward.

"Rayne. Rayne Phillips. Who are you?" I say.

She takes a step towards me. "Elise. I'm Elise. No one is supposed to come through that picture but Fitz and Willow."

I look down. "Willow is dead."

She drops to her knees. "No." The basket tips, spilling dark berries to the ground. I bend and pick them up.

"She is," I say.

"How?"

I grip her basket and try not to cry. "Lucifer. He took her light. Who are you?"

She smiles at me. "The guardian. I was a sister to Willow."

257

I frown at her outfit. "Why are you dressed like that?"

She laughs. "I am frozen. This place was made for Willow and Fitz. It's where they could come and be with each other without the world to interfere."

I shake my head. "I don't understand."

She smiles. "I sacrificed myself for her. She saved my life, so I came here for her. One of us must be here for the magic to remain. I hold the picture open, like a portal."

"Can anyone come through?"

She shakes her head. "No. You have to have true love for Willow or Fitz to be able to do it. Only love for them will permit a person's entrance. The love must be the purest kind of true love."

I pass her the basket. "This is like a fairytale."

She snorts. "There is no such thing as a fairytale. They are old tales, told over generations. Sometimes they get twisted, but they're always just stories."

I raise an eyebrow. "Either way I need to get out of here. But not in the weapons room at Fitz's. I need out another way."

She laughs. "You need Willow's portal."

"Where does is come out?"

She shrugs. "My house."

I stop and think. "Wait, so you leave when they come here, and then the rest of the time, you're here?"

She nods. "Yup."

"If she's dead, you won't be needing to stay then?"

She shrugs. "I'll have to ask her and see what she wants me to do. She and Fitz may want to stay here forever."

"She's dead, Elise."

She shakes her head. "Her light is gone. That doesn't make her dead. Witches don't die, per say. They shift. She's not in human form, but she is still here, somehow. Make no mistake about it. She is here. This place can't exist if she doesn't also exist."

I cover my eyes and shake my head. "I can't do any more riddles right now. Please, just tell me how to get out of here."

"The star, of course. The way you got in. The star on the left is his, and the star on the right is hers."

I look up at the two stars in the sky, one on either side of the moon.

"Just reach up and press your finger on the right star."

I look at her and nod. "I'll come back to free you."

She shakes her head. "No. I need to stay here. I need to keep the secrets here safe."

I am confused, but I look back and press the right star. Instantly, I am in a small room. It's a tiny living room, cozy like my house. I walk to the front door, expecting to see a world like no other with magical pixies fluttering about. Instead, when I step out, I see a busy street with cars and trucks zooming past. I am standing on a sidewalk in a city. It's dark and noisy. I turn back to the door but it's locked. I realize I'm holding a sword and have a dagger on my belt. I look like a freak. I turn and walk. I have no phone or keys or car. I wish I were back with Elise.

I look up as I walk. "You wanted me to meet Elise. You wanted me to have Ellie's weapons. Now what?"

There is nothing. Figures. The dead sparkle and float around me but say nothing.

I ran, I got my weapons, and I saw the weird magical portal where Fitz and Willow lived. I don't know what else could possibly happen, but I feel pretty ready for anything.

I walk until I see a bus stop. I look at the map.

I'm downtown Boston. "Fuck."

An old lady looks at me and shakes her head. My face flushes red and I continue on. I need a payphone. I need to stop jumping into the ocean and losing my phone, or leaving it behind.

I could call Mona, but she would have no way to come for me—if she even remembers me. Damned Constantine.

I could call Michelle, but her phone is probably in with a nun. The Earth Witches won't help me and the Water Witches brought me to Wyatt. They clearly have some directional issues. I don't trust Fitz, not yet. I don't have anywhere to go. I'm exhausted. I can feel my body doing its twitchy thing. I have to call someone before I randomly kill.

I wish Wyatt were here.

Instead, I phone Constantine, dejectedly.

"Really?" he answers in a gruff voice.

"I need you." I almost squeak it out.

"You ran away." He sounds pissed, as usual.

I snap. "You put me in a cell, and you ate three Water Witches."

He chuckles. "Someone has been learning about her past."

"I'm in downtown Boston at the corner of Water and Congress and freezing. I got my sword back. You know… the one you drove into my side."

"Be there in a minute, my love." He sounds fierce. He hangs up and I frown. How the hell is he here? I roll my eyes. Sneaky bastard.

The minute feels like an hour, and the cold wind doesn't improve my mood.

By the time the huge black SUV pulls up, I can't feel my fingers.

He grins and pulls up to the curb. I jump in and crank the heat. He frowns at me. "Pretty certain the rule about one's console in a vehicle is that guests to the vehicle don't touch the console."

I roll my eyes. "That's just the stereo."

His dark eyes are searching me.

I shake my head. "Unharmed."

"No new evil?" he asks.

I shake my head again and huddle into the hot air blowing from the dash.

"Can I die of frostbite or exposure?" I ask.

He laughs. "The only things that can kill you are the devils, the evil, and of course the beheading. But I have seen you thin as a rail, starved, dehydrated to the point your eyes are dried shut, and bleeding from malnutrition and sickness. You have the ability to suffer endlessly. Even after all of that, someone still has to cut your head off."

I sigh. "How exciting. So are you going to tell me about the first time you met me? Not as Ellie but as the other me?"

He glances at me sideways and pulls away to merge back into the traffic.

I grin. "You can't storm out of the room. I have you trapped, Constantine. Now spill."

He laughs. He's beautiful when he smiles and laughs.

He drives out of the city. "Are you hungry?"

I nod. "Yeah. Starved."

He pulls of the highway and drives to the McDonald's in Chelsea. I glare at him. "How rich are you?"

He shrugs. "I don't know exactly. Do we count land, or the money that's yours that I keep safe for you?"

I tilt my head. "Stop messing with me. For real... how rich?" He has money that's mine? Interesting.

He shakes his head. "Few hundred million, I suppose. Why?"

I point as he pulls into the drive-thru.

He laughs. "You've never eaten here, have you?"

"No, of course not. She never permitted things like this." I can't say her name.

His dark eyes sparkle. "You're in for a real treat." he says, laughing.

"You're cheap."

He holds up a finger. "No, impatient. Now shut up and let me order you dinner."

I listen to him order things I can't even imagine. Filets and shakes and diet soda and fries. She would have a stroke.

He pays a lady in the window and charms her with smiles and his dark magical eyes.

They pass us bags of food. Bags. For two people.

I have to put some of it on the floor. They pass us a tray of drinks and a stack of napkins that seems like it should be for a family of eight. The food actually seems like it's for eight people.

"Thank you, my dear. Have a pleasant evening."

She blushes. "Have a good night."

He drives. "Hurry. Pass me the fries. They don't taste good once they've cooled."

I frown and pass a hot packet of fries. "No-my-God, you eat this a lot, don't you?"

He stuffs his face and talks with several fries hanging from his lips. It's comical. "Yeah. It's addictive, I think. Have something. I recommend the fish filet."

"You have money that's saved for me?" I ask.

He frowns. "Yes, of course. I invested your dowry for you, just as I said I would when I received it."

His lips glisten from the hot oil. He chews and sips the diet soda. "Only the second time though."

"You got paid to marry me?" I am offended.

He nods. "Not the first time. You were a poor orphan the first time we met."

I sigh. "Good to see things have changed."

The SUV stinks.

I wrinkle my nose. "This stuff smells terrible."

He laughs. "Have some."

I take one of the four fry packets and stuff some of them in my mouth. It's salty and tasty. Instantly, my mouth waters for more. Soon, I look like him. Stuffing food into my face and drinking. She would be ashamed of me.

He speaks plainly, "The first time I saw you, you were in the Van Helsings' castle. I went to their castle to exact revenge for my uncle Vlad. They had murdered him mercilessly. You were a sight to behold."

I blush and stuff the delicious fish filet into my mouth. The sauce is a miracle.

He shakes his head. "Not a good sight. I'd never seen anything so disgusting and horrid in all my life. It was cruelty times a thousand. As a vampire, I have always done things that were unsavory. I've eaten children, raped women, killed whole villages. The early years are something I can never forgive myself for."

I want to be disgusted, but I understand the hunger. I nearly shrug it off before I scold myself mentally.

"What I saw when I entered that tower made me sick; the image haunted me for years. I couldn't be with you, not without thinking about it. I rescued you from their evil clutches and ran with you. I never got my revenge for what they did. I ran. You weighed nothing more than a few pounds of bones and ripped skin."

I gag a little and put my fish down.

He winces. "Sorry. At any rate, it was bad. You were full of poison and dying. The first couple devils had cleansed their evil in you. You were brimming with it. I brought you to my castle in the mountains and hid you. It took half a year to get you to the point I could be near you without seeing the images of horror. You fell in love with me quickly."

I laugh. "I wonder why?"

He smiles brightly. "I was your champion. It turned out that you were an orphan, raised by a mother who was rejected and considered a witch. You had lived alone with her in the forest. She had died, and the Van Helsings took you. I was taken by you, no doubt. You were a little vixen. You tempted me for some time with sex and love and not in that order. I couldn't do it though. I always saw you the way you had been."

I felt a tear slip down my cheeks. The memories are locked away, but I see a flash of something. His face. The pity in his eyes is devastating.

I bury my sorrow and open another burger.

He looks at me. His face hardens. "I fell in love with you. I have loved you ever since."

I shake my head. "How did I die?"

He presses his lips together and furrows his brow. "This is something I've been meaning to talk to you about. The twenty-first birthday isn't just a guideline for when the evil has to be eaten." He looks panicked. My stomach curdles from the fast food.

"What?" I frown.

He nods. "You have an expiry date. You die on the eve of your twenty-first birthday, sacrificed or not. The deal Lucifer made was soul for soul. He and Lillith would either give their souls for the soul of their child—or they would give their child for their souls. The grim reaper comes for you, if they're not dead by then. He came and stole you from my bed, from my arms, the eve of your twenty-first birthday."

The air sparkles with the dead. My stomach rumbles. I feel tears choking me in my throat. He sees my face and pulls over. I leap from the SUV. I bend forward and heave and gag until all the

McDonald's is gone. Sweat and tears mix, dripping from my face.

Everything feels slow and hopeless. It feels so big, and I can't grasp any of it. Definitely, not any hope.

I will die anyway.

Even if I get the devils, I die. I feel a mound of napkins pressed into my palm. I grip them and try to cry and throw up at the same time.

I wipe myself and sit on the step up into the SUV. The cold wind doesn't wash me clean.

I die anyway.

It doesn't seem fair.

His warmth is around me. He scoops me up and puts me back into the car. He grabs the bags of McDonald's and tosses them into the ditch.

I scowl. "Hey."

He glances at me. "What?"

"Don't litter. Willow will kill me from the grave. Littering and eating that trash."

He chuckles and then stops himself. "From the grave?"

I look down and the tears are back. I cover my face with the napkins and sob uncontrollably.

He holds me tight and kisses my forehead. "You stink. You always stink now. Ocean, sweat, old clothes, throw up, and fish filets."

I laugh/cry. "I just don't know what to do or who to trust. This world feels too big and too overwhelming. Wyatt seems like he's genuinely on my side, and Fitz and Willow had a secret world, and you. You're in it for yourself, it seems, and then you're nice to me. I don't know what to think."

He grips my arm, not hard but firm. He lifts my face. "When have I been in it for myself? I have lived over seven hundred years and loved you for nearly all of them. I get a meager year or two and then you die. Every time. I wait for the signs you've been born again. Then I track you like a bloodhound. I am lucky to get a year or two. Last time, I found you before the change. I made sure you and I would get at least four years. Only this time, I find you handfasted to a Van Helsing."

I look up at him. "But you betrayed me."

He shakes his head. "No. I have never betrayed you, Ellie."

I pull back. "Rayne."

He closes his eyes. "Sorry. You were Ellie when it happened, in my defense. I never betrayed you. We ran out of time before we found the way to end it. You made me promise I would do anything I had to in order to get the information about how to stop it. Trading you for information was the only way. I knew you would die in a couple months, anyway. I traded you, and they told me about the deal Lucifer made and about the seven devils."

I frown. "Why would they tell you that?"

He grins. "Fitz. He wanted it to end too. He never saw it as fair. He and Willow had started their little romance, and his family suspected something. He needed something to convince them that he was still team Van Helsing. I gave him you, and he gave me the answers. I knew this time we would succeed."

I shake my head. "I remember panicking. I remember the feeling of the betrayal."

He looks sick. "Compulsion. You knew about Fitz and Willow. You knew where I had all my darkest secrets and things we couldn't let them torture out of you. You made me compel you to forget everything, except the fact you loved me and that we were happy. You remembered the story we made up for you. Well, with a few additions I thought would be fun. Like my office." His corners of his lips play with the possibility of a smile. He shrugs. "Anyway, I think you still remember it all. The alley and the marriage and the old house that stood just where my new house stands."

I feel the confusion on my face.

He nods and sighs. "Pretty much how you're supposed to feel."

"Can you remove it? The compulsion?"

He shakes his head. "You handfasted. If I didn't know any better, I would say young Wyatt knows more than he is letting on. I would almost guarantee that he knows that handfasting you keeps you in the dark. It also prevents you from living off my sins, which is better for everyone."

I want to shake my head and say no, but I have a horrid sinking feeling it's true. All of it.

I think for a second and then nod. "We need to go to Burlington. I want Mona, and that's where the witch is who can break the handfasting."

He leans in and kisses my forehead. "I'm so sorry. We have so little time."

I climb in. "You knew who I was all along?"

He nods. "I wanted to tell you who you were, but Lillith forbid it. She said the only way to succeed was to let you grow like a normal kid. You needed love and purity for the quest. It's all of us against Lucifer this time. The Witches, Van Helsings, me, you and Lillith."

He closes my door and walks around to his.

He climbs in and looks like he's exhausted. "The Nixie. They've been trying to help you piece it all together. They want you to succeed. It's what Lillith wants. Them and the Witches. Well, the Earth and Fire Witches. The Air Witches want you to die and take the sin."

He starts the SUV and drives.

As always, I feel overwhelmed. "Why do they want that?"

He sighs. "I don't know. They're difficult. Made of the Angels. Almost no Fae in them. Earth and Fire and Water all have a lot of

Fae in them. The Air Witches are puritans. They have only Angel with a tiny bit of Fae in them. It's how they fly. Because of it, they don't have the same attachment to the Fae. They love Lillith. I don't know their exact reasoning. Angels protecting Angels, I guess."

"Can I borrow your cell?"

He hands it to me without asking me why. I think he would give me anything in the world. I wish he could give me more time.

Chapter Twenty-Six

The small house looks the same. I bang on the door one more time, but nothing. She wasn't at the Italian restaurant, and she isn't home.

Constantine turns to smoke and slithers under the door. He smiles as he opens it.

I shake my head. "This is so wrong. Although, I'm already going to hell."

He shakes his head. "Not if I can help it, you're not."

Her small house is dark but looks the same. My eyes let me see every detail. The room is clean. It looks so much like my house, I almost tear up. In the far corner, I see a sliver of dim light in the wall, behind the big chair. "Here," I whisper. I push the wall where the light is. Nothing opens it. He turns to smoke again and slips through the tiny crack.

He doesn't open the door. I don't hear anything.

I press my ear against the wall and wait.

I hear a scream and a thump behind the wall.

I bang on it. "Constantine!"

The wall pushes in. The waitress is standing face to face with me when the door opens. I step back. "Hi."

She glares at me. "Hi." She sounds super excited that we're here. Constantine is behind her in the brick stairwell.

"So you're dating a vampire and handfasted to a Van Helsing. You have quite the social life, Sin Eater." She crosses the room and sits down.

"You knew?" I'm surprised.

She shakes her head. "I never knew until recently. Willow did a remarkable job covering you in protection. No wonder Wyatt never knew what you were."

I sit on the opposite sofa. It's comfy and reminds me of Willow.

"You don't think he knew?" I know there is hope in my voice.

She shakes her head. "He would have never handfasted with you if he did. Handfasting is something for soul mates. It makes it so your soul can find its match, no matter what. No death and no birth or rebirth can separate the handfasted. It also guarantees that whatever sin you eat, he shares the burden. The burden and blessing of either party is shared in the magic of it."

I glance at Constantine. He looks grim.

"So, will he die?"

She shakes her head. "Not exactly. He'll rot. He'll rot the way you do. The darkness and magic will fill him and corrupt his soul. It's not pleasant, let me tell you. Not to mention, he'll end up in purgatory when he does die."

Terror and guilt ravage me. "How can I heal him?"

She shrugs. "Kill Lillith and Lucifer and the five devils. Have you fed yet, cleansed a devil?"

I nod and look down. "But Wyatt killed seven Nixie and gave me their light."

She gasps and looks horrified. "Oh my Goddess. How disgusting. How could you let him? They are our people, Rayne."

I can't stop the tears. "I had no strength. They each swam up and offered their neck to him." I heave and shake.

"She didn't ask for it. They gave themselves. It was their right." Constantine wraps himself around me. The defensiveness in his tone is unmistakable.

She wipes away a tear and fans her face. "No, you're right. It is their right to do as they wish with their light. They cleansed and saved you. Their light would have pushed out the evil. It would have disbursed back into the earth."

I look up. "What does that mean?"

She smiles. "You're clean again."

I shake my head, "No, the Earth Witches said I was evil. I bring a stain with me."

She shakes her head. "That's from Lucifer. His blood is your blood this time."

I frown. "What? No, I was born to a virgin."

She smiles. "Maybe she wasn't a virgin. Maybe she was raped by him or was his lover. He is known to enjoy both. I can feel the stain of him on you. It's not evil; it's just him. Now that Willow's protection is off of you, I can feel it."

I sigh and wipe away the tears. "Can you break the handfast?"

She looks sick. Her breathing increases, as panic and fear fill her expression. She nods. "Yup. He can't be touching you though."

Constantine kisses my cheek and pulls away.

She grabs a candle. It's black.

"Is there any cost I should know about?" I remember the discussions we've had on costs.

She looks like she's going to cry but shakes her head. She isn't making me feel confident. "Nothing I can think of. You know Wyatt has the evil he ate. You know the tracking is going to stop. I can't think of anything else. It hurts." Her voice sounds broken.

I shrug. "Can't be worse than anything else I've ever done or eaten or suffered through."

"I would expect pain. I've seen it done once. It was bad."

She lights the candle with her breath. It's a black candle. It lights up the dark room.

There's a knock at her door as she lights it. "Wanna bet that's your boyfriend?"

I furrow my brow. "Huh?"

She grins. "He can sense you're here. I bet he knows why. Why else would you come here? He probably has been following you for weeks." She has no idea.

The door shakes with the banging.

"He's going to break the door down." Constantine walks toward it.

"He will be able to see you, vampire. I can't cloak you. Only her and me."

He looks back at me. His dark eyes consume me, and then he's smoke. The smoke trickles out the window to the right.

She looks at me. "Ready?"

I nod. I'm terrified. My hand is shaking in hers.

She kisses my hand and pours the wax from the black candle over it. I wince from the pain of the burning wax.

She blows the wax with her mouth, speaking something in a low mumble. The wax hardens. She holds my hand and closes her eyes. She chants. I've seen Willow and her crazy friends do it before. She squeezes my hand. The pain starts there.

I let out a scream and flinch. It's sudden, and I don't know how to deal with the intensity. I squirm and try to get away, but her magic holds me.

The pain is like having my fingers pulled off slowly. She picks the black wax off and drops it onto the coffee table. It feels like she is skinning my hand, but the skin is attached to my heart. I scream until my voice is gone, and even then manage to make noise. My eyes burn from the tears flooding them. I try to pull my hand back, but she holds it tightly.

"Please, please, please," I chant too.

She is crying, just as I am.

She chants and picks the wax off.

The door banging has turned to screaming. I only hear it while I inhale for my next scream, which is hoarse and nearly silent. There is thrashing on the doorstep. I hear his pleas. I hear him screaming my name from the front step.

She collapses onto the floor as the last piece of wax drops to the coffee table. She is out of breath and sobbing. The dead fill the room. Their whispers become cries. They're telling me that she has taken in some of my soul. She must consume the wax. It will clear her debt for bringing more darkness to the world.

She picks up the pieces of the wax and puts one into her mouth.

"What are you doing? Don't listen to them," I ask through the crying.

"Taking my blame for destroying something made of love. The dead are right."

"Will it hurt you?" I sob.

She nods. "It's the cost."

"My soul is full of sin. Please don't. Please, don't eat that." I try to grab the pieces of wax but with one small movement of her hand, I am thrown against the wall. "You lied!" I cry out.

She shakes, taking the black wax into her mouth. She heaves as each piece is consumed. Her eyes don't look like fire anymore. They look dead.

I'm pinned but thrashing to be released. The door knocking and screaming is happening again.

Her tears turn black as the wax.

She coughs on the last piece and collapses onto the table.

I drop to the floor.

My arms and legs twitch from exhaustion and pain. I crawl to her like a wounded dog. My hand is completely burned. It's red and raw. She is barely breathing.

"You can suck our sin from her. She's a witch; you can't kill her. Take the sin."

I look up to see Wyatt in the doorway. He's holding his hand too.

"I'm sorry," I whisper.

He shakes his head. "I should never have handfasted with you, Rayne. This is all my fault."

I grab her face and press her stained black lips against mine. The nastiest taste flows from her lips.

"Stop when the taste changes."

I suck until it tastes sweet, but I don't stop. I take a long pull.

"STOP!" Wyatt screams.

I jump back and drop her on the coffee table again. She moans and looks at me.

I wipe the black greasy tears from my lips and shudder.

Wyatt helps her up. "You must run."

She nods and tries to stand.

I'm shaking. The sweetness of her was amazing.

She looks at me. "Run. The guards are down," she whispers. I look at Wyatt. His eyes betray his guilt.

"What have you done?" I whisper.

He clenches his jaw and looks back at the doorway that's slightly open still. "They came for you at Fitz's. He's dead. He fought my mother for you. A light filled the house and suddenly Fitz was dead."

I look down and fight the tears that are suddenly choking me. I don't know why, but the idea that Fitz died fighting for me shakes me. All the bad thoughts I had about him.

"Take me to my lair." Her words are weak.

I look at her. "Did I do this? Did I hurt you?"

She swallows hard and nods. "You just weakened me. I'll be fine in a couple days. You can't kill me, Rayne. It's okay." She is out of breath.

I look at the door. "Are they waiting for me outside?"

Wyatt nods once, "I'm so sorry, Rayne. I didn't know they followed me. Not until it was too late."

I'm trapped. Panic has set in.

"Hide her. Seal yourself in."

She nods. "Call the dead, Rayne. They'll fight for you."

Wyatt frowns at her and lifts her up. He walks down into the lair and then comes back up. The door closes and seals with a flame.

The air sparkles; the dead want me to run.

I shake my head. "I can't."

Wyatt gives me a weird look. I stand. My sword is in the SUV. I pull the small dagger from my belt and look at him. "What am I expecting?"

He looks grim, "Mother, Father, Maggie, Sarah, and a few others."

"Your fiancé?"

He nods.

I take a breath. "My memories have your mother doing some very fancy shit."

His eyes turn cold. "You don't stand a chance against her."

I close my eyes and let the sparkles become the only noise I hear. "Help me. Please fight for me. I don't know what you can do, but please help me."

The air gets thick and the sparkles become snaps of light, like electric charges in the air.

"What is this? You have magic?" he asks.

I shake my head. "I don't know." I honestly don't. I need to see Constantine. I need him to remove the stupid memory blocks from me.

The quiet of the house becomes overrun with the sparks. I watch as the front door creaks open. I stand ready with only my small dagger.

His mother walks in, dressed just as she was in the memories I have of her. Leather pants and a leather shirt. She looks like someone from the Matrix. She has on big boots and a sword. She smiles at me. Suzy Homemaker is gone. The homicidal schoolteacher has been replaced by a ninja. Her hair is pulled back into a tight bun. Her lips are dark red.

"That's a lot of leather for one lady." I look behind me to see Constantine. I smile. His jaw is set. He looks pissed.

I glance back at Gretel and smirk. "You want this fight?"

She looks at Wyatt. "Which side are you on, boy?"

He looks lost and scared for the first time ever. His cockiness is replaced by real fear. He shakes his head. "We can end this. Let's help her find the devils and Lucifer."

She laughs. In the doorway, I can see others dressed similarly.

Constantine taps me on the shoulder. "You'll want this." When I look back at him and take my sword, his eyes flash. Instantly, I'm held by them. Pressure fills my head. I grip it and cry out. Memories flood my mind. Old memories. Things it's impossible for one human to remember.

My sword becomes an extension of my arm.

I feel a growl run up my throat. Slowly, I turn my head to the left and make eye contact.

She smiles wide. "Finally. I was wondering when the simpering girl would be gone and the true Sin Eater would join us." She glances at Constantine. "Naughty of you, Basarab."

He speaks through his sneer. "I am going to rip your heart out, Gretel, and dine on it later."

Wyatt smiles grimly. "She doesn't have a heart."

I look at the clear standoff between the three of us and ready myself. I tap the floor with my sword. "Enough. Let's end this."

She steps down the stairs and opens the door for us. She puts an arm out. "My sentiments exactly."

She walks out onto the grass where seven of them stand. I walk toward the doorway. Constantine is smoke again. I smirk at Wyatt and pass him my dagger. "You look like your dad did when he was young."

He frowns. "No I don't. I look more like my mother."

I glance at the man he thinks is his father and laugh. "That's not your father, Wyatt. Your real father was an Angel. Your mother used to be a very naughty Van Helsing."

She glares at me from the grass. I smile back.

His face becomes a storm of anger. He looks at her. "You lied to me?"

She doesn't lose any of the crazed emotions on her face.

I turn to Wyatt and take his hand. It burns my skin, but I ignore it. "He was a wonderful man."

He looks sick and confused. "Let's do this." My heart is breaking for him. I know exactly how he feels.

I nod. Constantine has already become smoke. He appears

behind one of the Van Helsings and bites savagely into his neck. I dive through the door and kick my legs off the grass. I leap into the air and kick Sarah in the face. She stumbles back as his mother stabs something into my upper arm. I slash my sword across her forearm.

A whip wraps around my waist. I pull it and use the man who wields it as a shield.

Constantine is eating his second person. Wooden stakes stick out of his shirt, smoking. He rips one out and stabs it into the throat of the person he's eating.

Sarah shoots me with something. It does nothing. I pluck it out of my stomach and throw it at her.

Gretel smashes me in the face with the butt of her sword. I feel my nose break. I wince but duck and kick her legs out from under her and return the favor with my fist.

Wyatt is fighting the man who isn't his father. He looks savage.

I feel a sharp pain in my lower back. I fall. I feel a stabbing sensation. Sarah has me down. Her dagger is stabbing me psychotically. Gretel is bleeding from her nose and lips.

She laughs when she sees Sarah attacking me. Blood coats her teeth.

I try to flip Sarah but I can't. I'm hurt. Wyatt tackles Sarah off of me. His own mother stabs her sword into him. He punches Sarah in the face and knocks her out. He rolls off of her and lies in the grass.

I dig my fingers into the grass and try to pull myself to him.

I hear the sparkles and the feel the thick air. "HELP ME!" I scream into the night.

Gretel turns back to me and holds her sword up over me. Fire shoots from the ground and makes a circle around me. The flames reach ten feet. I watch as she tries to bring the sword down on me. The flames leap at her. She screams. In the flames, I can see Constantine. He is fighting savagely. He looks like he's having a good time.

Through the flames, I see Wyatt crawling to me. He's bleeding from his stomach and clutching it. I scream and reach for him. "HELP HIM! CONSTANTINE, HELP HIM!"

Instantly, Wyatt is gone.

Wyatt and Constantine are gone, and I am lying in a ring of flames. I can breathe knowing they're safe.

Gretel is charred and bleeding. She watches me for a moment. Hatred and disgust are all over her face.

I feel the dead cocooning me in the fire. They fear her. I feel a sharp poke in my arms and a whoosh of air and suddenly I'm flying. It feels like being home.

Chapter Twenty-Seven

His touch is remarkable.

He kneads the skin and rubs the oils in. "Did you miss this?"

I laugh. "That your fingers never tire or remembering who you are?" If I didn't want him so badly, I could fall asleep.

He coos, "I would like to think my never-ending massages are nothing compared to the fact that you remember me now."

I smile peacefully and let the kneading relax me. "Well, asking me during a never-ending massage is a bad idea."

"You remember it all?" he laughs.

I nod. "I do. I remember being all of them. I remember my first life as Liana with Mother and Father. I remember the second life, when I was Ezara and I lived with my father mostly. I remember my parents challenging God. I remember them telling him to try to live through the pain of sacrificing a child. If he did, they would consider his proposal. I remember being born as Maggie and hearing about the poor boy Jesus. He was born of a virgin and sacrificed by his father in a show of good will. I remember meeting you in the tower and you saving me."

His hands stop. He presses his body into mine. His warm skin against mine is amazing. "I love you. I have always loved you."

I open my lips to return the sentence but I cannot. My words get stuck in the truth.

I haven't always loved him. I feel my body tense with shame and guilt. He has done everything for me, waited hundreds of years for me, died a thousand deaths every time I die. How do I repay him? Fall in love with a Van Helsing. A child. Just as when my memories reminded me of my love for Constantine, they now betray me and remind me of my love for Wyatt.

His cocky smile and dark-blue eyes burn in my mind. I feel tears welling in my eyes. My heart will be broken, no matter the choice I make.

"What is it?"

I shake my head. "Worried about Mona. The reason we never separated was the Van Helsings. They will take her and make her bait."

He kisses my neck and I feel disgusting. "I had Tom pick her up yesterday and bring her here."

I nod. "Thanks."

"My love, shall we retire to the bedroom?"

I shake my head. "No. You go. I need to see Mona."

He kisses my back. "She'll be there tomorrow."

I push my aching body off the bed and wrap the huge blanket around me. He sees my face and lifts my chin. "What is this look?"

I shrug. "Confusion."

He frowns, "You have your memories. We know all there is to know. We have a year and a half until your twenty-first birthday. We know we have to kill the devils, Lillith, and Lucifer; we know the Nixie can take you to her; we know Lucifer is looking for you; we have the answers, my pet. After all this time, we finally have the answers."

His dark hair and dark eyes help me forget the other reasons I have for not wanting to make love to him. It really is only one reason. One person.

I look down on the scars filling in and fading on my arms. "I'm still Rayne. I'm still me. The memories of the other lives can only take so much room in my brain and heart, before the life I have now takes over and becomes the most important."

He bends his face and kisses my lips. Instantly, tears drip from my eyes. "You love him still?"

I murmur, "I love you too."

He steps back and walks from the room.

I bend over and cover my face in shame.

I grip my towel and walk out of the massage room, slipping down the hall to my room.

Mona jumps up and runs to me.

I instantly feel better.

I glance over and see Michelle on the bed. She squeals and runs over.

"Oh my God, you guys are both here. I miss you both."

Michelle smells me. "You smell like citrus and lavender."

I shrug. "I had a hippie for a mom. What can I say?"

Mona grabs me my fleecy PJ's from the closet. "Super creepy how he has all kinds of clothes for you already, huh?" She brings me my clothes. She smiles when she hands me a brand new pack of granny panties, organic unbleached cotton. I know she brought these.

I shake my head. "Not so much. We have been married twice before."

Michelle raises an eyebrow. "Damn, girl. What the hell are you doing in here?"

I feel my face attempting to brighten and laugh but I feel sick.

Mona sighs. "She still loves Wyatt. Look at that face."

I moan, "Tell me you two have drama or something, please. Anything. I feel like everything is always about me."

Michelle jumps on the bed and lies back. "I had priest sex."

I gasp and pull on my granny panties and fleecy PJ's.

Mona covers her eyes. "No-my-God. Priest sex? Why?"

She bats her long lashes and grins like the Cheshire cat. "Well, his name is Randolph. He's from Germany. He had only recently become a priest. I was doing my confession and he got a huge boner." She holds her fingers out in a very large measurement. I grimace. Mona looks horrified. "And I told him he was a sinner. He was wasting the gift God had given him. He got all-cute and blushed and said he had never had a woman before. I told him he should try it just once, as a test of his faith. To see if it was really what he wanted."

I shake my head. "Dude. You sound like a creepy old man luring him with candy. I'm pretty sure you're going to Hell. That was so evil."

She laughs. "Rayne, girl. I met my Christian. Now I am talking Advil and a cold bath. Not even kidding. But oh my God. Fabulous. Now that was a religious experience, let me tell you."

I laugh and Mona looks like she is about to either cry or rock in the fetal position.

I frown. "What about Benny?"

She looks offended. "I was on a mission from God, Rayne."

I point. "God is ashamed of you. I'm ashamed. Tots ashamed. You're going to Hell. You know that, right?"

She smiles wickedly. "I'll be in good company. Since when do you say tots?"

I stick my tongue out at Michelle and then look at Mona.

"Drama?"

She shakes her head. "I got B's in almost all my classes. So that sucked. My mom wrote me an email, and said not only did her and Dick break up, but that she wants me to move home and go to school there."

She looks upset.

I grimace. "It's all my fault."

She smiles. "No, it isn't. I told her to go eff herself and that Dick was a perve and that he totally perved on me like twice."

I feel rage. "What?"

She nods. "Yeah. Twice. He let me know if I needed help with becoming a woman, he would be more than happy to help me out. Barf. I kicked him in the balls and told him to get lost. Anyway, she cried and said she was sorry. She's sending me a bunch of money for Christmas." She rolls her eyes.

I'm sickened. "I'm probably going to eat him, if you're cool with it?"

She nods. "Oh yeah. No issues here."

Michelle wrinkles her nose. "Nasty."

I rub my belly and smile. "No, the meaner, nastier, more evil ones taste better."

Michelle pulls up a bag of candy and throws it on the bed. "Wanna watch Christmas movies?"

I frown. "What day is it?" I feel like Scrooge.

"December 18th. You've been a busy little bunny these last couple weeks, dude." Mona grabs the remote for the TV and presses a button on the wall. A huge TV spins around.

My jaw drops. "Oh my God."

She turns on the TV and Michelle opens the snack bag. I curl up with them and we watch The Grinch, with Jim Carey. Michelle twirls my hair while Mona and I play scrabble on her iPad.

The movie ends and they are both asleep. I realize the dead can't take me in this room. I'll never sleep.

I slip from the bed and out the door.

My feet pad along the hardwood.

I creep to the dark door. I touch it and know the memories are real.

I turn the knob and creep into the dark room. I smile when I see my chest, for the real reason. I kneel before the chest and look back at the door. I push into the wooden carvings and push in the right handle on the side. I lift the lid and smile down.

I pull down the hidden compartment and pull out the letter. The red wax seal is still intact.

I hold the paper to my chest and hug it tightly. If I smell hard enough, the chest has a lingering scent of her.

I trace my fingers along the seal. I crack it and open the letter.

In the dark my eyes can see every word perfectly. Her writing is stunning. Flowery and beautiful.

Tears leak from my eyes. I remember her face. I remember her love. I try to make it more important to me than the look she gave me when she left me. She left me to die.

I fold the letter and feel the love she has expressed in it. Love and a plan.

I close the secret compartment and turn around. He's standing in the dark watching me. "Keeping secrets?"

I shake my head and hand it to him. "Read it, if you like."

He shakes his head. "I don't need to. I know you. You'll be blathering on about it in no time."

I laugh bitterly. "I'm sorry."

He shakes his head. "Keeping you in the dark was the only way to keep the guards and protection upon you. It was a gamble we had to take. I just never imagined you would fall in love so easily."

I shake my head. "I never. He weaseled his way in there, trust me. Thank you for saving him and bringing him here."

He gives me his business-only face. I've seen if before, when he was angry with me. "What's the plan?"

I shrug. "She wants me to kill the devils and then come for her. It's pretty simple."

He laughs. "Nothing with your family is simple, Rayne. Nothing. The devils' deaths should have been simple and yet they are still alive."

"Then we leave now and go find them."

He smirks; it's sexy and makes my knees weak. "Just us?"

I shake my head. "No. We need the team of us. A one-man show has never gotten any of us anywhere."

He looks annoyed at the shot.

I walk past him but stop before leaving the room. "Why did you make it so the dead can't get to me in my room?"

He turns. "The ring of fire that protected you did this." He holds out his hand. I see an ugly scar on his skin. He never marks for longer than a second. I've seen him pull out stakes and the hole fills almost instantly.

"What is it?"

He smiles. "The dead can do nasty things when they want to, Rayne. They have their own special magic."

"Will that heal?"

He shrugs. "I don't know. I've never been wounded by hellfire before. I've only heard about it in legend."

I shake my head. "What am I to the dead?"

He leans over and brushes his lips against mine. "Their savior." He is smoke, and I am alone with my questions.

"You're an ass. We leave in the morning." I storm to a guest room and let the dead take me.

Chapter Twenty-Eight

'You're dead, Rayne. You were born dead and every night when you sleep, you are dead again. You've always been dead and I just forgot to tell you. You're dead because I killed you.'

Her words slip from her lips as tears flow around them.

She looks up at me and smiles. *'I killed you Rayne and I will kill you again.'*

Her eyes are gray like mine and filled with light. She is sitting on a lily pad in a white gown like the Nixie. Her long, dark hair flows around and moves, like it's part of the air.

I reach for her. "Mother," I call out but I'm falling away. She puts her head back down and chants some more.

'You're dead and I will kill you again.'

I wake calmly and remember the feeling of falling.

I blink and look around. I can still hear the chanting and the whispers. It feels like I'm being watched.

I haven't slept that good, since I was in my dorm room. I stretch and relax for a moment. I grab the letter from under my pillow and hug it. My dream was weird, as always.

I get up and leave my room.

The hallway is silent.

I creep down the hall to my room. Mona and Michelle aren't there.

It isn't that I don't trust Constantine. It's that he's mad at me. I recall that resulting in dead friends before. I race down the stairs. I hear something. I stop and listen. It's laughing. Wyatt, Mona and Michelle.

I turn and follow it. The house looks like a Christmas movie. Decorations are everywhere. It's elegant and overwhelming. I remember our Christmases together.

I smell bacon and eggs. My mouth waters. I walk in to find them sitting around the small kitchen table. Food is everywhere. I glance at Maria and smile. I rush and hug her.

She pulls me back. "I think you forget me, Miss Ellie." Her Spanish accent is just as strong, six hundred years later.

I shake my head. "No, never." She is my maid from before. I hug her again.

I look up to see Michelle, Wyatt and Mona eating.

I kiss her on the cheek and walk to the table.

Wyatt grins."Those are some PJ's, Rayne."

I blush and tuck my hair behind my ears. "Yeah, well, it's morning. I'm not one for mornings."

Michelle chews a piece of maple bacon and raises her eyebrows at me. "Where did you sleep last night?"

My eyes dart to Wyatt. I gulp. He grins. "She slept in the guest room next to mine."

I frown. "You checked on me?"

He nods. "Of course. I was worried. How are your wounds?"

I hold my arms out for them to inspect. "Looks good, huh?"

I glance over at his. "You?"

"I heal fast."

"Faster when someone gives you some of his magical blood." I turn to see Constantine strolling into the kitchen.

Wyatt forces a smile across his lips. "Yeah, and I've been itching like a heroin addict all morning."

Constantine snorts and looks at me. "Did you break the news to them yet?"

I look at them. Wyatt's eyes fill with fear.

"We leave today. To kill the five devils." Wyatt looks relieved but confused. I can see he's about to speak up. I continue before he can, "So pack light. Bring only essentials and no cell phones." I look at Michelle mostly. She looks insulted.

Mona tilts her head. "Dude."

Michelle twirls her hair and watches Constantine. "What counts as essentials?"

I sigh. "I'll pack your crap."

Mona looks upset. "What about Christmas?"

I look back at Constantine, who thinks for a moment. "We can do it in Switzerland; I have a house in the Alps. A chateau." He glances at Maria who nods. "Si. I will prepare the house. I will leave tomorrow."

Constantine nods. "Expect us the twenty-fourth." He looks at Mona. "One day, maybe two."

She smiles brightly. "Okay."

Wyatt looks conflicted.

"First holiday without your family?" I ask.

He nods. "Yeah. It's going to be weird." He stretches and rubs his hands through his dark hair. I want to touch it. I want to pull it a little.

He looks at us and takes a deep breath. "I've made my choice. I think we are on the right path. I think the best thing for the world is ending your parents. My mother is driven by revenge, not her duty to God."

He glances at Constantine. I feel like I'm missing something.

"Okay, well let's eat and then we'll head out." I look at Constantine as I sit next to Wyatt and start putting food on my plate. "You have a private jet?"

Constantine cocks an eyebrow. "Of course, my love. I'll call to have it put on standby. New Orleans and then Rio De Janeiro."

I frown. "What about Caracas?"

He shakes his head. "No. Willow isn't the only one who has people searching. I have had some of my people searching. None of the five devils live there. New Orleans, Rio, Capetown, Karachi, and Ciudad Juarez. We will go to Rio first and then hit Ciudad on the way out."

I frown. "You think that we can kill three devils in a week?"

He smiles. "The location was the issue, not the killing. I have addresses, lovers, favorite restaurants, everything. Modern-day technology has basically made it impossible for them to hide. Tracking them down this time was a snap."

"When did you get all this?" I ask.

He looks hurt. It's an act. "You think I would keep something important from you?"

I nod.

He laughs. "I got the majority of it in the last few days. My people followed the witches. Tom and the car will be leaving here in an hour." He turns and leaves. I know he's off to have his own breakfast. When we get to New Orleans, I'll have to find my own special snack.

Wyatt passes me the orange juice. I smile at him. I can't help myself. I know I look like a moron around him.

We land in New Orleans, and I am instantly hungry. I climb off the jet and let the air lead me. The dead whisper to me, and they lead me to the left. I walk away from everyone else. The man at the back of the plane smiles at me. I grab him by the collar of his huge jacket and pull him into my face. The dead don't come with me. They don't like him. I suck him fast and hard. I remember how to do it so fast no one even notices me when I do it. He will look like he had a heart attack. They always do.

I prop him against the wheel and walk back to the group. Constantine looks annoyed. He and Wyatt both caught me. Mona and Michelle are oblivious.

"Seriously? That couldn't wait?" Wyatt's dark eyes burn down on me.

I shake my head. "Really evil. Breaks into old people's houses. Duct tapes them and does bad stuff to them. He kills them and lives in their houses."

Wyatt looks over. "Wow. All that from a kiss, huh?"

Constantine. "You obviously haven't fallen victim to her kiss of death."

Wyatt stands up taller, towering over Constantine. "I have. I just don't let her win the battle. Makes her fight harder for it." He winks and walks past us.

Constantine's hands turn to fists. I grab his arm and point. "Best behavior."

His nostrils flare. "If only you could see the man you make me and the monster you make him." He rips his arm from my hand and stalks away.

I hate hurting him. I also hate when he says cryptic shit.

I grab my bag and follow them inside the airport.

When we leave the airport, Tom is waiting for us in a black SUV Constantine rented. We drive with Wyatt's head out the window. I almost had to duct tape Constantine's face shut, when he noticed the dog-like skill Wyatt has for tracking monsters.

Wyatt laughs. "I imagine this was far more attractive when done on a horse. Left, Tom."

I frown. "I thought you had addresses?"

Constantine gives me an annoyed look. "He left and went on the bus. They followed the bus and lost him."

I sigh. Mona passes me the iPad. I have nothing but vowels.

"Aioli," Constantine whispers and points to the L in the corner. "Triple word score."

I pass it to him. He takes it grinning.

Wyatt screams, "STOP!" Tom slams on the breaks just as I feel it. It's a sickening feeling inside of me. He's been gathering sin again. I can smell him in the air. It's not one man's sin, it's hundreds.

I grab my sword and jump from the SUV.

I sprint. My body is being pulled. It's the weirdest feeling. I want him. I want to eat the sin.

He doesn't see me. His sweater is the same. I realize it isn't a sweater. It hides his wings. It's camouflage.

He turns and instantly he is something I have never imagined. His black wings shoot out his back and spread. He hisses at me. His teeth are sharp and jagged.

He points. "You dare to challenge me?"

I stand ready with my sword. His arms and legs are longer than before. His hands are claws. The beauty of his face is worn down and gnarled. He's full of sickness.

He charges me like a bull.

I leap into the air and feel my back ripping. I float back down to the ground.

Shock covers his face. "No. No. It's not possible. IT'S NOT POSSIBLE!" He looks up to the sky. "YOU HAVE BETRAYED ME, FATHER!"

He charges and I slide my sword into him. He screams and claws my arms up. I remember the way it's supposed to be. I'm supposed to behead him. I've wounded him and the sin is seeping out slowly. I can feel it in the air around me. I pull my sword and spin. I hear the slicing sound as his head tumbles onto the ground.

I glance back at them. "Did that get a little Luke Skywalker for anyone else?" They don't move or speak. I frown. "What? I know I let a bit get away, but I think he took the rest." I smack my lips and taste the air. "There is very little here. He took the rest. I'm sure."

Wyatt points at me. "Your back."

I look behind me. The light is so bright, I drop my sword. My eyes squint. They're huge. They glisten in the dim light of the night. I drop to my knees on the cold cement.

"You're an Angel. Real Angel," Mona whispers.

I reach behind and touch the white feathery wings extending from my back. They're huge.

"How do I make them go back in? What do I do?" I hear the panic in my voice. I'm in an alley in a well-populated city with huge white wings.

Constantine is suddenly in front of me. He holds my face. "Just breathe. Calm. When you're calm, they'll go away. I've seen them once before. Not on you, on another Angel."

Tears are blinding me. I should be celebrating. I killed a Devil. His body has turned to black feathers. They're blowing down the dark alley way and getting stuck in the wetness on the street. Puddles of black feathers are everywhere.

"He was like me." I am shaking. Seeing his feathers makes me sick. I wonder if one day, I will be nothing more than a puddle of white feathers.

Constantine looks scared. Wyatt looks lost. Michelle looks slightly envious and Mona is in awe.

I try to calm myself. I try taking breaths. Nothing is happening.

Wyatt walks toward me. His footsteps are soft. He kneels and leans in and kisses me. I wince into his kiss as my back burns where the wings conceal themselves again.

Constantine growls.

I lean back and look at them both, "What am I?"

Wyatt looks back at him and makes a face. Constantine nods. "You're the real daughter of Lillith and Lucifer. No human birthed you. Not this time."

The End!!

Stay turned for the Four Horsemen, due out in the fall of 2013

Tara Brown is a Canadian author who lives in Western Canada with her husband, kids, cats and a naughty beagle. She can always be reached at tarbrow@hotmail.com or her author page on Facebook https://www.facebook.com/TaraBrownAuthor

She also writes erotica under the name Sophie Starr, with a debut novel coming this fall. Her facebook page is https://www.facebook.com/pages/Sophie-Starr/197415180427028

Other books by Tara Brown

The Devil's Roses
Cursed
Bane
Hyde
Witch
Death

The Born Trilogy
Born
Born to fight
Reborn

Imaginations
Imaginations
Coming Soon- Duplicities

The Blackwater Witches
Blackwater
Coming Soon-Book 2
A New Dawn, A Blackwater Short Story

The Blood Trail Chronicles
Vengeance
Coming Soon- Vanquished
Coming Soon- Valiant

The Light Trilogy
The Light of the World
Coming Soon- The Four Horsemen

The Single Lady Spy Series
The End of Me
Coming Soon- The End of Games

Stand Alones
The Lonely
LOST BOY
My Side
The Long Way Home
Coming Soon- P.I.'s Like Us
Coming Soon- Bullets Made of Blood and Bones

Printed in Great Britain
by Amazon.co.uk, Ltd.,
Marston Gate.